Safe Haven
Where Hope Lives

Safe Haven
Where Hope Lives

Elizabeth Stiles

There are only two ways to live your life. One is as though nothing is a miracle. The other is as though everything is.
Albert Einstein

The question is not, "Can they reason?" nor "Can they talk?" but "Can they suffer?"
Jeremy Bentham

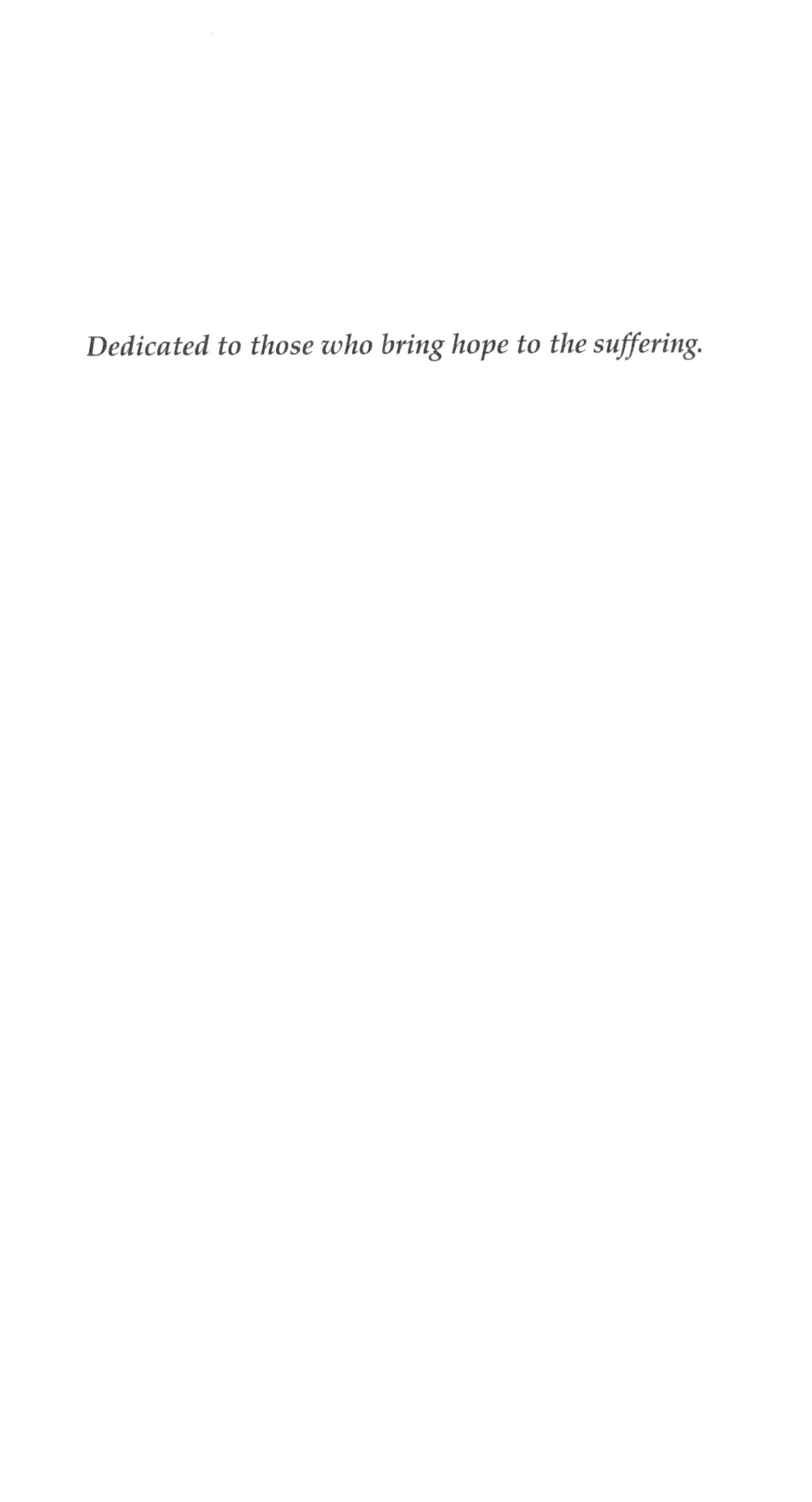

Dedicated to those who bring hope to the suffering.

Table of Contents

PART I

Chapter 1
June 21ˢᵗ, 1995

On the eve of Michael Russo's fortieth birthday, his life would take a turn. Not a bend in the road, or gradual curve, but a hairpin on a one-laner edging a cliff. He should have seen the warning signs, but so focused on the fresh layer of asphalt in front of him, he could not foresee what lay ahead.

He'd arrived at the studio at 6:45 that morning, met with his team to discuss last-minute changes, on set before 8:45. By 9:20, he'd summarized the headlines and then skimmed his notes for the Mayor Daley interview while Harvey entertained viewers with the weather forecast. After wrap-up, he'd met with the producers to discuss upcoming stories, headed to Dagwood's for his standing order, then sat at his desk reviewing changes Shannon had made to the contract.

He'd just bitten into his pastrami on rye when a dozen elementary schoolgirls, dressed in pleated plaid jumpers and saddle shoes, flooded his office. He swallowed the chunk of crust lodged in his throat and glanced at Jane, who stood in the doorway hugging a clipboard.

Was it this morning she'd reminded him the girls from St. Fabian's summer school program would visit for career day?

Jane arched a "did you forget" eyebrow. He returned a "deer in headlights" look. She volleyed a "you'll be fine" smile and leaned an "I'm here if you need me" pose against the door.

He straightened his tie, cleared his throat, and then explained the day in the life of a morning news anchor. Confident he'd conveyed his duties in an age-appropriate manner, he asked for questions. They stared as if his head were on backward.

A soft voice rose from inside the huddle. "I do." The kids parted like the Red Sea.

A girl with knobby knees and crooked pigtails stepped forward and looked at him with the most curious green eyes.

She pulled back her shoulders, lifted her chin, and asked the same question Meg had asked before she closed her eyes and never opened them again. "Are you afraid of anything?"

His mouth went dry, his mind blank. "I… ah…"

Salvation came from a compassionate voice behind the group. "Girls," their teacher said. "Please ask Mr. Russo questions about his career, not his personal life."

A slender girl, face overtaken by glasses, fired her hand high. "Do you know what today is?"

"Your birthday?"

She corrected him with a roll of her eyes. "The summer solstice. At exactly 4:34 this afternoon, the sun will stop and change directions."

"The sun stops? I didn't know that. Does anyone have questions about—"

"How old are you? 'Cuz you look younger on TV."

"Did you really meet Michelle from *Full House?*"

"My dad says you're not a real news reporter like Peter Jennings. Mom says it doesn't matter 'cause you're hot."

Jane clapped her hands, snapping the girls' attention. "Who wants to be on TV?"

A round of cheers. The teacher herded them down the hall.

Michael sank back in his chair and blew out a breath. "That did not go well."

Jane plopped *The Chicago Sun-Times* on his desk. "You did fine."

"They stared at me as if—"

"You had mustard on your face?" She handed him a napkin.

He wiped his chin and frowned at the yellow stain. "What would I do without you?"

"Hopefully you won't have to find out."

"You're going with me. It's in the contract. Non-negotiable."

Her face lit up. "Next month I'll be the administrative assistant to the primary anchor of *The Chicago Nightly News.*"

He flipped through his contract, noting Shannon's red lines. "Paperwork's not signed yet."

"Only a formality." She tapped her nails on the clipboard. "About tomorrow."

"How bad?"

"The usual. Black balloons and streamers, over-the-hill banners, look who's forty posters. Just smile and act surprised." She pushed a manila envelope across his desk.

"What's this?"

"Anna faxed the listing information and directions to the farmhouse in East Haven. She and the real estate agent will meet you at three. It's an hour drive, so leave by two. Questions?"

"Plans tonight?"

"Rollerblading with Rita."

He raised his brow. "That's your third date."

A blush warmed her cheeks. "Fourth."

"Well, be careful. I'd hate for you to break a leg. Or your heart."

She swung around and pushed past Harvey, who'd wandered in wearing his "Electricity is Really Just Organized Lightning" T-shirt.

Harvey had been the meteorologist for *Wake-Up, Chicago!* since its inception in 1985, hired the day after Michael was chosen as news anchor. Last year, Shannon attempted to replace Harvey with a younger model—one with more hair and height, proper style and tact, better curves, and longer legs. But Harvey was the station mascot, a teddy bear in a clown suit with a loyal following. Upper management wasn't willing to part with him. Yet.

Harvey snatched the powdered doughnut left from the morning team meeting and bit into it. "Great interview with the mayor. You're gonna make one hell of an evening news anchor." He plopped into the chair across from Michael. "I'm going to miss you, my friend."

"I'm only moving five floors up."

"The show ain't gonna be the same, Mikey. We were the perfectly matched odd couple. Like Felix and Oscar. Ernie and Bert. Turner and Hooch."

"They'll find someone great to replace me."

"Like that thirty-something Brad Pitt doppelgänger from the *Morning Buzz?* 'Cause that's who they're interviewing."

"Jake Jones?"

"Saw him walk out of Shannon's office an hour ago." Harvey popped the rest of the doughnut in his mouth and swallowed. "How's Anna?"

"Good." He interlaced his fingers behind his head, closed his eyes, smiled at the image of Anna shuffling around his Lincoln Park loft in her Hello Kitty pajamas, hair messed. "Really good."

"Don't you got that premarital counseling session with her priest tonight?"

Anna's image faded. His smile faltered. The chair snapped back in place. "At seven."

"Would love to be a fly on the wall when he discovers you're an atheist."

Michael rubbed the ache in his temple and tossed his glasses on the desk. "Say, Harvey. What do you know about the summer solstice?"

"It's the day the sun's path reaches its northernmost position, stops, then reverses direction."

"Actually stops?"

"Technically, no. It's not the sun, but the Earth moving relative to the sun. Why?"

"Something one of the kids said."

"Hey, about tomorrow." He dusted powdered sugar off his shirt. "The roasting wasn't my idea."

Jane popped her head into the room. "Shannon wants you in her office."

Michael stood, hesitated. Shifted his gaze from Jane to Harvey.

"This is it, Michael," Jane said, beaming. "What you've wanted since you walked in the door ten years ago."

Harvey slapped him on the back. "You're headed for the big leagues, my friend."

Michael slipped into his suit coat, picked up the contract, glanced at his watch.

Jane adjusted his tie. "Go! I'll call Anna and tell her you'll be late. She'll understand."

***

Shannon—like a wooden match, slender and stiff, with a head full of fiery-red hair—paced behind her mahogany desk, phone cradled between ear and shoulder. She motioned Michael to take a seat. He set the contract on her desk and rehearsed how he'd react to her offer.

Shannon hung up, whisked the door closed, then eased into her chair. "I'll get right to the point," she said, tenting her fingernails. "We've hired Jake Jones as our evening news anchor."

His tie became a noose. Words log-jammed in his throat. "I thought..."

"Jake was always our first choice. We were just waiting for things to fall in place."

He gripped the chair arms. Forced himself to breathe. "You were stringing me along until—"

"Don't take it personally, Michael. Broadcast news is a fickle business."

Michael pushed up from the chair and paced the room. "So now what? I'm stuck at the morning news desk?"

She clicked her fingernails together. "We've decided to revamp *Wake Up, Chicago!* We're interested in attracting a younger audience. We'll need anchors who can relate."

Michael flattened his hands on her desk and leaned forward. "You're firing me because of my age?"

"Not firing. We just won't renegotiate your contract when it expires in three months." She swiveled in her chair. "Look, we'll give you an opportunity to spin it anyway you want. Make us out to be the bad guy."

"Big of you." He threw his arms in the air. "So that's it? Ten years of loyalty and you repay me by showing me the door?"

She twisted her lips. "Let me talk to Marty. Maybe he can get you a job in field reporting."

"Don't fucking bother." He shredded the contract and threw confetti over her desk. "I quit!"

Chapter 2

Somber skies dominated Chicago's skyline. A foggy haze engulfed the city and cloaked buildings in stagnant gray. Without the accustomed Lake Michigan breeze, subway stench and exhaust fumes choked streets.

Michael merged onto I-90 West and, weaving in and out of traffic, hammered Stella's gears like Andretti, slowing only for the occasional toll. Stella, his '65 Shelby Mustang GT350, seemed to sense his seething anger. She responded without hesitation, devouring road and rage without complaint.

Outside the city, the fog lifted. Sunlight glinted Stella's windshield. Michael slipped on his Oakleys, cranked Collective Soul's "The World I Know." Tapping rhythms on the dashboard, he sang. With each verse and passing mile, anger dissipated toward resolve.

Fuck the job. He'd reinvent himself. Do something different. When he'd graduated from NYU with a master's in journalism, he was determined to become an investigative reporter. Seek out injustice, uncover political scandal, bring the message of truth to the masses. He'd let broadcast journalism derail that goal.

Time to pursue his dream. Get back on track.

Without his income, he and Anna would have to put their house plans on hold. Anna would understand. Always did.

Stone Temple Pilots' "Interstate Love Song" streamed through the speakers. Michael coasted the exit ramp, turned south on Route 47, and smiled. Barren road. He punched the accelerator. Stella responded with a raw, throaty growl.

With her V8 heart, Stella was a tsunami on wheels. Her sexy curves and Wimbledon White body sported Guardsman Blue rocker stripes and Le Mans top stripes. But it wasn't her impressive horsepower or iconic looks that bonded them. It was nostalgia. Stella held the few good memories Michael had of his dad.

Entering a 25-mph zone, he downshifted and rolled to a stop at the first intersection. Cloud shadows drifted across Stella's hood. He glanced at his watch. Fifteen minutes late. He retrieved the listing from his briefcase, focused on the grainy photo. Behind a stand of pine, he could make out a section of gable roof, a hint of a window, a fieldstone chimney. Underneath the picture, a one-line descriptor. *Quaint two-bedroom farmhouse on forty acres located on a quiet country lane.* Directions scrawled across the bottom. *Turn right at the Citgo station two miles west of town, follow Hope until it ends.*

Why this town? This house? What had caught Anna's eye?

He eased Stella through a tunnel of oaks down Main. Victorian-styled houses painted in pastels framed the street. Bikes lay abandoned on manicured lawns. Wind rustled leaves and snapped sheets.

Driving through historic downtown, he read a few of the canvas awnings over storefronts. Dillon's Hardware, Roxy's Diner, Sally's Resale Shop.

Occupying the heart of town, an antique Catholic church with thick stone walls, leaded glass windows, and massive oak doors.

The traffic light at First turned red. An old man, sitting on a bench outside Harold's Feed Store, tipped his hat. Michael nodded in reply.

He and Anna had lived in and around big cities their entire lives and were ready for a simpler life. A switch from roller coaster to Ferris wheel. But East Haven seemed more like a merry-go-round.

On the outskirts, he spotted the Citgo station, turned right, and drove through endless rows of tasseling corn and miles of soybeans. Gravel crunched and dust billowed. Hope ended, edging a forest of withered pines. A "House for Sale" sign, planted precariously among a ditch of weeds, pointed toward a rutted driveway.

"This isn't a Ferris wheel," he muttered, maneuvering Stella around several tire-eating potholes. "It's a tilt-a-whirl."

The two-story farmhouse wore the color of neglect. Wood shake siding, formerly cornflower blue, bled stains of rusty nails. Gutters sagged, shutters dangled, and spider cracks webbed windowpanes.

Michael thrummed the steering wheel, then parked Stella next to a yellow Miata sporting an Illinois vanity plate stamped *BRN 2 SEL*.

He opened his door and stepped into a puddle. A blanket of dust coated Stella's hood, and mud splattered her side panels. He threw his suit coat onto the passenger seat, wiped his wingtips on a carpet of dandelions, and climbed the crumbling porch stairs. A copper blonde in a dark suit and billowy silk scarf emerged from the doorway.

She slapped her hand against her chest. "You're Michael Russo."

"Yes," he replied, smoothing his tie.

"My Grams watches your show every morning. She calls you 'The Face of Chicago.'"

"Ahh…thanks. I think. Listen. Ms.…"

"Adams," she said, blinding him with her teeth. "Katie Adams."

"I believe there's been a misunder—"

"Where are my manners?" She shook his hand and pulled him into the entryway.

Anna appeared wearing the smile he'd fallen for two years ago. They'd met at a benefit for Healing Hearts, a non-profit supporting victims of domestic violence, a foundation she'd started after resigning as a prosecuting attorney. The moment she'd walked on stage to deliver the keynote, he became mesmerized. Her passion, her enthusiasm, her ability to believe in something wholeheartedly, captivated him.

She slipped her hand into his. He pressed his lips against her temple, closed his eyes, and inhaled lingering hints of lilac. For several heartbeats, she was all that mattered.

Katie clapped. "Why don't we start in the living room?"

Michael ran his fingers across paisley wallpaper peeling from plasterboard and eyed a light bulb dangling from exposed wire.

Anna shrugged. "Can't hurt to look."

Katie yanked the heel of her peep-toe pump from a crack in the plank floor, then teetered one-footed while slipping it back on. "I was telling Anna the widower who owned the place died last year. Kids are settling the estate." She glanced at the water stains on the ceiling. "Needs a little TLC, but you can't beat the location. Best soil in Kane County. Borders a twelve-hundred-acre forest preserve. And there's a pond behind the barn." She drew back the green velvet drapes shrouding the picture window.

Once the dust settled, he and Anna stepped forward. Crabgrass grew rampant. An old fieldstone wall, surrounding an aging barn, lay in ruins. Ivy covered the wooden framework of a rusted windmill. A galvanized gate, leading to a meadow of ragweed and chicory, sagged on its hinges. A skeletal swing set haunted the yard.

Anna squeezed his hand and bit into her lip. She wasn't seeing the same images. At least not in the same light. He and Anna viewed the world through different lenses. Where he saw problems, she saw possibilities. Something else he loved about her.

Katie sneezed twice and then spun on the balls of her feet. "Let's check out the kitchen, shall we?"

Anna tugged his hand and pulled him away from the window with her magnetic smile.

Katie gripped the antique glass doorknob and leaned into the swollen five-panel door. "You're going to love this kitchen, Anna. A cook's dream."

Or nightmare, depending on one's tolerance for canary yellow.

Katie ran her hand over the butcher block center island as if modeling on The *Price is Right.* "All appliances are included. The Wedgewood is vintage—dual ovens, built-in warming drawers, four gas burners. The Kelvinator refrigerator is in mint condition." She waved her hand at the hanging cast-iron skillets. "And the kids are leaving the kitchenware."

He turned the spigot above the sea-foam green porcelain sink. Pipes jumped. Rusty water belched from the faucet and swirled the drain.

Katie shut off the water and, wiping hands on her skirt, said, "Why don't we head upstairs?"

They followed into a bedroom the size of the closet in his loft. "It's small," she said, as if in apology. "But it'd make a cute nursery."

The vein in Anna's neck pulsed. The floorboards groaned under Michael's shifting weight. A fly buzzed as it battered the window.

Katie cleared her throat. "The house just needs aired out." She slammed her palms against the window frame several times and shoved it above her head. "There." She clapped her hands as if cleaning chalkboard erasers. "All fixed. Now Anna," she said, roping their arms, "wait until you see the master bedroom."

After Katie dragged Anna away, Michael walked to the window. A forty-year-old man with furrowed brow reflected back at him. He rubbed his cheek and frowned. When had the coarse gray hairs outnumbered the thin black ones and fine lines etched themselves around mouth and eyes?

A breeze ruffled the gauzy curtains. He looked through his reflection and focused on the barn—weathered paint, pockmarked wood, battered shingles. A picture on a postcard or puzzle. The image of a dying American dream.

Katie still had Anna trapped, so he headed out the back door, past an overgrown garden, and followed a dirt path. He pushed the barn door open. Metal wheels squealed along a rusted track. A swirl of sunlit dust. The barn smelled of sweet hay and sun-soaked grain. Of frayed rope, worn leather, axle grease, and machine oil.

He shuffled his shoe in the fine layer of chaff coating the plank floor. A draft rippled spider webs hanging from beams. Rusted shovels, pitchforks, and rakes cluttered a corner. A mouse squeezed out from beneath a Duckwall apple crate and disappeared behind a kerosene lantern.

Michael slid the bolt on a plywood door, tugged on the hammered copper handle. The warped particle board splintered and snapped like brittle bones. Inside the closet: an extension ladder—splattered with russet paint, an old Radio Flyer wagon, metal pails stacked like nestling dolls, an axe, an open sack of bird feed.

Anna slipped through the barn door and into his arms. "How's 'The Face of Chicago'?"

"Completely smitten." He brushed his thumb across the smattering of freckles complementing her fair Irish complexion. "Where's Katie?"

"She locked up and left after I told her we weren't interested." She glanced up through sweeping lashes. "Are we?"

A swallow darted through the door to a nest of grass and mud tucked into the rafters and peeked down as though awaiting his answer.

Anna slid her hands up his arms. "How was work?"

He planted his hands on her hips, hesitated. Why spoil the mood? "Never a dull moment. How was your day?"

"Guess what charity *Chicagoland Magazine* named one of the best non-profit organizations?"

"How many guesses do I get?"

She slapped his chest with the flats of her hands.

"Ouch." A chuckle escaped. "So proud of you. We'll celebrate."

She toyed with the birthstone on her chain. "Speaking of celebrations, we threw a surprise baby shower for Joyce. It was amazing! All the adorable booties and onesies, the bunting bags and swaddling blankets, the…" She tilted her head, peered into his eyes. "You have no idea what I'm talking about, do you?"

"No clue."

"Why did you let me ramble?"

"Love hearing your voice."

Color warmed her face. "Joyce glowed with excitement."

"Understandable."

Anna stepped out of his arms, turned around, and inspected the barn. Maybe this was a good time to confess his employment status.

"Something happened at work," he said. "I need to tell you…"

She slipped off her sling-back pumps, climbed the rickety ladder, and disappeared behind the hay bales.

"Anna, be careful. What are you doing?"

"Looking for a place to celebrate."

"In the loft?"

"Ever hear of a roll in the hay?"

"Sounds prickly."

She reappeared, dangling panties. "Where's your sense of adventure, old man?"

"You're deflating my ego."

"Join me. I'll blow it back up."

All thoughts of joblessness dissipated. He scrambled up the ladder, threaded a coil of her auburn hair around his index finger. "You are one sexy woman, Mrs. Russo."

"Ms. O'Leary," she corrected, unbuckling his belt.

"Still don't understand why you won't change your name after we're married."

She slid her hand inside his pants. "Do you really want to argue right now?"

"Oh, god, no."

The corner of her lips curved up. "Thought you didn't believe in God."

"Right now, I'd believe in unicorns."

"What about a one-legged turkey?"

"A one-legged what?" He followed her gaze. A turkey, perched atop a hay bale, cocked its head and stared through beady eyes. "How fitting," he said. "A peeping Tom."

Chapter 3

Basking in the afterglow of a blissful orgasm gave Michael confidence. "Listen," he said, tucking Anna's hair behind her ear. "About work. I ah…"

Anna anchored a thigh across his hip, nuzzled her face against his neck, and brushed her fingertips dangerously close to his reset button. He clutched her wrist, but it was too late. Damage done. Only one way to repair it. He flipped her onto her back and framed her head between his forearms. God, that smile.

"You were saying," she said as he kissed her jawline. "About work."

"It can wait," he replied, nudging her chin up with his nose. A hint of lilac rose off heated skin.

"Turkey still watching?"

"Flown the coop, so to speak." His lips found the delicious curve of her throat.

"Did you hear a rooster crowing?"

He growled against her neck, then lifted his head. "When?"

"Right when you…um…" Her face flushed, masking freckles.

He glanced at his watch. "Why would a rooster crow at 4:34 in the afternoon?"

"Shit!" Anna pushed him off, leapt to her feet, and shimmied into her skirt. "We're going to be late."

"Our appointment isn't until—"

"I promised my parents we'd stop by before our consultation with Father Mulcahy. I need to shower."

"Why?"

"Because," she said, buttoning her shirt, "I smell like sex."

"My favorite scent." He propped himself against a hay bale. "We can reschedule."

"No, we can't. We're lucky Daddy could get us an appointment on short notice. Where's my underwear?" She dropped to her knees and searched loose hay, skirt edging thighs.

She caught him ogling. "Why are you sitting there?"

He interlocked his fingers behind his head. "Enjoying the show."

She threw his shirt in his face.

"Anna," he said, holding up her panties. "You're thirty-six years—"

"Thirty-five," she said, snatching them.

"Your parents are controlling your life."

"They are not."

"You're allowing them to plan your wedding. Correction," he said, wresting into his pants, "our wedding."

"We've been through this a million times."

"Why not get married on the beach?" He tucked his shirt into his pants. "Or fly to Vegas."

Anger reddened her face, then paled in disbelief. "You're backing out on me."

"Just rethinking the whole Catholic church fiasco."

"You promised—"

"That I'd meet your priest and discuss options."

"My parents were right." She sank onto a hay bale. "We'll never get past this."

He lifted her chin to meet his gaze. "I intend to prove them wrong."

She flashed a half-hearted smile.

He plucked a piece of hay from her hair. "We can drop by your parents' house for a few minutes before our meeting."

He'd have to discuss his employment news with her after church.

As he descended the ladder, a breeze filled the barn with the sweet scent of clover and the laughter of a child. Laughter that reminded him of a six-year-old who'd once trusted him with her life.

"Faster," Meg had begged, while he swung her in circles.

He'd gripped her hands tighter, bent his knees, and quickened the pace. Meg's willowy body soared above the ground, her blond hair a flag in the wind.

"I'm flying, Mike. I'm flying." She giggled. "Don't let go."

"I won't. I promise."

"Michael?" Anna squeezed his hand. "What is it?"

"Nothing." He kissed her forehead.

Holding hands, they walked up the path. Anna's gaze settled on the window of the tiny bedroom. The lines between her eyebrows deepened, the bow of her lip tightened. The look. Flirting with ideas. Visualizing possibilities. Entertaining hope.

"The house has character," she said.

"Suppose we could renovate. Give her a facelift."

"She's full of potential. Just needs a little love. A second chance."

That smile would be his undoing.

***

Michael drove through the historical district of Evanston and parked Stella in front of Anna's parents' Irish-inspired country house. Side-by-side, they traversed the flagstones toward the massive mahogany door bearing a Celtic cross.

Anna ironed her skirt with her hands. "How do I look?"

"Sexy as hell, Mrs. Russo."

She flashed him a warning look. "Play nice."

"Where's the fun in that?"

The door swung open. Grace O'Leary stood as if balancing a book on her head. Her porcelain skin and tailored black suit showed neither flaw nor wrinkle. While Anna's features were soft perfection, Grace's jaw and cheekbones were sharp and unforgiving. Only the arch of their brows and the curve of their noses hinted resemblance.

"Aine," Grace said, using the Gaelic. "You're late."

"Sorry." Anna air-kissed both sides of her mother's stoic face. "Traffic was a nightmare."

"New perfume?" Grace asked. Her steely gaze traveled over Anna's shoulder and landed on his face. "It's musky. Doesn't suit you, dear."

"Actually," Michael said, leaning in to give Grace a peck on the cheek, "I gave it to her."

"Colin," Grace said, turning her back on him, "Aine's here."

The O'Leary home entertained a museum feel. Elaborate oversized paintings. Heavy, lavish curtains cascaded from ornate curtain rods onto glossy wood floors. Ivory statues of Catholic saints perched on marble pedestals.

Colin sat in his leather recliner, reading the *Tribune*.

"Hi, Daddy." Anna bent to kiss her father. "How's work?"

"Ugly." He tossed his newspaper on the floor and pushed his bulk out of the recliner. "Had to preside over a child sexual abuse case. Bastards should be castrated."

"At least we agree on that," Michael said, extending his hand.

Colin anchored his arm around Anna's shoulders and clamped a massive hand around Michael's. "Michael."

He squeezed back. "Colin."

"Colin." Grace's incisive tone cut through the tension. "Get Michael a drink."

"A beer would be fine. Thanks."

"Aine," Grace said, folding the newspaper Colin discarded, "what happened to your hair? It's a bird's nest. Honestly, you need to—"

"Guess what, Mother? *Chicagoland Magazine* named Healing Hearts one of the top ten charities in the city."

"Congratulations, dear." She brushed a speck of hay off Anna's suit coat. "You know your father could get you a job in any prestigious law firm downtown."

Anna threaded her arm through Michael's and held on as if restraining a pit bull.

He inhaled, deep. "Anna's happy running her foundation."

Grace smiled. "I only have her best interests at heart."

Anna set her free hand on his bicep. "Michael and I looked at a house today."

"I didn't realize you were searching. What neighborhood?"

"East Haven."

"East Haven?" Colin handed Michael a goblet of Merlot. "That's too far from Divine Child."

He stared in confusion at the wine. "Why's it matter how far we live from Divine Child?"

"Divine Child has the best Catholic schools in Chicago."

"But we've decided—"

"To keep looking." Anna squeezed his arm.

"Aine, honey. You don't know the first thing about house hunting. I'll make an appointment with Sean at Mulligan Reality. I'm sure Michael's too busy to look at every house on the market."

"We should get going," Anna said. "Don't want to be late for Father Mulcahy."

"He's looking forward to meeting you, Michael. Colin's told him all about you."

"Then I'm sure we'll be best friends in no time."

"He assured Colin that even though you're agnostic—"

"Atheist."

"—he'll perform the marriage ceremony. Colin and I were married at Divine Child, as were both sets of Aine's grandparents. We can't break tradition."

"For Heaven's sake, no."

"Michael," Anna said, pulling on his arm. "We need—"

"Father Mulcahy christened Aine, gave her first communion, and presided over her confirmation. He'll be the one to marry her."

"Good thing I asked her before he did."

"He'll welcome you into the church when you're ready."

"How thoughtful."

"Of course, you'll have to promise to raise your children in the Catholic faith."

"Which won't be an issue since Anna and I agreed we won't be having kids."

Colin's glass slipped from his grasp, shattered against the fieldstone hearth. Red wine bled into the plush white area rug. Grace didn't flinch.

Michael set his untouched goblet on the mantel. "Let's go, Anna. Mustn't keep the good Father waiting."

He'd reached the door when Anna cried out. "Mom! Get Dad's pills."

Colin, clutching his chest with both hands, wheezed.

Anna slid Colin's arm around her shoulder. "Michael! Help me."

He ducked his head under Colin's other arm and helped settle him into his chair. Grace, hands trembling, returned with a vial.

Anna placed a tablet in Colin's mouth. "It's okay, Daddy." She knelt next to his chair, enfolded his hands with hers. "Give it a minute…that's it…slow, deep breaths."

Colin's breathing normalized. He eased back and nodded. Anna stood, swung around to face Michael. Her soft blue eyes had hardened to marbles. She pushed past him and marched out the front door.

He slipped his hands into his pockets and followed.

She turned. "You had to push it, didn't you?"

"They started it."

"Dear God, Michael." She threw her hands in the air. "How old are you?"

"Old enough to know I'm being manipulated."

"You know my father has a heart condition. Why would you—"

"Wait." He shook his head. "You're blaming me?"

"Why couldn't you just let it go?"

"Why the hell haven't you told them we don't want kids?"

"I'm their only child. The only one capable of carrying on the O'Leary bloodline. Our history. Our heritage. It's not an easy subject to broach."

"Here's a novel idea. Why don't you tell them what *you* want?"

"Because I'm—"

"Afraid to? For god's sake, Anna. Tell them the truth. That you don't want to raise a child in a world filled with hatred. One with so much pain and suffering."

"That's your truth, Michael. Not mine."

"But we'd agreed…"

"We did. But something happened today." Her eyes scanned the second-story windows, and when she spoke again, her voice softened. "I know this sounds trite, but I've been having these thoughts."

"What thoughts?"

"That my child…our child, might help change the world."

"I don't understand. What happened?"

"Does it really matter?" she said, her eyes pools of blue. "You're not going to change your mind."

Icy pins pricked his feet. "I can't—"

"You mean you won't. There's a difference." She twisted off her engagement ring and placed it in his hand.

"Anna, please. Let's take time. Think this through." Who was he fooling? Nothing would change his mind. Or hers.

"We were both wrong." She looked at him without a trace of that smile he lived for. "It wasn't my parents or God who tore us apart."

Chapter 4

"Looks like a lot of work," Phil said, climbing into the driver's seat of the Smith Bros. moving van.

A stiff breeze knocked a dangling gutter against rotting wood shakes, blew a loose shingle from the balding roof, and stirred an earthy decay. Dandelion parachutes swirled around the old farmhouse. Snow in a globe.

With the heel of his shoe, Michael snagged an oak leaf cartwheeling the rutted drive. "Should keep me busy."

Phil adjusted the bill of his Blackhawks cap, rolled a toothpick across his lips. "Got a cousin in the construction business. Works pretty cheap if you're interested."

"I'll keep it in mind."

After the moving van backed down the drive, Michael retrieved a shoebox from Stella's passenger seat and carried it into the house. Except for his office furniture and mattress, he'd sold his furnishings to the cardiologist, subletting his loft. Everything he'd amassed fit inside the forty U-Haul boxes pyramided in the center of the living room. Nothing of value other than the contents of the shoebox he clutched.

It'd been four weeks since he'd quit his job and lost Anna. Three weeks since he'd drained his savings and bought the forty-acre East Haven farm. Two weeks since he'd declared himself an investigative reporter. A week since doubt and remorse settled in.

The bare bulb hanging in the entry flickered, then fizzled. He blew out a breath and mumbled, "What a fucking mess."

He climbed the stairs. Loose floorboards creaked. In the tiny bedroom, he set the shoebox on his desk, then opened a large box and pulled out his framed Master's of Journalism Degree, hung it from the bent nail on the wall. Set the picture he'd taken with Woodward and Bernstein on top of his bookshelf.

He dug back through the box and found *The Reporter's Handbook*, *The Journalist and the Murderer*, *Mass Media and American Politics*, and his dog-eared *The Elements of Style*. He organized his desk—paper tray, pencil holder, blotter; then his top drawer—paper clips, staples, highlighters. He turned on his ThinkPad, opened a Word document, slid his fingers over the smooth curves of the home row, and stared at the blinking cursor. Where to begin?

His mom's voice echoed. "Look around you, Michael," she'd said, watching him struggle to write a paper in fifth grade. "The world's filled with untold stories. Pick one that tugs at your heart."

The late afternoon sun cast a rectangle across the top of the shoebox. He walked to the window and studied the barn that stood as if holding the weight of the world on its shoulders. What was it about that old barn?

He headed outside, wandered down the path, and rolled open the door. A small rooster with iridescent black and orange plumage collided with his shins. It somersaulted backwards, then clawed to its feet and cocked its head. A cloudy film coated its beady eyes. The rooster charged again. He stepped aside and watched it scurry up the path.

Inside the barn, among the rafters and bales, nothing had changed, but something was different. A smell of hope, if hope had a smell.

A gust whistled through gaps in the planks. Outside, the windmill blades clunked to life. Swings clanged against metal frame. The meadow gate squeaked on rusty hinges.

A broad-shouldered man sporting a buffalo plaid flannel shirt and a dense but neatly trimmed beard appeared in the doorway. He dragged off a black knit cap, revealing dark, shoulder-length hair. He had the smooth brow of a thirty-year-old, yet his eyes reflected age-old sadness.

"Frank Mackenzie," the man said in a rumbling tenor voice. The inky tattoo of a dove peeked out from beneath his shirt cuff. "Everyone calls me Mac."

"Michael Russo," he replied, shaking the offered hand.

"You're not a farmer."

"That obvious?"

"No calluses," he said, releasing Michael's hand.

"I'm an investigative reporter," he replied tentatively, as to convince himself rather than Mac.

Mac scratched his beard. Sunlight glinted his wedding band. "So, you bought Neil Buchler's place."

"All forty acres."

"Plenty of room for the kids to run."

"No kids."

"Wife?"

"Just myself. You?"

Mac slipped his hands into the back pockets of his jeans. "Same."

"Live close by?"

"Small place in town."

"Did you know Neil?"

"Came by a couple times a week to check on him. Promised I'd take care of the birds until someone bought the place."

"You mean the one-legged turkey and the blind rooster?"

"You've met them?"

"More like they've met me."

Silence filled the barn. Mac shuffled his boot along a worn plank. Michael scanned the rafters searching for something to say.

"She's a beauty, ain't she?" A hum rolled in Mac's throat. "Hand-hewn oak timbers. White pine pegged siding. Mortise and tenon joints. They don't make them like this anymore. Gotta be 150, give or take a decade." His gaze traveled along the ridge between the gables. "Think of all she's witnessed. Births, deaths, struggles for survival. She guards secrets."

"You know barns?"

"I've helped restore a dozen or so. A passion of mine."

Michael pounded his palm against a support post. "Think she can be saved?"

"Framework's solid. Have to pull up floor planks to check piers and sills. The loft needs reinforced, boards replaced, but no sign of termites." He craned his neck, inspected the ceiling. "A few broken rafters. Some water damage. Probably needs a new roof."

Mac retrieved the extension ladder from the storage room, walked it onto his shoulder, and headed out the door. Michael followed. After anchoring the feet on level ground, Mac slid the extension up to the overhang. He jump-tested the first rung several times before barreling up the aluminum steps and onto the roof.

Having little familiarity with ladders, Michael eased up slowly and sat on the edge of the roof. He lifted his face and marveled at the darkening blue stretch of canvas above. He'd lived in the city so long, he'd forgotten the sky wasn't the shiny color of steel or the chalky hue of concrete; it didn't end at the ceiling of clouds but began.

The roof vibrated underneath Michael's hands. Mac traversed the ridge like a tightrope walker, then negotiated the battered shingles and sat next to him. "She needs a new roof. I'd be happy to help."

"Appreciate the offer, but I'll probably just leave it to its own demise."

The last of the sun's rays cast towering shadows across the rolling landscape and splashed the horizon in pastel pinks, hazy purples, and smoky blues. They sat silent while a chorus of crickets ushered in twilight.

Mac toyed with his ring. "Nothing more powerful than a God-painted sunset to reflect upon life's choices." He lowered his head as if to hide the sadness in his eyes, but could not mask the pain in his voice. "Time to head home," he said, pushing to his feet.

"Thanks for stopping by," Michael said, once he'd hit solid ground.

Mac slipped on his cap, nodded, then walked up the path.

The wind stilled. The swings stopped swaying, the mill blades quit turning, the crickets ceased chirping. Silence descended upon the farm.

"Hey, Mac."

Mac turned at the top of the hill.

"That offer to help still stand?"

He could hear the smile in Mac's reply. "Anytime."

"Can't pay much."

"Not in it for the money. But if you feel the need to compensate, we'll figure something out."

"Where can I find you?"

"Around," he replied, before darkness swallowed him whole.

Michael closed the barn door and then wandered up the path around the side of the house. Headlights bounced up the drive. Harvey emerged from his Bimmer clutching a bucket of KFC and a six-pack of Bud.

The rooster darted from the dead bushes and barreled straight into Harvey, multiple times, before clamping its legs and wings around Harvey's pant leg. "What the hell, Mikey," he said, trying to shake the rooster off. "Is he your guard dog?"

"He's miffed you're carrying his deep-fried cousin."

"Ha, ha. Funny. Could you get him off me, please?"

He removed the rooster from Harvey's leg and deposited the squawking bird into the bushes.

"No garage?" Harvey said, inspecting the exterior of the house. "Where's Stella going to sleep?"

"The barn. Apparently, it's not going to collapse anytime soon."

Harvey handed him the beer. "Brought some brew."

"Watch your step," Michael said, ushering him inside.

"Nice place, Mikey. Straight out of *Better Homes and Gardens*."

"Thanks." He cracked open a beer, handed it to Harvey. "Not sure where to hang my House Beautiful award yet."

"Where's your furniture?"

"You're looking at it." He moved two of the sturdier boxes for a makeshift dining table and then snagged a chicken wing from the bucket. "Haven't had a chance to unpack the fine china. Good thing you brought finger food."

Harvey gnarled into a chicken thigh. "Saw a Jeep back out of your drive."

"That was Mac."

"Old MacDonald?" He chuckled. "Old *Mac*Donald had a farm. E.I.E.I—Forget it," he said, when Michael didn't laugh.

"He's not a farmer, and he's not old. Has what some women might call rugged good looks. The strong, silent type." He swirled his beer, took a sip. "Says he isn't married but wears a wedding band."

"Maybe he gets hit on all the time. Wears a ring to keep the girls at bay. I should be so lucky," he muttered.

"Maybe his wife died. And he can't bear to remove the ring. Anyway, he's a nice guy. Seems…lonely." He finished his beer and popped another. "How's work?"

"They're moving me to *News at Noon*. Consolation prize."

"At least you get to sleep in." He sucked grease off his thumb. "How's Jane?"

"Miserable. Shannon's assistant quit, so they replaced her with Jane. Asked her out to lunch yesterday to cheer her up, but she already had a date with Anna."

His heart retreated deeper inside his chest. He swallowed the chunk of chicken lodged in his throat with a swig of beer. "Did you see her?"

"Couldn't take my eyes off her. You really messed up big time, my friend." He wiped grease from his mouth with the sleeve of his "Weather Forecast for Tonight: Dark" T-shirt, reached into the bucket, and pulled out a breast.

"So, how long are you going to play Oliver Wendell Douglas?"

"Oliver who?"

"*Green Acres*. Jeez, Mikey, you grow up in Antarctica?" He guzzled beer, belched. "Look. I get it. You needed a change. But how long before you realize this wasn't your best idea?"

"Could be tomorrow. Could be next year." He studied the pattern of water stains decorating the plaster ceiling. "Maybe this was the worst mistake of my life. Or exactly what I needed." He handed Harvey another Bud. "Let's give it some time."

Harvey stayed until they'd sucked the chicken bones dry and hammered the last beer, sometime around midnight. Michael scrounged through the boxes until he found his toiletry kit, set it on the large box labeled 'bedding', and hauled it up the stairs. He brushed his teeth, stripped to his boxers, pulled out a frayed quilt, and then collapsed onto his mattress, too exhausted to bother with sheets.

Despite the warmth of the day, night had brought a nip of cold air and a silence so deafening it kept him from sleep. His stomach churned. Chicken grease in a clogged drain. He flipped over onto his back and stared at dangling ceiling wires.

Wind whistled through the screen, snapped curtains. He rose and walked to the window. Dim light slipped through the cracks in the barn's siding. He groaned at his forgetfulness, then draped the comforter around his shoulders and headed outside.

He wandered down the path, cool soil sifting between toes. The scent of honeysuckle drifted. Hundreds of stars pricked the inky sky, beacons of light from another world.

A soft glow emanated from the loft. He climbed the ladder and searched the rafters. A pull chain dangled from a bulb affixed to a beam. As he reached for the chain, his foot caught on hay bale twine. He fell, hit his head, rolled onto his back.

Thoughts of Anna flooded. That pattern of freckles along her collarbone. The sweet lilac scent of her skin. Her lilting laugh. The warmth of her breath against his neck. And that smile.

Whether he moved 60 miles from Anna, or 600, he couldn't escape memories of her. He enveloped himself inside the quilt and drifted to sleep, holding tight onto everything Anna.

Chapter 5

The warmth of the sun stirred Michael from sleep, its rays streaming the loft like spun gold. He pried open his eyelids, half expecting to see Anna's face hovering. Instead, the one-legged turkey stared down at him.

He shook his head as if to clear it and blinked. Long and hard. "Still here?"

A purring escaped its throat.

He sat up and massaged his nape. "What the hell am I supposed to do with you?"

It puffed up its feathers and shook.

"Thanksgiving's in four months. Suppose I could fatten you up. There'd only be one drumstick, but since I'm a breast man myself—"

It hissed and flew to the floor.

"Sensitive about the leg, huh?" He scratched his stubbly jaw and chuckled. "Great. I'm having a conversation in my underwear with a turkey."

He cocooned himself inside the comforter, walked up the path, and entered the house through the back door. A distorted buzz from the entry. The doorbell works? Go figure. He squinted through the peephole.

Mac clutching a brown paper bag in each arm.

Michael opened the door.

Mac glanced at Michael's bare feet. "Bad time?"

He wiggled his dirty toes. "Headed for the shower."

"Brought you some staples. Flour, sugar…I'll come back later."

"Now works." He stepped aside, gestured for Mac to enter.

Mac's gaze traveled along the gaps in the hardwood floor, the cracks spidering plaster walls, the water-stained ceiling.

"Needs a lot of work," he said, leading Mac into the kitchen.

"It's home. A chance to start over." Mac set the bags on the counter, his gaze transfixed on the Wedgewood oven.

"You cook?" Michael asked.

"Dabble. You?"

"Made lasagna once. Didn't know to cook the noodles first." Michael slid open a drawer—wooden spoons, metal spatulas, dull knives. Held up a fork with bent tines. "Neil's kids left the kitchenware."

Mac pulled a cast-iron skillet off the wall. "Go clean up. I'll make breakfast."

***

Michael stepped out of the shower, cracked the door to let steam escape and, shaver in hand, waited for the mirror to clear. Mac's tenor voice drifted up the staircase in a pitch-perfect rendition of Billy Joel's "She's Got a Way." Michael's mind added the subtle piano chords that underscored the haunting lyrics, then wandered to the night he'd met Anna.

He'd lingered near the bar, away from the lights of the dance floor, sipping courage from a whisky glass. The din of conversation and clattering of plates waned. Anna approached the podium. While she graciously thanked the board of directors, her staff, and everyone for their generous donations, Michael searched the ballroom for the slender man with the wiry-red hair who'd accompanied her at dinner. He was out on the terrace, behind a statue of Zeus, showering gratitude on a magnetic blonde for her charitable gift with more than words.

The room erupted in applause. Chandeliers dimmed, and tiny lights twinkled overhead. The orchestra struck up Sinatra's "Fly Me to the Moon."

Anna walked to the center of the dance floor in a silky-blue gown that flowed over her curves like water. She fiddled with the button on her opera glove, shifted uneasy in silver heels, and scanned the crowd. Couples converged onto the floor, engulfing her in a whirlpool of taffeta and tails.

He buttoned his tux, wove around half-empty tables, drifted between waves of dancers until he found Anna alone, lost at sea. He stood behind her, captivated by the cascade of curls tumbling over bare, jutted shoulder blades. The curve of spine. Sway of hip. Scent of lilac from heated skin. "Ms. O'Leary."

She turned, looked at him through a sweep of dark lashes.

Spellbound by the ocean of blues that swam in her eyes, his tongue knotted.

"Mr. Russo. Thank you for coming. I hope you're enjoying yourself."

He conjured a response but stumbled over the words. Too many adjectives, not enough verbs.

She tilted her chin. "You look—"

"Old," he squeaked in a pubescent voice. He cleared his throat. "I mean older. Than I do on T.V."

"I was going to say more handsome but now that you mention it." A teasing smile.

While he searched for his voice, her attention wandered the room.

"I was wondering, Ms. O'Leary —"

"Anna, please," she said, refocusing.

"Anna, could you put the thirteen-year-old boy who's invaded my body out of misery and dance with him?"

"I'd be delighted, Mr. Russo, but I promised the first dance to my fiancé. Someone must be holding him captive." Her gaze darted between the twirling couples toward the terrace.

He leaned to block her line of vision and offered his hand. "Maybe I could stand in? Until he's free."

The orchestra played the last notes of "Fly Me to the Moon." The couples politely applauded, then lingered on the dance floor while the piano led into "She's Got a Way."

Anna slipped her hand into his.

Mac switched to a hum mid-verse, drawing Michael from his reverie. Anna's image evaporated with the steam. The mirror cleared. He rubbed the stubble on his cheek, then dropped the razor into his toiletry bag, dressed, and followed the rich, earthy aroma into the kitchen.

Mac stood at the stove, his sleeves rolled, a rooster embroidered dishtowel over his left shoulder. He saw Michael and stopped humming. "You okay?"

"That song…"

"Reminds you of someone?" He grabbed an aluminum percolator off the back burner, filled a blue speckled enamel mug, and offered it to Michael. "She must have been special."

"That she was," he mumbled, before sipping. "Do you sing in front of people?"

"Only when I have to." He pulled a stack of pancakes out of the warming drawer, lowered the flames on the burners.

"You seem comfortable manning that stove."

"My grandma taught me on a Wedgewood." He ladled warm syrup over a plate of pancakes and handed it to Michael.

He picked up the bent-tined fork, sliced through the stack, and shoveled a forkful into his mouth. The cakey layers and sweet syrup melted. "Damn good," he said. "What's your secret?"

Mac smiled over the rim of his coffee mug. "Oh, Mr. Holmes, I would love to tell you, but then, of course—"

"I'd have to kill you."

They laughed.

"Sherlock fan?" Mac asked.

"When I was twelve, I checked out a copy of *The Hounds of Baskerville* from the library. Hid it underneath my mattress so my mom wouldn't confiscate it. You?"

"Have a first edition." He wiped his hands on the dishtowel and hung it over the sink. "Got some free time Saturday. Could help with the barn, if you'd like."

"Tell you what," Mac said, when Michael didn't answer right away. "In exchange, you can help me clean Hank's pasture."

"Hank?"

"Town veterinarian. Owns a small farm down the road."

"Sounds easy enough."

A chuckle escaped Mac's throat.

While Michael polished off pancakes, Mac penned a list of materials on an IGA bag. "Take this to Harold's, five miles south of town, off 72, just past St. Joe's Hospital. Ask for Charlie. That should get us started. I'll bring my tools."

Michael walked Mac to his vehicle—a topless Jeep, Renegade decals, side panels splattered in mud. "Thanks for breakfast," he said.

"Anytime." Mac jumped into the driver's seat, cranked the key until the engine caught.

"How'd you know?" he asked Mac. "That I'm starting over."

Mac jerked the gearshift into first, spun the steering wheel. "No furniture."

After Mac's Jeep disappeared in a cloud of dust, Michael tore the list off the IGA bag, grabbed Stella's keys, and drove to Harold's Lumberyard. He wandered down a row of building materials toward a steady beeping noise. The sharp smell of oily metal sliced through the clean scent of fresh-cut pine. The operator of a Hi-Lo placed a large stack of pallets onto a shelf, lowered the lift, and swung it around.

The driver's face was thin, young, and pale. A hard hat covered much of his shaved head. An inked falcon flew across his bicep, broken chains dangling from talons.

"Can I help you?" the boy yelled over the puttering engine.

"Looking for Charlie."

"Who's asking?"

"Michael Russo."

He appraised Michael through dark eyes framed in black liner. "Is Charlie expecting you?"

"Mac sent me."

The boy turned off the engine and jumped from the seat. Couldn't be over five-six in steel-toed boots. He yanked off gloves, exposing black fingernails and the words GOTH GIRL inked above knuckles. "I'm Charlie."

"Sorry. I thought…"

"Don't sweat it." She shoved her gloves in her back pocket. "What do you need?"

She scanned his list, then handed it back. "We'll deliver everything tomorrow."

"That soon?"

"Mac's got connections." She climbed into the Hi-Lo. "Tell Ben at the service desk. He'll set it up."

***

Sally's Resale Shop occupied the corner of Main and First. The front showcase featured a bronze Tiffany lamp, a green velvet chaise lounge draped in a white lace throw, an ornately framed oil painting of a fox hunt, a headless mannequin donning a roaring twenties flapper dress.

Michael opened the front door. A bell jingled. Candles flamed the scent of pinecones and rose petals. Wall-to-wall shelving overflowed with porcelain dishes, cut-glass vases, bone china tea sets, and ceramic mugs. The floor space packed with racks of clothes, shoes, hats.

Old Sally must be hiding somewhere in the chaos.

He maneuvered around crates crammed with mason jars, Christmas ornaments, and vinyl records until he found a woman leaning against a glass counter, leafing through a five-ring binder, a cigarette perched between her fingers. With her wavy blonde hair, wide-set eyes, and perfectly arched eyebrows, she reminded him of a thirty-something Lauren Bacall. She took a drag on her cigarette, blew smoke from the corner of her mouth, and batted it with a flick of hand. "Do you know how to cook?" she asked without taking her eyes off the page.

41

"Sorry, no," he replied, trying to divert his attention from the button on her blouse threatening to pop under duress.

"Too bad." She stroked the foot of her cigarette with her siren-red thumbnail. Ashes cascaded into a crystal bowl. "Nothing sexier than a man who cooks." She studied his face and pointed her cigarette-wielding fingers at him. "You look familiar. Been here before?"

"First time."

She sucked on her cigarette until her cheeks hollowed. She looked him over and blew out another round of smoke. "A resale virgin."

"Guilty as charged."

"You the one who bought Neil Buchler's farm?"

"Michael Russo. How —"

"Small town." She dragged a thumbnail over her glossy lip. "You don't look like a farmer, Mr. Russo."

"You don't look like a resale shop owner, Ms…"

"Sally." She took another hit from her cigarette, stared out the window at the Catholic Church across the street. "We all like to fool ourselves."

"It's a beautiful building. Are you a member?"

An amused smile played on her lips. She pulled her gaze away from the church. "God abandoned me a long time ago, Mr. Russo."

"Michael."

"Okay, Michael." She twisted her cigarette butt in the crystal bowl, stood tall, confident. "What can I help you with?"

"I'm looking for a kitchen table."

She tugged a tight woven mini-skirt over long legs, slipped bare feet into matching heels, and disappeared through a wall of stringed amber beads. "You coming?"

The cluttered chaos spilled into the back. A small clearing in the corner housed a twin mattress, a worn corduroy recliner, an old steamer trunk, and a threadbare oriental rug. On top of the trunk sat a half-finished puzzle, a bowl of Fruit Loops, a glass of pulpy orange juice. A dehumidifier hummed. The rich scent of leather and the mustiness of aged paper overpowered the aroma of vanilla.

"You read?" she asked, as they walked down a hall lined with bookshelves.

"Mostly newspapers."

She trailed a fingernail over book spines. "Most of these aren't worth much. But I have a few rare finds, collectables, first print editions. What do you do for a living?"

"I'm an investigative journalist."

"And what are you currently investigating?"

"Searching for inspiration."

"In East Haven?" She laughed. "Good luck."

At the end of the hall sat a table draped in a blue quilt covered with glittery stars. She pursed her lips and pulled up a frayed corner. A child, wearing a karate jacket and a motorcycle helmet, crawled out—a parakeet perched on his shoulder.

Sally knelt on the floor, ratcheted up the visor, revealing vacant brown eyes. "Sorry, Luke. Need to inspect the Millennium Falcon."

He flapped his hands.

"We'll build a new one. With a better hyperdrive."

He rocked on his feet, hummed the Star Wars theme song.

She reached for him. He jerked away. "Henry. Please—"

Michael cleared his throat. "Actually, that table won't fit in my car. Maybe bar stools?"

Sally closed the visor. "Go finish your breakfast. And don't forget to feed R2," she added as he ran down the hall.

While Sally picked up scattered Star Wars action figures, Henry pulled Fruit Loops out of his bowl and lined them along the edge of the trunk.

"How old is he?" Michael asked.

"Turned five June twenty-first. Diagnosed when he was three. High functioning but won't speak." The parakeet snatched the purple Fruit Loops the boy offered. "At least not to me." She dragged her attention away from Henry. "I've got a couple of stools behind the counter."

"Lead the way."

"They're wobbly, but they match." She shoved a box of Christmas lights aside with her foot, dragged out the stools. "Twenty bucks. I'll include the cookbook." She pushed the red and white checkered binder, ringed with coffee stains, across the counter. "A guy like you should know how to cook."

While Sally wrote up the sale, he browsed the glass corner cabinet. Hidden behind miniature mohair teddy bears and porcelain-faced dolls stood Barbie, decked out in a wedding gown, bow at the waist, pin-dot veil. The identical one he'd bought Meg on her seventh birthday. He'd saved money that summer cutting lawns to buy a Schwinn Sting-ray with the three-speed stick-shift in campus green, but Meg missed Dad, and Michael wanted to cheer her up.

Meg hugged him around the waist until he couldn't breathe. He'd looked at his mom for help, but she was too busy wiping tears to notice him turning blue.

Sally's reflection appeared in the mirror lining the back of the cabinet. "Do you have a daughter?" she asked, handing him the sales receipt.

"No," he said. "Can you cash a hundred?"

She handed him his change. His gaze caught on a picture of Henry in a crane stance tacked to a corkboard. Behind Henry, in the same position, Mac.

"You know Mac?"

"Doesn't everybody?" She handed him the cookbook. "Who knows? Maybe it'll give you the inspiration you're looking for."

***

Michael spent the afternoon scrubbing and scouring the kitchen. Around eight, he sat on a wobbly stool and took a bite of the pepperoni pizza he'd purchased at the Citgo station. The ball of rubbery cheese and cardboard crust lodged in his throat. He forced it down with a swig of Coke and flipped through the cookbook. Several loose pages, smudge prints, and oil stains, but the book appeared intact.

In the margin, written in faded blue ink, next to the directions on how to make meatloaf, were the words "best recipe in book." He'd cook them all and decide for himself.

Why not try something new?

He settled into his office chair. Moonlight spilled through the window, illuminating the shoebox. Mac's words came back to him. "It's home. A chance to start over."

He set the shoebox in his lap, ran his fingers over the edges, and lifted the lid. He rolled Anna's engagement ring between index finger and thumb. The diamond wasn't as bright, nor the gold as shiny, as the day he'd slid it on Anna's finger at the beach. He reached into the box and took out the frame that held his favorite picture of her. The one he'd snapped when she discovered the ring inside his sandcastle. He set the photo and the ring on the desk, pulled out his dad's dog tag, and ran his fingertip over the imprinted numbers and letters he'd memorized as a kid. RUSSO. JOHN MICHAEL 013345612. O POS. BAPTIST. He dropped the tag into the box and pulled out the blue velvet pouch with his mother's wedding band. The one Anna would have worn if…

He placed the pouch back into the box. His fingers brushed Meg's teddy bear. He ran his fingertips across its felt paws, over the rough stitching of its nose, under the smooth ribbon of silk around its neck, before sinking them into its thick curly coat.

Even now, twenty-seven years later, he can still hear her scream his name.

Chapter 6

A shrill cry startled Michael awake. "Damn rooster!" He punched his pillow, retried sleep, but the savor of last night's meatloaf lingered. His mouth watered, his stomach pleaded.

He flipped over. A searing pain pierced his low back. The consequence of hauling lumber and 50-pound bags of dry concrete mix to the barn yesterday. He forced himself out of bed, wrestled into a Chicago T-shirt and cargo shorts, and then stood by the window. The warming sky promised another sweltering day.

He swallowed two Advil with a swig of OJ and ate leftover roasted carrots and potatoes. With no TV or newspaper to command his attention, he sat on the front porch with his coffee and listened to the dawn chorus. A pleasant change from the constant grind of garbage trucks and annoying back-up beeps of delivery vans.

Mac's Jeep jounced up the drive. He parked in the weeds, cut the engine. "Brought reinforcements."

Charlie, dressed in a Nine Inch Nails T-shirt and grunge jeans, leapt out of the back, flashed a "hang loose" sign, strode toward the barn.

Henry, wearing his motorcycle helmet and karate jacket, slid out of the passenger seat, clutching an X-wing starfighter. Mac crouched in front of him, pulled off the helmet, tossed it into the Jeep. "Remember what we practiced."

Apparently, Sally knew Mac more than she'd let on. Could she be the ex? Henry, his son?

Henry approached, shadowed by Mac. With his bowl of wavy-blonde hair and wide-set eyes, no doubt Henry was Sally's son but bore no resemblance to Mac.

"Michael, this is Henry."

Henry, gaze downward, extended a limp hand.

"I met Master Luke," he replied, shaking Henry's hand. "In another galaxy."

Henry turned to Mac and displayed a series of hand gestures. Mac watched Henry tear off toward the barn. Although Mac's eyes remained soulful, a smile of contentment tempered the sadness.

"Hope you don't mind," Mac said as they followed Henry. "Sally had a few errands."

"He knows sign language?"

"I've taught him a few words."

They found Charlie inside the barn, sitting on an anchor beam, dangling her steel-toed boots. "She's Dutch," Charlie said, gesturing. "Trademark H frame. Square floor plan. Mortise-and-tenon joints. Purlins hold'n up the rafters. Don't see many of her kind outside of New York or Jersey. Timber's hand-hewn. 1850s?"

Mac hummed in agreement. "Thereabouts."

Charlie swung down, her awry shirt exposing a trail of small, waxy-white, circular scars along her spine. They weren't fresh marks, and their placement ruled out self-inflicted. What kind of monster uses a kid as an ashtray?

Either Mac didn't see the marks or already knew about them because his expression didn't change.

Mac pushed against a support post. "Need to pull floor planks. Reinforce the stone piers before we tackle the roof."

"I'll get the tools," Charlie said, skirting out the door.

"She's bright," Michael said.

"Headed to UIC in the fall to study architecture. Full scholarship."

"Her parents must be proud."

"You'd think." Mac glanced at Henry, who'd set his X-wing fighter on top of a lumber stack and stood—eyes closed, arm raised, hand stiff—as if to levitate the toy.

"Maybe he can use the force to jack up the barn," Michael said.

A smile encroached Mac's beard. "Wouldn't surprise me."

Mac constructed a fort in the corner of the barn with hay bales and used sign language to communicate with Henry. Henry saluted and crawled into the fort.

They spent the morning removing planks, patching post bottoms, and sills. Mac and Charlie worked efficiently, exchanging few words. She seemed to know what he needed before he asked.

While Mac worked, he explained the repairs and their necessity. He taught Michael how to use a power drill and a circular saw, how to hold a hammer and drive in nails.

Every so often, Mac would cup both hands, blow through the gap between thumbs, and create cooing sounds. He'd wait for Henry to mimic the sound, then return to his task.

By noon, the temperature had crept into the low nineties. Sweat dotted Henry's upper lip, trickled down Charlie's face, soaked through Michael's T-shirt; yet Mac, dressed in jeans and flannel shirt, appeared unfazed, just a slight sheen on his forehead.

Mac took Henry to the house to wash up for lunch. Michael headed to the picnic table in the shade of the maples. The weathered planks squeaked and bowed as he lay atop the table to stretch out his back. The maple leaves wilted in the heat, and the sparrows, who'd frolicked in the meadow all morning, sought refuge in the deep shade of the branches.

Michael cupped his hands to replicate Mac's cooing.

"It's a dove call." Charlie sat at the table, took a swig of water. "Mac taught him. It's their secret signal. Means all is well."

He sat up, placed his feet on the bench. "Mac says you're headed to UIC in the fall."

"If it weren't for Mac, I'd be headed to juvie." She wiped sweat from her brow with the hem of her T-shirt, revealing more waxy scars along abs.

"How do you know Henry?"

"Moved in with Sally at the shop two years ago. In exchange for rent, I take care of Henry after school."

Mac traipsed down the hill carrying a coal miner's lunch pail, Henry in tow.

"Does he ever sweat?" Michael asked, wiping forehead with crook of elbow.

Charlie guzzled water and pitched the empty bottle into the old oil drum. "Nope."

Mac unwrapped a sandwich with no crust and set it in front of Henry.

Henry lifted the bread and examined the peanut butter.

"Checking for grape jelly," Charlie explained. "Won't eat anything purple."

"Made meatloaf last night. Got leftovers if anyone's interested."

Charlie snatched the apple out of Mac's hand. "Mac won't eat anything that shits."

He tried to swipe the apple back, but she leapt out of reach. "Charlie devours anything not nailed to the table."

"Hey, a girl's gotta eat." She crunched into the apple. "Gonna head to the yard. Pick up what we'll need this afternoon. You can pay me when I get back." Mac tossed her the Jeep keys. "Later," she said before heading up the path.

"You cooked?" Mac asked.

"Sally convinced me to try." He pushed up from the table. "You want anything?"

Mac smiled at Henry, who was attempting to levitate his sandwich. "Got everything I need right here."

While Michael washed his hands in the kitchen sink, he watched Mac and Henry from the open window. Two sparrows fluttered from the maple, hopped along the table's edge, eyed Henry's untouched sandwich. A car door slammed, sending them skyward.

Sally, wearing a vintage floral sundress, pink heels, and cat-eye sunglasses, rounded the corner of the house.

Mac stood, slipped hands into back pockets.

Sally walked briskly, directly to Mac, as though intending to jump into his arms. Instead, she beat her fists against his chest. Like a mountain pelted by hail, Mac didn't flinch.

"You son of a bitch," she screamed, as if the force of words might move him.

Mac didn't respond and made no attempt to stop her assault. Feeling like a voyeur, Michael stepped away from the sink, but Sally's words sliced through the unforgiving heat.

"He's not your son. Do you hear me?"

In the wake of silence that followed, a low, steady wail surfaced.

Michael returned to the window. The sound came from Henry, who rocked on the bench, hands clasped against ears.

Sally knelt. "Oh, god, Henry. I'm sorry." When she reached for him, he jerked away. She looked at Mac and pleaded, "Do something."

Mac settled across from Henry, bowed his head. At first, he didn't appear to be doing anything, but then his smooth tenor voice rose above Henry's whimpers. By the time Mac finished singing the chorus of "Blackbird" for the third time, Henry had fallen into a trance.

Sally pushed to her feet. "Home, Henry." But Henry didn't budge. Mac removed his flannel shirt, set it on the table. Henry, clutching the shirt in one hand and his X-wing fighter in the other, slid off the bench and trailed Sally up the hill.

Mac dropped his face into his hands. His shoulders sagged as if an unbearable weight had been placed upon them. Undershirt stretched against taut muscles.

Michael walked down the path and stood behind Mac. The dove tattoo on his forearm, now fully exposed, had a broken wing. "You okay?"

Mac lifted his head and rubbed bare arms as if chilled.

"If you want to call it a day…"

He glanced at the barn. "She'll keep my mind off it."

Chapter 7

Michael stood at his office window and watched the predawn sky pale to blue gray. Mid-September and the maples blushed. The days grew shorter, the air crisper, the earth cooler. Autumn would soon color the farm.

He shut down his ThinkPad and switched off the desk lamp. Second all-nighter this week. Wasn't that he couldn't sleep. Just avoided it until his mind was too weary to dream of Anna.

He'd written a feature article on the architecture of barns in America and a special interest piece about life in rural America. Not exactly watchdog journalism, but at least he was sharpening his writing skills before tackling the injustices of the world.

And he was content with his initial efforts. Bernstein started out as a copy boy at the Washington Star, and Woodward was initially turned down by the Washington Post for his lack of journalism experience. Everyone had to begin somewhere.

In the kitchen, Michael added a dash of cayenne to the Hollandaise sauce while eggs sizzled in bacon grease.

Teaching himself to cook became a gratifying distraction. Kept his mind from wandering to Anna.

Sunday nights, Jane would visit, bring a bottle of Chardonnay. They'd demolish the wine while cooking whatever dish Michael chose. Jane and Anna developed a friendship after Michael had introduced them, but Jane wasn't one to interfere. He didn't know what Anna had told her about their breakup, but Jane never broached the subject. She was too busy lifting his spirits.

Michael polished off the Eggs Benedict, filled his Thermos with coffee, then laced up his Timberlands and ambled toward the barn. Over the last two months, he and Mac had secured support posts and anchor beams, replaced damaged boards in the loft. She was far from finished but stood a bit taller, leaner, prouder.

Restoring the barn proved cathartic. Kept hands busy and thoughts focused. Mac helped Tuesday and Thursday mornings, Saturday afternoons. They talked about everything from carpentry to cooking, yet Mac never discussed his relationship with Sally or Henry. Michael didn't press. Though curious, it wasn't his business.

Michael rolled open the barn door. The smell of fresh-cut wood greeted him. A thick layer of fine sawdust covered the floor. In the corner, a stack of plywood waiting to be cut to size. He tugged on work gloves and grabbed a tape measure.

While the saw blade bit through its third piece of plywood, Harvey appeared wearing his "I Like How the Earth Spins. It Really Makes My Day!" T-shirt.

"Expecting a flood?" Harvey screamed over the high-pitched whir of the saw.

Michael finished his cut, switched off the power. "What?"

"Noah? The ark?"

"Why aren't you at work?"

"Feeling under the weather, man." When Michael didn't laugh, Harvey said, "A weatherman, feeling under—"

"You never get sick."

"It's a mental health thing. Thought I'd take the day off. Stop by. See if you're done playing Bob the Builder."

"Could you hand me the square?"

Harvey stared at the tools on the floor. "I don't see a square."

"That metal thing, shaped like an 'L'."

"Then why's it called a square?" He handed it to Michael. "You throw out your razor, Mikey?"

"Don't like the beard?"

"It ages you." He rocked on his feet. "Got a date this weekend. She has a friend…"

"Thanks, but not ready." He scooped his Thermos off the floor. "How's *News at Noon*?"

"They hired a new anchor. Harper Rose. Blond with a southern accent."

"You don't like her?"

Harvey shrugged. "She doesn't get my jokes."

"Some people have no sense of humor."

"Speaking of which," he said. "That doctor you stole Anna from. The head of neurology at Providence."

"Duncan Kelly?"

"Saw them together at Denali's. They looked…cozy."

He shuffled his boot through the layer of sawdust. He'd been attempting to patch the gaping hole Anna left in his chest, without much success, while she, evidently, had moved on. With her wealthy, Irish-Catholic ex-fiancé, no less. He swallowed a mouthful of bitter coffee.

"Sorry, Mike. Thought you should know."

***

That afternoon, while Michael repaired a section of fieldstone wall, Anna wandered down the path in boot-cut
jeans. A light breeze ruffled her blouse and swept coils of
hair across her face. Her eyes were softer, freckles darker,
jut of chin more rounded than he remembered. He yearned
to tell her how beautiful she was, how much he'd missed
her, how empty he felt without her. Pride wrestled with his
heart and won. He dumped a bag of concrete mix into the
wheelbarrow.

"Hope you don't mind me stopping by," she said,
tucking a curl behind her ear. "I would have called first,
but..." She turned and gazed at the second-story window.
"Jane said you bought the farm."

He dug a trough through the mix with his shovel,
added a bucket of water.

"You're growing a beard."

"If you came to tell me about Duncan—"

"I'm pregnant."

He shook his head as if he'd misheard. "That's not
possible." His gaze darted to the ground and then back to
her face. "The chances of getting pregnant while taking the
pill..."

Her eyes went wide, her body rigid. "You think I
stopped taking them? So I could get pregnant?"

"I didn't say that."

"You didn't have to." She spun on her heels.
"You're an ass."

"Wait." He chased after her. "Where are you
going?"

"As far from you as I can."

"What are we going to do about it?"

She swung around. The anger in her eyes halted him in his tracks. *"IT?"*

"That's not what I—"

"For Christ's sake, Michael. Grow up."

He lowered his gaze.

"Oh, my god." Her tone changed to disbelief. "An abortion?"

"Don't assume—"

"You selfish son of a bitch." She glared through steely-blue eyes. "Well, guess what, Michael. It doesn't matter what you want. Because it's not your choice. Or my parents'. It's mine. I want this baby. We don't need your approval or support. And we certainly don't need you."

***

Michael lay on his mattress and stared at emptiness. Dark clouds stole the moon. Thunder rumbled. Scent of rain.

After Anna stomped off, he'd tried to focus on repairing the wall, but her words buzzed, angry bees in his ears. The cement thickened in the wheelbarrow, and the shovel broke. He slammed the barn door on his fingers, burned his dinner omelet, and then went to bed with swollen knuckles and an empty stomach in search of mind-numbing sleep.

He closed his eyes and concentrated on breathing. The inhale of cool air, exhale of warm. His thoughts would not settle. They clanged around his head like heavy wind chimes. He flipped over, kicked off the covers, and drove his face into the pillow.

Sleep arrived. The nightmare followed.

He faced a forest of towering pines. Evergreens so dense no moonlight penetrated their needle-laden branches. Behind him, a wall of black churning clouds bore down. He slipped between two trees. Damp moss and wet bark hung heavy. Darkness deepened.

The cries of a baby echoed the woods.

He sprinted blindly. Mangled branches clawed at his face and arms. His chest burned, and his legs caught fire. He stopped, doubled over, forced air into his lungs.

He spotted a clearing. Moonlight filtered through branches and cascaded toward the forest floor. He staggered forward. Blood trickled from a forehead cut. Sweat stung eyes. Icy pins pricked his feet.

Stumbling into the light, he dropped to his knees, focused on the tiny naked form lying face down on a pile of leaves. He slid his hands beneath the baby, turned her over in his arms.

Death stared with vacant eyes.

***

Michael sat on the back porch, clutching Meg's teddy bear. The rising sun evaporated the remnants of his nightmare along with lingering fog. He'd lived on the farm two months and, although he'd felt lonely, he'd never felt so...alone.

As if on cue, Mac lumbered around the side of the house; beard trimmed, hair slicked in a ponytail. He sat next to Michael, glimpsed the teddy bear, but said nothing, as if completely normal for a forty-year-old man to cradle a stuffed animal.

"Won't be able to help with the barn this morning. Something I need to attend to. I'll come back this afternoon." He studied Michael's face. "Feeling all right?"

"Didn't sleep." He fingered the ribbon around the bear's neck. "Ever been afraid to let go of something?"

"Sure."

"And you found a way? To let go?"

"Of the something? Or the fear?" Mac toyed with his ring and squinted into the sun. "Remember learning to ride a bike? The panic when the bike wobbled?"

He nodded. "Terrified I would crash."

"Or afraid of the pain that'd follow?" Mac scanned the yard until his gaze fell on the rusted swing set. "Do you recall the moment your dad let go of the bike and you were riding all by yourself?"

"The irrepressible grin."

"The swell of pride."

"I'd conquered the world." He gave Mac a fleeting smile and dug his fingers into the bear's curly coat. "It's more complicated."

"Is it?"

Mac stood, then disappeared from where he'd come, leaving Michael staring into the glass eyes of a teddy bear.

Chapter 8

Michael's hunch was correct. Anna's Audi was parked in her parents' drive. He bolted up the walkway, pounded on the door, and then hesitated over what he'd say to Grace or Colin if they confronted him. Had Anna informed them how he'd reacted? He shoved his hands into his pockets, stepped back.

The door swung open. Anna stood in the entry, hair in a messy knot, blotchy pale skin, red-rimmed lids. His heart sank at the anguish in her eyes. He'd rehearsed how to confront anger, not devastation.

She sniffled and tightened her robe belt. "Why are you here?"

"Umm…I came to apologize for…"

She bit into her swollen lip.

"God, Anna. You're a mess."

"If that's an apology, you're more of an ass than I thought."

"Yes—No! I mean no, that's not an apology. Yes, I'm an ass."

"We agree on something."

A strained silence settled. He peeked over her shoulder. "Where're your parents?"

"If you came to interrogate them, you're too late. They left for Ireland yesterday."

He shifted his weight, regrouped. "What I said yesterday. I was wrong."

"Always about you."

"Please, Anna." He took a bold step forward. "I need to tell you—"

"You've already said enough." The door swung toward his face.

He stuck his foot in the doorway. "Give me a chance to explain."

Her skin turned papery white. She gripped the door frame.

"Are you feeling—"

She clamped her hand over her mouth and fled inside. He followed her into the bathroom. Kneeling in front of the toilet, she pitched forward. He pulled her hair away from her face and rubbed her back while she puked. She slipped her hand into her robe and cradled her belly as if protecting the life inside.

Reality struck like an oncoming train. There was so much more at stake than his fear.

Anna sank back on her heels. Sweat slicked forehead and blush-colored cheeks.

"You okay? Is the baby—"

"She's fine." Anna wiped her mouth with the back of her hand. "Morning sickness."

He grabbed a Kleenex box off the counter. "Always this bad?"

"Sometimes worse. Dr. Kellan said it'd subside in a few weeks." She pulled out a tissue and blew her nose. "You've done this before."

"My mom. Chemo."

She wove the robe belt around her fingers. "You wanted to talk?"

"About Meg. Never told you the entire story."

"Let me get cleaned up."

While Anna showered, he studied pictures of her arranged meticulously in the upstairs hall. A toddler with a pretentious pout, a kindergartner with a toothless grin, a teenager with an awkward smile. Near her bedroom, a series of black and whites of Anna and her dad at the beach, building a sandcastle, searching for seashells, chasing seagulls. There was a spark in Colin's eyes as he watched Anna jump the waves. As if she were the moon that controlled the tide.

At the end of the hall hung a crayon drawing of a unicorn playing under a rainbow, Anna's name printed in block letters in the lower right-hand corner. The paper, which appeared to have been torn into strips and then pieced back together with Scotch tape, was protected behind an ornate frame as if a Rembrandt.

Anna emerged from the bathroom. Soft pink sweater, dark denim jeans. The heat of the shower left skin flushed and hair damp. The scent of lilac pulled him a step closer.

"I wonder," he said, when she met his gaze, "if our child will be as passionate and beautiful as her mother."

A whisper of that smile.

"Let's go for a walk," she said. "Get some fresh air."

The wind rustled the trees and skittered leaves along the street as they strolled in silence. Despite the nippy air, the sun warmed his face. He wanted to reach for Anna's hand, intertwine their fingers, but he'd lost that privilege.

At the neighborhood park, he led Anna over to the bench in an area designated a wildflower preserve. A breeze rippled ornamental grass tufts and stirred a sweet, earthy scent. He stood at the edge of the pathway, thoughts drifting to memory.

"I was thirteen when my dad left for his final tour. While he packed, we had a father-son chat. He told me I was old enough to take care of Meg until Mom came home from work. Said it was my job to watch over her, keep her safe."

He picked a pink coneflower and settled next to Anna. "We'd recently moved to Evanston. There weren't any kids Meg's age living in our neighborhood, so she always wanted to hang with me. Being shadowed by a seven-year-old didn't impress my new friends.

"One day after school, Jimmy Snyder came over and asked if I wanted to see the tree house he'd found. Made it clear my sister wasn't invited. Meg was in the living room, wearing her Sleeping Beauty Halloween costume, watching *Lassie*. Told her I had to run an errand. That I wouldn't be long."

He peeled a leaf from the coneflower's stem, rolled it between his thumb and forefinger. "Jimmy and I followed a dirt path through the woods. The tree house was wedged in the limbs of an old oak. Wasn't much. Several pieces of plywood held together by screws. We climbed two-by-fours nailed to the trunk, crawled along a thick branch about fifteen feet from the ground, pulled ourselves into the clubhouse through a hole in the floor.

"We were discussing how to rebuild it when I heard Meg call my name. She'd followed us. Jimmy taunted her. Meg pouted. Should've made him stop, but I was angry. Told her she was a baby for crying. For carrying that stupid teddy bear around and dressing as a lame princess. I yelled at her to go home."

He tore a flower petal and let it fall. "Meg wouldn't speak to anyone that night. I felt like the worst brother on the planet. After school the next day, she asked me to play hide-and-seek. Figured she'd forgiven me. Counted to one hundred, searched the house, but couldn't find her. The door to the backyard stood open. When I found her Sleeping Beauty costume stuffed in the trash can and her teddy bear abandoned on the steps, I knew where she'd gone."

"The tree house," Anna whispered.

He stripped the flower of the remaining petals and twirled the prickly seed cone. "Sprinted through the woods barefoot on pure adrenaline. Meg was standing on the branch, trying to reach the hole in the floor. I called out to her. She glanced down at me, lost her balance. Screamed my name as her feet slipped from the limb.

"I scrambled to her, brushed leaves from her face. She seemed so peaceful, I was afraid to touch her. Then her lids fluttered open. She coughed and winced. Said her head hurt. Blood trickled from her ear.

"I tried not to panic. Didn't want to scare her. Told her I needed to go for help, but she begged me not to leave. I slipped my arms underneath her, pulled her into my lap. She shook. Her skin turned chalky white, her lips blue. She told me she was cold, so I took off my sweatshirt and covered her. 'Promise me,' she said, 'you won't let go of me.' I held onto her tighter. 'Never. I swear.'

"She stared through the canopy at the blue sky and asked, 'Are you afraid of anything?' Then she closed her eyes. Never opened them again.

"I sat on the hard ground, shirtless and barefoot, clutching onto Meg. It was so cold that day. The kind of biting cold that freezes the breath in your lungs. Pricks your skin till it burns."

He twisted the stem around his fingers until it snapped, then let it tumble to the ground. "By the time the police found us, the sky had turned twilight. They pried Meg from my arms. I broke my promise. I let go."

Anna reached for his hand, but he stiffened and pulled away. He didn't want her pity and didn't deserve her compassion. If she touched him, if he looked at her, he'd never be able to tell the rest.

"When Dad came home for Meg's funeral, he hardly spoke. Mom locked herself in her bedroom for hours at a time. Dad went out at night. Got drunk. Passed out on the couch. One night, he didn't return. Headed back to Vietnam before his leave was up. Two days later, he stepped on a land mine."

He stared down at the broken flower, stripped of its petals. "If I hadn't said those awful things to Meg, she'd still be alive. Dad would have finished his final tour. Mom wouldn't have had to live through the pain of losing a child and a husband. Wouldn't have given in to the cancer."

Anna wiped her wet cheeks with her palm. "Michael. You can't believe that to be true."

"Fatherhood frightens me, Anna. Being responsible for another life?" He met her gaze. "Can you promise I can keep her safe and out of harm's way?"

"Truth is," she said, placing her hand over the gentle rise of her belly. "I can't."

***

As Michael and Anna walked the farm, he shared memories of Meg. How she'd cross her eyes while she sucked in a spaghetti noodle and got sauce all over her face.

The week she marched around the house in her new pink rain boots, refusing to take them off, even when she slept. The day she'd made an "ant crossing" sign and roped off an area in front of the house to protect a colony who'd built their home in the cracks of the sidewalk. He even managed a laugh.

He promised Anna he'd see a therapist. She stopped at the entrance to the barn, turned, and kissed him. "Even an ass," she said, leading him to the loft, "deserves a second chance."

***

Sunlight streamed through the loft window, highlighting the soft hair on Anna's neck. He ran his hands down her bare back, worried about how pregnancy would change their relationship, intimacy, sex.

And the cost of raising a child? Diapers, childcare, braces, college. He'd have to get a job. Delay his journalism aspirations.

Fatherhood? He'd never raised a puppy, let alone a baby.

Anna tugged the quilt over her shoulders. "How'd this get here?"

"Come up here when I can't sleep."

She snuggled into his side. Hummed against his neck. "What is it about this barn?"

"Mac says she's full of secrets."

"Mac?"

"Guy who's helping me with the restoration." The swallow swooped into the loft, hunkered down on her eggs.

"You know," she said, "it's possible she was conceived in this barn."

67

"As long as she's not born in a barn." He turned to face her. "How do you know she's a she?"

"Woman's intuition."

"What did your parents say?"

"Haven't told them."

He cupped the curve of her hip in his hand. "Let me tell them."

"My dad might grab a shotgun and force you to marry me."

"Do they allow firearms inside a Catholic Church?"

The blue of her eyes brightened. "You'll marry me at Divine Child?"

"If that's what it takes."

She peeked up at him through long lashes. "And promise to raise her in the Catholic faith?"

"I'd rather that choice be hers, but as long as she's not brainwashed into becoming a nun."

"Would it be so bad if she became the next Mother Teresa?"

"I was leaning toward Gandhi or Mandela."

Anna's stomach rumbled. "Our little human rights activist is trying to tell us she's hungry."

"Fried chicken and potato salad in the fridge."

"Colonel Sanders?"

"Chef Russo. Made from scratch."

"When did you become Julia Child?"

"Been teaching myself."

"This I've got to see."

She wrapped the quilt around her body, tucked it under her arms, and climbed down the ladder. Mac's throaty chuckle echoed the rafters.

Michael zipped his Levi's, peered over the edge.

Anna tightened her grip on the quilt and backed up against the stall.

Mac studied Anna as if she'd just hatched.

Her eyes went wide. "Frank Mackenzie?"

"Anna O'Leary." He glanced up at Michael, a smirk on his face. "So you're the Irish lass Michael's been pining for."

Michael clambered down the ladder. "You know each other?"

"Frank and I graduated from Divine Child the same year. Daddy mentored him when he became a member of the parish. Last I heard, he'd been accepted to Sacred Heart Seminary."

"And you were headed to law school," Mac said. "How are Colin and Grace?"

"They're—"

"Seminary?" Michael stared at Mac. "A priest?"

Mac dropped his gaze, shuffled his boot in sawdust. "Have a small parish in town."

"The Catholic church on Main?" He shook his head. "Thought you restored barns?"

"A passion of mine."

"But I told you I was an atheist."

"Guys," Anna said, pushing past them. "I need to use the bathroom. Can we discuss this up at the house?"

"You don't fit my image of a priest," Michael said as they followed Anna through the back door.

"What's that look like?"

"Effeminate, feeble, gray hair. Black shirt, white collar, sensible shoes." He set the leftover fried chicken and potato salad on the island. "You're not going to try to convince me there's a God, are you?"

"As long as you don't try to convince me there's not."

"Deal."

"Sorry for misleading you. Being a priest can get lonely. I needed a friend. Sounds selfish."

"Not really." He cracked open a Coke and handed it to Mac. "So you and Sally aren't...weren't—"

"Married?" He sipped. "No."

"And the ring?"

"To remind myself I'm married to the church."

"Then Henry isn't—"

Anna walked into the kitchen wearing his Speed Racer pajama bottoms and an undershirt, sat on a stool, and bit into a chicken wing. "Oh...my...God," she said, sucking the grease from her fingers. "I'm marrying a man who can cook."

"You're engaged?" Mac asked. "Congratulations! When's the date?"

"Depends on Anna's work schedule."

"Guess being an attorney keeps you busy," Mac said to Anna, who'd just sunk her teeth into a chicken thigh.

"Anna quit her job as district attorney. She runs a foundation for victims of domestic violence."

Anna gripped the counter. Her face paled. "Excuse me—" She fled the kitchen.

Mac scratched his beard. "How far along?"

"How'd you know?"

He patted Michael's shoulder. "Go take care of her. We'll work on the barn later."

Michael found Anna lying in the fetal position on his mattress. He sat on the floor and brushed his fingers against her forearm. "Bad?"

"Don't think she likes your fried chicken." Color rushed into her pale cheeks. "Can't believe I was half-naked in front of Frank Mackenzie."

"Small world," he muttered. "What was he like in high school?"

"Quiet, shy. Didn't socialize much. 'An old soul' Daddy would say." She sat up, hugged her legs, set her chin on her knees. "Grew up on his grandparents' farm. Moved to the city to live with his uncle after his mom died. Never talked about his dad. Everyone knew he wanted to be a priest. Didn't keep the girls from trying to change his mind. Has those eyes…"

She straightened her back. "Of course, he didn't have long hair. Or the beard," she said, pulling his whiskers.

"Don't like it?"

"Makes you look—"

"Old."

"I was going to say more handsome, but now that you mention it."

Oh, that smile. "I promise," he said, resting his forehead against hers. "I'll shave before our wedding."

Chapter 9

Michael breezed through the first ten questions of his pre-marriage inventory and then glanced at Anna. She sat next to him at the kitchen island — dressed in panties and one of his undershirts — biting the eraser end of a pencil, focusing on her page.

She'd been living at the farm for a week but hadn't moved her belongings. She wanted to wait until they told her parents. Everything.

The previous night, she'd arranged their first consultation with Father Mulcahy. A couple he was counseling had delayed their nuptials, so the church was available November 25th, Thanksgiving weekend.

Michael brushed his fingertips up the inside of Anna's thigh.

She smacked his hand. "I know what you're doing."

"What?" he replied, feigning innocence.

"Distracting me so you can copy my answers."

"This is easy. Why would I cheat?" The next questions dealt with family issues. *I am concerned that in-laws may interfere in our marriage.* A chuckle escaped. "I'm going to ace this bad boy," he muttered, darkening the agree circle. Sex and intimacy. *I am comfortable being naked around my future spouse.*

"What?" Anna asked when she caught him flexing his pecs.

"I didn't say anything." Next question. *Do you suspect your future spouse has had homosexual thoughts?* And the follow-up. *I am concerned that homosexual feelings or behaviors could have a negative impact on our marriage relationship.* "What kind of inventory is this?"

Anna exhaled an exaggerated breath.

"Sorry." *My future spouse and I have agreed that we will not have children.* "Little late for that," he mumbled. *We have discussed the expectations each of us have as to our roles as husband and wife.* "What did you put for number 54?"

"Father Mulcahy told us not to discuss our answers."

"Oh, right." He skipped that question. *Certain behaviors or habits in my future spouse annoy me.* This'll be good.

He leaned back, stretched, peered over Anna's shoulder.

She draped her arms over her paper. "You're cheating."

"No, I'm not."

She quirked her eyebrow.

"Okay. I'm cheating. I just…don't want to fail."

"It's not a test. You don't get a grade."

That doesn't mean he wouldn't fail. He slumped over the counter and read through the finance questions. They hadn't discussed finances. Anna had her job, a company car, health insurance, a retirement plan. He'd checked into acquiring COBRA insurance after he'd quit, but the premium seemed excessive, and he was healthy, so he passed. He'd liquidated most of his assets to buy the farm, and the balance in his 401K was dismal.

"Shit!" Anna jumped off her stool. "We're supposed to meet my parents for dinner in an hour." She dashed for the stairs.

He glanced at her page. Found number 55. *There are certain behaviors or —*

Anna swiped her inventory off the island. "Nice try, Ace."

"I've been thinking," he said, following her into the bedroom, "about getting an actual job."

She pulled a blue satin dress out of her garment bag. "Thought you wanted to be an investigative journalist."

He sat on the mattress. "With the baby coming, maybe I need something more stable."

"Give it time." She slipped the dress over her head. "Once you publish a few articles, you'll find your stride."

"If I got a job, I could get health insurance. Rebuild my portfolio. Save for college."

"College?" She plopped onto the bed and slipped into heels. "She isn't born yet, and you're worried about college?"

"She'll need a degree to find a cure for cancer or a solution to global warming."

"Get dressed," she said, heading for the door.

He dumped the contents of his laundry basket on the bed and searched for an undershirt.

"After we're married," Anna called from the bathroom, "I'll add you to my insurance. You can focus on your writing while you watch her."

He furrowed his brow. "Like Mr. Mom?"

"No." She returned to the bedroom, plucked an undershirt out of the pile and held it up. "Like a dad."

***

Anna thought that dropping the bomb on her parents at Luca's, their favorite Italian restaurant, might soften the blow. There's no way, she claimed, they'd explode in front of all those people. He explained the circumstances to Mac that morning as they worked on the barn. Mac advised to wear a Kevlar vest, in case.

"Promise," Anna said, pushing the wide end of his tie through the loop as the elevator ascended, "to be on your best behavior."

He pressed his index and middle fingers together and held them up. "Scout's honor."

She yanked his tie to form the knot. "Never a Boy Scout were you, Ace?"

"Would you believe Cub Scout?"

She tugged his collar and tightened his tie. A bit too much.

His neck veins pulsed. "Tiger Scout?"

The elevator chimed.

"Saved by the bell," he choked out, then caught up to Anna at the reservation desk.

A pageboy blonde wearing a fitted black suit and a familiar smile greeted Anna. "Ms. O'Leary. Your parents are seated in the back."

They followed the hostess around a two-story mirrored bar, through a set of towering marble pillars, past several tables crowded with crystal and silver. Clinking glasses and clattering plates punctuated muffled conversations. The aroma of warm bread and sweet tomato sauce mingled.

As they approached the O'Leary's table, a flash of disbelief registered on Grace's stoic face.

Michael captured Anna's arm. "You didn't tell them I was coming?"

"Didn't want to give them time to prepare."

"Might've been a good idea to share."

"Aine." Grace held out her hands. Colin stood.

Anna slid her hands into her mother's, air-kissed her cheeks. "Mother."

"That dress doesn't do much for your color, dear. Or your figure."

"Grace." Michael bent to kiss her cheek. "As always, a pleasure."

"Michael," she replied. "You appear…healthy."

Anna wrapped her arms around Colin. "Hey, Daddy."

He returned her hug and kissed the top of her head. "How's my girl?"

"I'm good."

"Michael." Colin shook Michael's outstretched hand. "Anna didn't say you'd be joining us."

Grace postured. "We assumed, when she asked Colin to make reservations for four, she'd be bringing Dun—"

"The view is stunning," Anna said, glancing out the oversized windows at Lake Michigan.

Colin ordered a bottle of Cabernet. While the waiter filled their glasses, Michael rehearsed the lines Mac helped him prepare. Once the waiter retreated, Michael reached for Anna's hand. "Colin. Grace. Anna and I are getting married."

Grace blinked. Colin's gaze shifted from Michael to Anna. Their expressions showed no surprise, so he forged ahead. "I realize we don't see eye to eye on what's best for

Anna, but we were meant for each other." He and Mac admitted that last part was cliché, but were hard pressed to come up with an alternative. "To make peace, I've agreed to wed Anna at Divine Child."

Grace sipped her wine and picked up her menu. "I'm thinking the Australian Black Truffles."

"Mother." Anna spoke in a loud whisper. "Did you hear what Michael said?"

"I'm done listening to what Michael wants."

Anna plucked the menu from Grace's hand. "Then listen to what I want."

"Order the duck. It's what you always want."

"Stop telling me what I want."

"Fine." Grace shrugged. "Don't order the duck."

Anna stood and threw her napkin on the table. "What I want, mother, is to marry Michael and raise our child on the farm. If you want to be part of our lives, you'll accept that."

Grace stared wide-eyed at her daughter. Anna stared back, unblinking. The muffled conversations faded. The clinking and clanking of dinnerware ceased. A couple at the next table shifted their gaze between Anna and Grace as though watching a chess match.

Colin slapped his hand against his chest.

"Anna," Michael said.

She didn't move.

"Anna." He tugged on her arm. "Anna—"

She swung her anger in his direction. "What?"

"Your father."

Anna and Grace turned their heads toward Colin.

He clutched his heart. "You're pregnant?"

Tears spilled over Anna's lashes. "Sorry, Daddy. Didn't mean for you to find out that way."

Colin's eyes turned glassy. His gaze swept the room. "I'm going to be a grandpa!"

Several of the wait staff and patrons nearby clapped. Colin couldn't wipe the grin off his face if he tried. Grace remained cordial throughout the evening.

After goodbyes, Anna and Michael waited for the valet. He unknotted his tie and hummed a tune.

"Why so chipper, Ace?"

He patted his chest. "No bullet holes."

"Don't celebrate yet. Mother doesn't give in that easy."

"I'm well aware of that fact. Not why I'm celebrating."

"What's up?"

"Just earned my first merit badge."

***

Anna and Grace spent October planning the wedding, while Michael worked on the house. He'd hired a handyman to replace the leaky pipes, update the electrical system, and repair the boiler. He and Mac fixed the front porch, removed the shutters, and patched the roof. Jane and Rita pulled out dead shrubs and planted pink peony tubers that would create an ornamental hedge around the perimeter of the house next summer. Harvey helped move Anna's couch, TV, dresser, and bed frame to the farm. It wasn't perfect, but the house was becoming their home.

Since Anna wanted to convert the spare bedroom into a nursery, Michael set up his office in the living room with his desk facing the window overlooking the backyard. Grace volunteered to help Anna decorate the nursery. Michael volunteered to stay out of their way and occupied himself in the barn while they debated primary or pastel.

Mac taught him how to build a cradle using the original white pine barn siding. While Michael fine-sanded slats, a dove cooed from the rafters. Mac cupped his hands, answered the call.

"How's Henry?"

"Busy. Between school and therapy, haven't seen much of him." He handed Michael a piece of fine-grit paper. "Written your vows yet?"

"Struggling with that."

"You're a writer."

"If only it were that easy."

Mac ran his fingertips over the rail. "A coat of linseed oil and a few layers of varnish, and she'll be ready for occupancy."

"Don't be rushing things, Mac. Got five months to figure out the whole fatherhood thing."

"Worried?"

"What if I make mistakes?"

"You fix 'em."

"Not talking about putting her diaper on backwards or her shoes on the wrong feet." He set down the crib and stared into the loft. "What if she gets sick? Or hurt?"

Mac stood. "I'm going to check the shingles. Make sure they're bonding. They don't set right, you'll have all kinds of issues down the road." He hesitated long enough for Michael to catch the invitation in his eyes.

Mac inspected the roof, pressing on shingles with his boot. A satisfied hum rattled in his throat. He sat on the edge of the roof and dangled his feet. Michael settled next to him.

The late afternoon sun washed the tops of the maples in vibrant oranges and bathed the meadow in warm yellows. A breeze flittered the leaves of the giant poplars. Clouds snailed across the brilliant blue sky. The deep vibrating purr of Hank's old John Deere provided a soundtrack.

"Farming is grueling work," Mac commented, as they watched Hank's tractor inch across the field, churning up rows of fresh, brown dirt. "A farmer can spend countless hours preparing the earth, planting seed, fertilizing soil, tending sprouts, ridding the fields of weeds and pests, but he never knows the weather. An entire crop gone in the blink of an eye. Yet he still sows. Season after season."

Hank's tractor sputtered and stalled. A cloud drifted over the sun, casting them in shadow. The wind held its breath, and the trees stood stock still. The Earth grew silent. Then the old John Deere roared back to life, and the world continued.

"Knowing does not create faith, Michael. Not knowing does."

***

An electric blue November sky backdropped coppery oaks and crimson maples crowning the hilltop. The mercury clung to fifty, and the smoky aroma of burning leaves tempered the tang of rotting crab apples.

Michael swigged from his water bottle and inspected Hank's pasture. The noonday sun had evaporated the last of the dew, and manure piles dotted the landscape like giant gopher mounds.

Mac hoisted a bucket of cow manure onto the tractor-trailer as if it were weightless. They'd been shoveling shit for three hours, yet he showed no fatigue.

"You neglected to tell me when we made our pact," Michael said, wiping dung from his muck boot in the grass, "how grueling this would be."

"Understanding requires experience."

"Would've taken your word for it. How'd you get this gig anyway?"

"A few of my parishioners can't afford veterinary care for their pets. In exchange for his services, I help around the farm." Mac pitched his shovel blade under a fresh pile. "He tends my flock. I look after his herd."

A dozen black-capped chickadees skimmed the field, perched on the low rung of the split-rail fence. "Storm's comin'," Mac said.

There wasn't a cloud in sight, and no rain in the forecast, but Michael had stopped trying to figure how Mac knew things. He nodded and replied, "Better get a move on."

Mac placed an empty bucket in front of Michael and sang the first verse of "With a Little Help From My Friends." Michael sang backup the best he could.

By the time they crested the hill, they'd filled twenty-five buckets, the rolling green pasture now pristine and landmine free. Sunlight filtered through the trees, casting dappled shadows. The breeze stirred the earthy scent of meadow grass. Michael hummed in satisfaction.

Mac came from behind, set his hand on Michael's shoulder. He inhaled deeply and scanned the field. "Another thing you have to experience to understand."

Hank opened the gate, ushered in the herd. A Guernsey lifted her tail and christened their clean carpet of grass.

"However short-lived," Michael muttered.

Mac's Renegade bounded up the hill. Charlie had come home for the weekend and borrowed Mac's Jeep. She skidded to a stop, engaged the parking brake, and ran toward them. "Henry's missing." Her gaze swung from Michael to Mac. "Ed's back."

Chapter 10

Mac floored the Jeep, spraying grass and dirt skyward. Tires chewed earth. Michael gripped the passenger seat, and Charlie held fast to the roll bar. Mac curled his fingers around the steering wheel, squeezed his knuckles white. He sat rigid, eyes fixated on the horizon.

The wind shifted, swaying pines. In the distance, lead-bellied clouds gathered the scent of rain.

Mac screeched the Jeep to a halt in front of Sally's. Charlie dashed toward the park. Michael and Mac raced to the front door.

The shop looked like the epicenter of an earthquake. Overturned bookshelves. Shattered china. Smashed display cases. A mechanical voice sounded from the rubble. "If you'd like to make a call, please hang up and dial again."

Glass crunched under Mac's boots. He stepped over a one-armed mannequin, pushed aside an upended dresser, and waded through a minefield of jumbled Christmas clutter. Michael followed through the beaded drape.

Sally, dressed in a red halter dress with white polka dots, hunched in a corner, clutching a red shoe with a broken heel. Mac knelt, lifted her chin. Rivers of mascara muddied her face. An angry welt marred her cheek. She looked at Mac with red-rimmed eyes.

"It's okay," he said, catching a tear on his thumb. "I'm here."

"Ed—"

"Gone." He gently pried the shoe from her hand, examined the finger-shaped bruises on her wrists. "Where's Henry?"

"He took off when…" Her chin trembled.

Charlie burst into the room. She bent over, hands on knees, sucked in a breath. "Water tower."

"Oh, god." Sally staggered to her feet.

"Stay here," Mac said. "I'll bring him home."

Mac slammed his hands against the metal bar of the emergency exit. A gust caught the door, flung it against the building. He sprinted into the alley, Charlie and Michael at his heels.

Dirt and debris sprayed Michael, momentarily blinding him. He dodged a toppled garbage can rolling into his path. A plastic grocery bag kite-sailed, snagged on a branch. Church tower bells clanged the six o'clock hour. Call to prayer.

A crowd had gathered around the 160-foot goliath, a towering sentinel protecting East Haven. They stared up, mouths agape. Henry paced the metal walkway, flapping his hands. The wind ruffled his hair, battered the belt of his karate jacket. In the distance, lightning streaked. Thunder snarled.

Mac shouldered through the throng, scaled the access ladder. Michael started after him. Charlie grabbed his arm. "You could make it worse."

Mac dashed up the grated stairs two at a time.

"How'd you find him?" Michael asked.

"Henry climbs trees to watch birds. Lately, he's been obsessed with migrating geese. Figured he'd try and find a way to get close to them."

As if summoned, a flock of geese skirted above the tops of the elms, winging away from the approaching storm.

Henry watched the birds, then climbed the first rung of the safety rail, leaned forward, arms spread.

Comments rose from the crowd.

"He thinks he can fly."

"What if he jumps?"

"I can't watch."

Mac stepped onto the walkway, crouched next to Henry. He took off his flannel shirt, held it out. Henry craned his neck toward the receding flock, then stepped down from the rail, took the shirt, and held it against his face. Mac pivoted on the balls of his feet, turned his back to Henry, who wrapped his arms around Mac's neck. Carrying Henry piggyback, Mac descended the stairs.

A collective sigh emanated from the crowd. Lightning split the sky, scattering them.

Michael, Mac, Henry, and Charlie took shelter under the awning of Roxy's Diner. Hail pelted the canvas, bounced off concrete like popping corn.

Goosebumps prickled Michael's skin, raising the hair on his forearms. A chill settled into his bones. Temperature must have plummeted twenty degrees.

Within minutes, the hail morphed into a cold, driving rain. Henry slid off Mac's back. "Charlie," Mac said. "Could you —"

"Come on, squirt," Charlie said, opening the door to Roxy's. "It's French Fry Friday."

Henry trailed Charlie into the diner, clutching Mac's shirt.

Mac's hands trembled; his complexion pallid, ghost-like.

"You okay, Mac?"

"Will be." His gaze wandered up the street toward Sally's. "You have questions—"

"That don't require answers. But I do need coffee." He rubbed his arms and scraped mud off his muck boots onto the cement. "Don't think Roxy will appreciate the smell or the mess."

"Head to my place. Fresh beans in the Mason jar above the fridge, next to the grinder. Pot's on the counter. I've gotta check on Sally." He glanced at the swollen clouds and ran into the downpour.

"Mac!"

Mac turned. Rain streamed off the tip of his nose, his beard; plastered undershirt against his chest. "Behind the church. Door's unlocked," he hollered, then disappeared into the alley.

At 6:40, the rain subsided. Michael walked to St. Columbia, passed through wrought-iron gates, wandered along a wet cobblestone walkway under a canopy of drippy oaks until a quaint white stucco cottage appeared. A fieldstone chimney rose from a slate roof covered in soft-green moss.

A flower garden, weathered by autumn, surrounded the house. Withered vines clung to statues of saints. Bird feeders hung from barren fruit trees. Dried sunflower heads drooped on wilted stalks.

He climbed the stone steps toward an arched plank door. Nailed above the entry, a brass crucifix. Under Jesus' watchful gaze, he stepped into the entry.

A plastic bird poked out the trapdoor of a carved wooden clock with cast-iron pinecone weights, cuckooed. Seven times. He removed his muck boots and stood, sock-footed, on cold tile.

The lingering scent of fresh baked bread pulled him into a narrow kitchen. Whitewashed cabinets, hardwood floors, robin's egg blue appliances with chrome accents. An oak kneeling bench positioned beneath a window overlooked the garden.

Michael scrubbed his hands in the porcelain sink, dried them on a dishtowel, found the beans, set to work. He stood by the window as the brewing coffee filled the kitchen with a heady aroma. The rain intensified, pelted the glass, raced down the pane. A pair of chickadees sheltered on the sill.

A Bible lay open on the kneeling bench, a string of rosary beads lining its gutter. He read the highlighted passage: *"As far as the east is from the west, so far has He removed our transgressions from us."*

The edge of a photo peeked out between pages. Curious, he pulled it out. A picture of Henry sitting on a park bench surrounded by ducks. Printed on the back in Mac's handwriting — *June 21st, 1990. Henry's fifth birthday.*

The front door swung open. The photo fluttered from his hand, slid beneath the bench. Mac, leaving a trail of water, strode through the kitchen, headed down the hall. "I'll just be a minute," he called back.

A door slammed. A faucet squeaked. Water flushed through pipes.

Michael retrieved the photo, slipped it back between the pages, and filled two coffee mugs.

Mac walked into the kitchen barefoot, wearing a fresh flannel shirt and jeans. He dried his hair with the towel around his neck, took the mug Michael offered.

"Thanks," Mac said. "Let's sit by the fire."

The living room was warm and cozy. Inviting. A winged chair and ottoman in a leafy-green fabric crowded the corner. The light from a Tiffany lamp fell over cove plaster ceilings, crown moldings, distressed wood-paneled walls.

Mac added a log to the fire, set it ablaze. Wood popped and crackled. The aroma of syrup drifted. "Sugar maple," he said. "Reminds me of my grandparents' home." He sat on the edge of a barnwood coffee table facing the fieldstone fireplace, gesturing for Michael to do the same. They sipped coffee, warmed in the silence of flames.

A large tapestry, depicting a man in a brown frock surrounded by a flock of birds, hung over the mantle. The glow of the fire highlighted coppery tones.

"St. Francis," Mac said. "Patron of animals."

"How's Sally?"

"Resting."

"Did he—"

"Rape her?" He shook his head.

"Did she call the police?"

"After Ed trashed the place, he broke down. Apologized. Promised he'd dry out, get his act together if she'd take him back."

"She wouldn't do that, would she?"

"Ed's mercurial, manipulative. Sally's convinced herself she did something to deserve it."

"Anna counsels victims of battered woman syndrome. Maybe she can talk with Sally," he suggested. "How'd you meet?"

Mac stared into the fire. "I was assigned to St. Columba July of '89. While unpacking books in my office, I noticed a woman arranging the window display across the street. I've been attracted to women before, but there was something exotic, extraordinary."

Michael raised a brow.

Mac glanced at him sideways. "A man has temptations, desires, regardless." Cradling his mug, he leaned forward. "She caught me staring and waved. Embarrassed, I shied away. Over the next few days, I lingered near my window, out of sight, just to get a glimpse. She wasn't a parish member. I'd discovered she lived with a trucker in a trailer park on the outskirts of town.

"By the end of August, I knew what time she arrived at the shop, that she went out for lunch on Tuesday and Thursday, closed early on Fridays. Figured as long as she stayed in her world, I in mine, my infatuation would diminish."

He stared into his mug. "I'd been working late when Sally staggered into my office, eyes puffy and red from crying, blood trickling from a swollen lip. She'd had a fight with her boyfriend. Wouldn't file a police report. She'd hit him first. Had it coming, she said.

"As I cleaned the blood from her face, she reached over, stroked my lip with her thumb. One thing led to another and…" He tapped his ring against his mug. "I felt ashamed. Breaking my vows to God. In his house, no less. I told her I'd made a mistake. She slapped me. Grabbed her clothes and left.

"For days, I struggled with guilt. Wandered the streets of Chicago, drunk and broken. Got a tattoo," he said, rolling up his sleeve to expose the dove with a broken wing. "A reminder of my fall from grace."

He stood up, set his coffee on the mantle. "After I'd sobered up, I decided to confess at the Holy Table in front of my peers. While getting ready for the meeting, a lanky guy wearing dirty jeans and snakeskin boots walked into the church. Reeked of vodka and motor oil. Said he wanted to make a confession. Told him he'd have to come back the next day, use one of the confessional booths. He tipped up his cowboy hat, spit tobacco at my feet, sneered as he said, 'I'd prefer to do it right now. Face to face.' Apparently, his girlfriend admitted, under duress, that she'd had sex with another man."

"Ed," Michael mumbled.

"When I asked why he wanted to confess, he said, ''Cause I'm going to kill the son of a bitch who fucked her.' Thought he'd ask for absolution before he committed murder."

"Does he know it was you?"

"Sally says no, he's clueless."

"Bet he makes one hell of a father."

"Ed skipped town last year. Couldn't handle Henry's meltdowns. Sally moved into the shop."

"Which is why you've taken Henry under your wing."

Mac toyed with his ring. "There's a chance Henry's my son."

"Did you ask Sally?"

"Claims she was pregnant when we slept together. Said the fight they had the night she came to me occurred after she told Ed the news."

"And you believed her?"

"Had my doubts. But as Henry grew and bore no resemblance, the likelihood of fatherhood became less hope and more a dream. A dream I had to relinquish. Until Henry's fifth birthday." He studied the tapestry as if searching for frayed threads. "I'd discovered Henry had developed a few of my...quirks."

"Did you tell Sally?"

"She's sticking to her story. Refused DNA testing. Somehow, she'd found out I'd consulted an attorney."

"The day she came to the farm. That's why she was so angry. What'd the lawyer tell you?"

"Unless Ed denies he's the father, I have no legal rights to petition the court for paternity testing. Something called a legal presumption in favor of Ed."

"Now what?"

Gripping the antique brass handle of the iron poker like a sword, Mac jabbed logs. As if awakening a sleeping dragon, flames flared, heat rose, wood hissed, spit. Mac stood his ground. The fire dwindled, lost vigor. The dragon slumbered.

"Wait until Ed blows up again. Protect Henry from the fallout."

"If Sally allowed the DNA testing and you found out Henry was your son…"

"I'd leave the priesthood, seek joint custody. Show Henry the meaning of unconditional love."

"And if he's not?"

His gaze rolled over the tapestry. "Wouldn't love him any less."

Chapter 11

Brisk wind whistled the pines and twisted the coppery-brown leaves of autumn. Waves of geese winged across the expansive November sky. Michael trekked to the house from morning chores just as the sun nudged the tree line.

When he'd left Anna an hour ago, she was on her way to the shower. But as he entered the back door, she had yet to make it to the kitchen. He sprinted up the steps, two at a time.

Anna lay naked on the bed, sleeping on her side, her skin flushed from the heat of the shower. A damp lock of auburn hair curled around the swell of breast. Michael sat on the mattress edge and absorbed everything Anna. Her gentle curves had always captivated him, but the changing landscape of her body fascinated him. What must it feel like to carry a life inside of you?

Anna's eyelids flittered like butterfly wings, revealing vivid blues.

"Didn't mean to wake you."

"You didn't." Anna smiled at her bump. "She did."

"Kicking?"

"Tumbling."

"Maybe she'll be an Olympic gymnast."

"Or astronaut."

"What if she's a he?"

"He'd better like pastels, cause I'm not repainting the nursery." She rolled onto her back. "What do you think of Gabriella?"

"She'd be five before she could say her name."

"We could shorten it to Ella or Brie."

"Brie Russo. Love the sound."

Anna splayed fingers over arc of belly. "She's thrilled with the farm."

"Having secret conversations without me?"

"Jealous?"

"A little."

"You'll get plenty of bonding time when I'm back at work." She propped on her elbows. "Mac called. Sally agreed to move in with Ed if he stayed sober through the holidays. Promised Mac I'd try to talk her out of the idea."

"If anyone can, it'd be you. Hungry? Omelets?"

"Oatmeal, please." She sat up, hugged her knees. "We're meeting Mom to shop for cribs after the ultrasound."

"An afternoon with Grace. Sounds wonderful."

"She's trying. You could too."

"Won't be nominating her for mother-in-law of the year."

"Daddy wants us to stop by after our meeting with Father Mulcahy."

"Such a perfect day." He kissed her forehead. "Get dressed, mama bear. Your porridge awaits."

Michael cracked an egg against the frying pan. Anna walked into the kitchen, picked up the article he'd clipped from *Backyard Farmer,* and sipped her coffee. "You can't be serious."

"It's our first Thanksgiving as a family. Thought we'd start a tradition."

The bacon grease spat and sizzled the egg white. Anna's nose crinkled. "Who, may I ask," she said, peering out the window at the turkey hobbling along the side of the barn, "will play executioner?"

"Guys at the feed store said it'd be my initiation to farm life."

"And what, city boy, do you know about slaughtering turkeys?"

He shrugged. "How hard can it be?"

She stared at the turkey, who stared back in apparent curiosity. "I'll remind you, you said that," she replied, walking out of the kitchen.

"What about breakfast?" he called after her.

"Lost my appetite."

***

"Did you see the look on Daddy's face when we told him Brie's due date was St. Patrick's Day?" Anna said, handing Michael her coat. "You'd have thought he'd won the lottery."

"Grace isn't exactly thrilled with the name. She said, 'Who names their child after French cheese?'" He hung Anna's coat in the front closet. "Where'd she get your name?"

"Aine is Irish for splendor, radiance, brilliance. She appears in folktales as the best-hearted woman who ever lived—lucky in love and money."

The closet doorknob broke off in his hand. "At least Grace got the love part right."

Anna grabbed the lapels of his sports coat, drew him close. "Don't care about the money part. And neither will Brie. All we need is love." She kissed him, slipped out of her heels. "Coming to bed?"

"I need to finish up a piece I'm working on. Won't be long."

Moonlight spilled across his desk. He retrieved the grainy black-and-white from his pocket, shrugged out of his sports coat, and sank into the chair. If he squinted, he could make out the bow of lip, curve of nose, shell of ear. At twenty weeks, she looked like a tiny being—hands balled into little fists, heels pressed into Anna's womb.

"So you don't see any issues," he'd asked Dr. Kellan, clutching half a dozen pamphlets on birth abnormalities.

"She has all the necessary parts, growing in all the right places and, according to measurements and calculations, all the correct sizes." She snapped off her gloves. "Relax, Dad. She's perfectly content floating in her amniotic sea. You've got about 140 days to figure out the art of diapering."

The flow of water sounded in the pipes. He propped the sonogram between his favorite photo of Anna and the framed picture of Meg, then switched on the gooseneck lamp. Pulling a fresh piece of paper from the top drawer, he scripted across the top of the page: *There are a million reasons I love you, Anna.* He drew a line through it and wrote underneath: *When you walked into my life.* Scratch that. *You are my best friend, the love of my life, my soul mate.* Cliché. He balled up the paper and sank a three-pointer into the wastebasket. *When I look in your eyes, Anna,* he scrawled along the top of a new sheet, *I see my life.*

Three lines in, the wind battered the window, scattering his thoughts. Darkness descended over the farm. Silence settled into the house. Vowing to try tomorrow, he turned off the lamp and climbed the stairs to join Anna.

***

The Monday night before Thanksgiving, Anna abandoned Michael for Jane Austen. He'd decided to prepare for tomorrow's impending execution by rereading the how-to article from *Backyard Farmer*. Satisfied he could do it—despite his aversion to killing anything—he crawled into bed next to Anna, who'd traded *Sense and Sensibility* for the comfort of pillows. The sheets were cold. A chill crept through his bones. He scooched closer to Anna, slid his hand around the slope of her belly, hunkered into the warmth of mother with child.

Seeking sleep, his mind ticked through a checklist of items he'd stored in the barn: A killing cone from Hank's Feed Store, a large scalding pot, a hanging rope, an oversized cooler, two buckets: one to catch blood and feathers, the other for entrails—

A thump against his palm. A thump so strong, his fingers vibrated. A thump that tickled and terrified him. He pressed his lips against Anna's nape and smiled. And as he held the life of his daughter in his hand, sleep found him.

***

The rooster's call startled Michael from a pleasant dream. He cursed into his pillow, turned on his side, and smiled at the sight. The sexy sway of Anna's naked backside bathed in sunlight.

He sidled up and kissed the curve of her shoulder.

She moaned and arched against him. "What time is it?"

"Nine." He ran his hand up the inside of her thigh.

She caught his fingers before they reached their destination. "You're procrastinating."

"Not what I'd call it."

"Time to man up. Get the job done."

"That's what I'm attempting," he said, punctuating his statement by pressing the hard evidence against the curve of ass.

"Your persistence is admirable, but your timing sucks." She threw the comforter on the floor and bolted toward the bathroom. "Our budding gymnast thinks my bladder is a springboard for tumbling routines."

The rooster spouted off again as if to remind him the day wasn't getting any younger.

"Don't suppose your parents would prefer fried rooster over roasted turkey?" he called out.

"For Thanksgiving?" she yelled over the whoosh of water swallowed by the toilet.

"Yeah, didn't think so," he muttered.

He wrestled into a pair of worn Levi's, found an old Chicago sweatshirt, and wandered to the window. Frost weighed down the blades of grass and coated dead leaves. Rotted pumpkins dotted the abandoned garden. Withered corn stalks snapped like matchsticks.

His hand trembled. The same hand that held his daughter. For days, he'd prepared for this. So why, on the morning of execution, second thoughts? He closed his eyes and chased away his dithering with a chuckle. It's just a stupid turkey.

Anna emerged from the bathroom in her terrycloth robe, hair piled on top of her head. She opened the closet and rummaged through her clothes. "Sally finally agreed to talk to me. I'm meeting her at the shop at ten." She held up a maroon sweater dress, scrutinized, and then exchanged it for a flowy wrap skirt. Her face looked pale, her freckles more pronounced.

"You okay?"

The center lines of her eyebrows creased. "A little achy."

"I can stay—"

"Go." She hung her skirt on the closet hook, draped her bathrobe over the chair back, and stepped into the bathroom. "I know where to find you."

In the kitchen, he collected the necessary tools: His new Victorinox curved skinning knife and five-inch boning blade, a roll of Bounty, several heavy-duty plastic bags, a cutting board, and three large bags of ice. He shoved his feet into his Muck Boots, placed the items into the old Radio Flyer, and wheeled them out to the barn.

He filled the scalding pot with water, placed it over the blazing fire pit, headed into the barn armed with his killing tools and a fair amount of determination. The turkey stood in the corner of its stall, knee deep in straw. Its glassy eyes darted between Michael's face and the butcher knife.

Michael stepped forward.

The turkey fanned its tail feathers and made a low throaty growl.

He set the knife down and showed empty hands. "Just want to talk."

It puffed its feathers and shuddered.

"Not falling for it, huh?"

The turkey stuck out its chest and yelped.

"Look," he said, channeling Clint Eastwood. "We can do this the easy way, or the hard way. It'd be a hell of a lot easier if you'd roll over and play dead."

It stood its ground as if it had a fighting chance.

Michael figured his best move would be to lunge for the turkey's leg, yank, and flip it upside down. He hadn't anticipated how strong-willed a sixteen-pound, one-legged turkey could be. When the squawking and cursing finally stopped, and the hay settled, it wasn't the turkey's leg he had clutched, but its neck.

The turkey appeared to have surrendered. Its waddle faded, body limp, wings splayed. Its black, glassy eyes had dulled and rolled in their sockets until they gazed upon Michael's face.

Something within those eyes. Other than fear. Something beyond acceptance of fate.

A cry swept through the barn door. A scream so terrifying, it shook Michael's soul. He released the turkey and bolted from the barn.

Anna stood before the bedroom window, bloody hands against glass.

Chapter 12

The squeal of Stella's skidding tires at the ER jerked Michael from panicked stupor, the drive a blur of lights and sound.

Shock receding, a deluge of sensations inundated him. The salty taste of Anna's tears. Her sticky blood on his fingertips. The loss of weight and warmth when they pulled her from his arms.

"Your wife," Dr. Grey explained, "has placental abruption, a serious complication in which the placenta detaches from the uterus. She needs immediate surgery."

"She'll be okay?"

He nodded.

"The baby?"

Dr. Grey twisted the Rolex from his wrist, exposing a patch of pale skin. "We'll do our best to repair any damage so you can try again. Sit tight. This may take a few hours."

Michael called Grace, then paced. Of the 726 linoleum tiles covering the waiting room floor, 562 were smoky gray, 131 inky blue, 33 mustard yellow. There appeared no logic for their placement, no pattern, no design, as if someone randomly chose their fate. He pivoted in squeaky boots, counted again.

"Mr. Russo." Gina, the unflappable receptionist, stood with one foot on mustard, one on blue.

"Anna?"

"Not yet."

"How long has it been?"

"Ten minutes since you last asked." Her gaze shifted to the clock. "Gonna be another hour or so. Grab a coffee in the cafeteria. If there's any news, I'll come get you."

The bright lights in the gift shop snagged his attention. He ducked under a cluster of pink and blue balloons, walked by a display case of silver rattles and picture frames, cut down the aisle of curly-coated lambs and plush baby blankets, then stopped at the floral station near the back. Red roses, yellow daisies, pink carnations, leafy green stems filled the cooler.

An older gentleman peeked out from behind sunflowers. "Can I help you?"

"Peonies?"

"Not this time of year, I'm afraid." He pushed the wire-framed glasses over bump of nose and peered at Michael through magnified lenses. "But I have Ranunculus, identical in texture and shape."

A vase of slender flowers, each with a single funnel-shaped ivory petal, sat on a glass shelf inside the cooler. "What are those?"

"Calla lilies."

"I'll take one."

"Would you like me to add baby's breath? Wrap it in a blanket of tissue paper?"

"Just the lily, thanks."

He left the gift shop and ventured down a long corridor of darkened offices ending at a heavy oak door. Ran his fingertips over the gold nameplate, slipped into the dimly lit room. The sharp scent of furniture polish cut through stagnant air. The icy atmosphere stung like sweat bees. A back-lit cross loomed above the altar. He eased into the last pew.

Flames flickered across the dark panel walls, illuminating an oversized oil painting of Christ, a lamb slung around the back of his neck. Jesus studied Michael through curious eyes. *Why have you come?*

A wedge of light entered the chapel and then disappeared. Mac—wearing a black shirt with a Roman collar, pleated pants, Oxford shoes, hair tucked into a bun—touched his chest and signed the cross from bended knee. He settled next to Michael.

"How'd you know I was here?"

"Came to visit a parishioner. Saw your car. Asked the nurse, followed your trail."

"Then you know. About…"

Mac nodded.

"So, this is the place," Michael said, "where people come to pray for miracles. Make bargains with God."

Mac toyed with his ring.

"How am I supposed to tell Anna the baby she loved more than life…" He rubbed his nape. "This may kill her, Mac."

The chapel door opened. Gina stood in the doorway, her silhouette haloed in light. "Mr. Russo. Dr. Grey is out of surgery."

Gina led them into a consultation room, closed the door. Colin sat on a bench, clutching a weeping Grace.

Dr. Grey's face was a mix of inscrutable emotions. "Mr. Russo." He pulled off his surgical cap. "Your daughter is alive."

Michael shook his head. "But…how?"

"Anna regained consciousness briefly before delivery. Pleaded with us to save Brie."

He glanced at Grace, continued. "Upon delivery, Brie was in acute respiratory distress. We suctioned fluid from her airways, revived her with a bag mask. Inserted an endotracheal tube and connected her to a ventilator. Performed cardiac massage, administered epinephrine to elevate heart rate, artificial surfactant to help her lungs work."

"She's going to live?"

"Heart rate and pressure are dangerously low. Without mechanical assistance, her internal organs won't receive adequate oxygen." He stared at the pale patch of skin on his wrist. "It's only a matter of time."

"There's nothing you can do?"

"The survival rate of preemies born at twenty-two weeks is less than one percent. We've done everything medically possible."

"When can I see Anna?" He waited for an answer, but no one looked up.

Grace's cry pierced the silence. Colin clutched her tighter.

"After we delivered your daughter," Dr. Grey said over Grace's stifled sobs, "Anna began to hemorrhage. By the time we found the source, it was too late." He set his hand on Michael's shoulder. "I'm sorry, Mr. Russo. Anna passed in surgery."

"No. That can't be. She…"

The air became too thick to breathe, the light too dim to see. Dr. Grey spoke, his voice muffled, his words jumbled. He rambled about the age of viability while Michael searched Colin's face for signs of a horrible misunderstanding. But the pain etched across his brow, the agony in his eyes dashed all hope.

He turned. Waited for Mac to wake him up from this nightmare. But Mac stared down at a mustard tile, as if his gaze could change it to slate blue.

Dr. Grey cleared his throat. "We've moved your daughter into a private room so you can hold her while she passes."

The lily fell from Michael's hand, tumbled to the floor, the edges of its delicate petal already tinged with death.

"I want to see her."

Dr. Grey slid his hands into the pockets of his lab coat. "Gina will escort you to your daughter's room."

"Anna. I want to see Anna."

***

Gina left Michael and Mac standing in front of Anna's room.

Mac set his hand on Michael's forearm. "Want me to go in with you?"

Michael shook his head and pushed through the door.

The room was sterile, chilly. The air smelled sharp and thin. Anna lay on a steel table, a white sheet tucked under arms. He knelt, intertwined their fingers, and pressed her hand against his mouth, warming her skin with his breath.

"Anna," he said. He waited for her to squeeze his hand, take a breath, whisper his name. Waited for her eyelids to flutter, chin to quiver, tears to spill down cheeks.

He closed his eyes. Prayed to a God he didn't believe in. Asked for a miracle that would never happen.

"I'm sorry," he sobbed, "that I left you. Sorry, I failed you."

When he could no longer endure the unforgiving silence, he forced himself to stand, let go of Anna, and walk away forever.

"Michael," Mac said, chasing. "Where are you going?"

"I can't be here."

"You need to make arrangements."

Michael quickened his pace and rounded the corner. "Put Grace in charge."

"What about Brie?"

Michael stopped in front of the emergency room doors. An image of his thirteen-year-old self clutching onto a dying Meg surfaced on the glass pane. Icy pins pricked his feet. The door glided open. A cold gust froze tears. "Tell Colin to bury her in Anna's arms."

***

Michael peeled out of the parking lot onto 72, tires squealing. He pointed Stella west, gunned past sparse traffic, and raced empty miles toward the setting sun.

Speeding under the blood-red sky, memories flashed.

Anna's pale face. Limp fingers. Cold skin. Dr. Grey's somber voice coming from Anna's bloodless lips. *'Hold her while she passes.'*

He leaned on the horn as if to exorcise the haunting images and punched the accelerator. Stella gathered speed. Yellow lines blurred.

A doe, stunned by headlights, stood motionless. He swerved onto the shoulder. Slammed brakes. Rear tires slid on loose gravel. Stella skidded to a screeching stop. Dust swirled in high beams.

The deer swiveled her head, looked at him as if he'd invaded her space, then flashed the white of her tail and bounded into the woods.

He hunched over the steering wheel. Slowed his racing heart. Choked on the smell of burnt rubber.

A glow emanated from Stella's dashboard. The gas gauge hovered at quarter tank.

Up the road, an illuminated billboard promised cheap gas. Cheaper alcohol. Only two miles. He licked his dry lips, rifled the glove compartment for his wallet. Shit. He pounded his palm against the steering wheel. Left it on the kitchen counter. Under the liquor cabinet. He pulled into the eastbound lane, sped home.

The farmhouse was dark. Cold. Quiet. A coffin. He twisted the cap off a bottle of Jack. The warm liquid cascaded down his throat, sloshed in his empty stomach. Lighter fluid.

He stumbled into his office, turned on the gooseneck lamp, and sank into his chair. Pulled out the vows he'd started writing and read aloud, *"When I look in your eyes, Anna, I see my life. My world. My home. Falling in love with you was the single most remarkable thing I've ever done. I don't want to do life without you by my side."*

He lit a match and watched flames dance along the paper's edge and then dropped it into the metal wastebasket.

He downed more whiskey, snatched the sonogram off his desk, studied the blurry image inside Anna's womb, safe and sound.

The sonogram slipped from his fingers, fluttered into the smoldering wastebasket. He picked up his favorite picture of Anna. Wind-blown hair hid her cheeks, oversized sunglasses her eyes, but nothing could hide that smile. Tears stung his eyes, burned his throat. He took another pull, dragged his sleeve across his mouth. Fuck. That smile.

A shaft of light emanated from the open barn door. He slipped Anna's picture into his sweatshirt pouch, grabbed Jack by the neck, headed out the back door.

The night was frigid, a soulless black swallowing up the sky. Not even the moon braved the darkness. Embers glowed in the fire pit. Was it this morning he'd set out to butcher the turkey? Using his boot, he kicked the bucket over. Water splashed onto hot coals, hissed, then smoked.

Inside the barn, fluorescent lights hummed and glowed. He slammed down more Jack, surveying all he'd accomplished the last four months. All that work. For what?

The sharp, glinty blade of the axe caught his eye. He wrapped his fingers around the smooth wooden handle, flexed his muscles, and swung the axe through the air like a baseball bat. Wielding the heavy steel felt liberating.

The turkey stuck its neck through the stall slats, eyed Michael. As he approached, it backed against the wall. He tightened his grip, raised the axe and, without hesitation, drove it downward.

Splintering pine sent the rooster flying into the rafters. Michael lifted the axe above head. The turkey cowered. The blade swung down.

Cleaved the cradle in two.

PART II

Chapter 13
November 22nd, 1995
8:00 a.m.

Sunlight reached through the barn window, smacked Michael's cheek. He winced, clamped eyelids, unglued tongue. Sour whiskey permeated pores, hung on breath.

Propped on elbows, he focused on his immediate surroundings. Splintered pine littered the straw-covered floor. Images emerged, pulsed rhythms with the throb in his temples. The Jack. The axe. The crib.

And death hit him like a bullet shattering glass. Yesterday's joy, now sorrow and despair. Anna's smile fading…

He slipped his hand into his sweatshirt pouch, came up empty. Shit. Anna's picture. He rifled through straw on hands and knees.

"Looking for this?" The sharp edge of Grace's voice skated along frayed nerves. She stood before him, dressed in yesterday's suit—skirt askew, blouse wrinkled. Her eyes red-rimmed, the skin beneath them sallow, but her stoic face showed no emotion. She let the bottle of Jack slip. It landed with a thud and rolled between his hands.

He sank back on heels, prepared to face judge and jury.

She swiped her hands together and appraised his disheveled appearance. "As much as I'd love to lecture you on your appalling behavior, we don't have time. Gabriella's life is at stake. Get your ass up. I'm driving you to the hospital." She pivoted on the balls of her feet and exited the barn.

"Wait." He staggered after her. "She's alive?"

"If you'd been anywhere near your phone and sober, you'd know."

"You've seen her?"

She marched up the path, heels digging into earth, but it didn't slow her. "We were by her side all night."

"Which is where I should have been," he bit out before she could.

"You'll have all the time you need to wallow in guilt after you sign the documents."

He followed into the house. "Documents?"

"After your cowardly getaway, Colin called Duncan Kelly. He arranged for Gabriella's transfer to a state-of-the-art, level three, Neonatal Intensive Care Unit. Can't move her without your approval."

Nausea curled his gut. Bile burned his throat. He steadied against the counter, wiped cold sweat from his nape. "I need to—"

"No time." She swiped her purse off the desk and stormed toward the front door. "The neonatal transport team is waiting."

He grabbed his wallet off the counter. His gaze caught the heart magnet tacked to the refrigerator. Beneath it Brie's sonogram, corners singed.

Michael approved the transfer to Lakeview Hospital. Colin accompanied the neonatal transport team in the ambulance. In no condition to drive, Michael rode with Grace.

Sixty-four minutes of awkward silence, coexisting with headache, nausea, and guilt.

Andrea, an administrative nurse with a soft smile but a firm grip, greeted Grace and Michael at the NICU reception area. "Gabriella arrived safely," she said, leading them into a private waiting room. "The attending neonatologist, Dr. Webber, will be with you shortly."

Grace perused the room, while Michael studied the photographs that lined the walls. Pictures of a willowy man with a balding head and graying goatee, grinning at miniature babies cradled in his slender hands. A quote painted on the wall above the frames—*Having a premature baby is like getting one of God's miracles in the midst of their creation.*

Michael, standing by a window overlooking the hospital courtyard, grappled with thoughts. Somehow, she'd survived. But for how long?

Grace handed him a bottle of water, then rummaged her purse and placed two Advil in his hand like a penance. She watched him swallow and goaded him to drink as if he were six.

Dr. Webber entered, introduced himself, and gestured toward the cluster of cushy chairs in the center of the room. He tugged up the pleats in his pants and settled next to Michael.

"Gabriella is one tough little girl. A fighter," he said. "The transport team connected her endotracheal tube to a high frequency oscillatory ventilator and added nitric oxide to speed the rate of oxygen into her bloodstream. By the time she arrived, her heart rate and blood pressure had normalized.

"We've inserted a special IV called a venous catheter into her umbilical stump to deliver antibiotics, as well as fluids and nutrition, then transferred her into an incubator to regulate her body temperature. We increased the dosage of artificial surfactant to help keep her airways open. She's hanging on with all her might." He smoothed his goatee. "Questions?"

Michael leaned forward, rubbed his hands. "Dr. Grey said she had less than a one percent chance of surviving."

"Don't put much stock in statistics. Each child is unique, capable of defying the odds. Not going to lie. Micro preemies are susceptible to serious medical conditions and complications. The next few days are crucial. My primary concerns are underdeveloped lungs and risk of infection. Our neonatal team is monitoring her every breath." He pushed to his feet. "I'm sure you're eager to see your daughter."

"Right now?" Michael jumped up, tipping over Grace's Styrofoam cup. Coffee sloshed over the parenting magazines lining the acrylic table. He grabbed her beverage napkin and blotted up the spill. "Isn't it too soon?"

"Bonding improves the immune response."

"I have to make a few calls," Grace said, excusing herself.

Dr. Webber escorted Michael to the reception area. Andrea sprang from behind the desk and handed Dr. Webber a note.

"Excuse me a minute."

A nurse, toffee-colored hair swept into a ponytail, stood behind the desk flipping through a file. With her smooth, fair complexion, she couldn't be older than thirty, but her eyes reflected the weariness of too many tragedies.

"Sorry," Dr. Webber said on return. "Need to check a patient." He motioned for the weary-eyed nurse.

"Sara, this is Michael Russo, Gabriella's father. Sara is one of Brie's nurses. She'll take you back and answer any questions."

"Mr. Russo." She smiled tersely. "Follow me."

At the sanitation station, he scrubbed his hands raw for the prescribed three minutes and then trailed Sara.

"We often refer to gestational age in the NICU," she said. "The typical pregnancy lasts forty weeks. Most preemies are between twenty-four and thirty-six weeks."

"Brie's only twenty-two weeks."

"She's our youngest. This way." She led him through sliding glass doors.

The NICU was a cacophony of noise and movement. Nurses hovered, monitors beeped, alarms buzzed, ventilators whooshed, machines hummed. A bank of computer screens flashed green numbers, blinked red lights, and framed jagged lines that dipped and spiked like a mountain range.

"It looks chaotic, but everyone here is a dedicated specialist." He shadowed Sara through a maze of staff and machines. "Parents can stay twenty-four/seven, but we encourage breaks. Once you understand our diligence, you'll feel comfortable leaving. Gabriella's pod," she said, skirting the nurses' station, "is around this corner."

Colin sat, shoulders hunched, in front of a quilt-covered incubator. The stubble on his face did little to mask pale skin. The whites of his eyes had a grayish tinge and his lids drooped like a basset hound's. He tried to speak, but his words died from exhaustion. He pushed to his feet as if he'd morphed into a ninety-year-old man, patted Michael's shoulder, and lumbered away.

Sara removed the quilt. Brie lay on her back, connected to a half-dozen tubes and wires. She was the size of his outstretched hand, her foot smaller than his thumb. Anna's engagement ring could fit around her wrist. Her ten tiny fingers and ten tiny toes were all perfectly formed. A soft layer of dark fuzz covered the crown of her head. Purple veins spidered beneath translucent skin like the nervures of a leaf. Her mouth was taped closed around an endotracheal tube, her eyelids fused. A sticky substance coated her body. Ribs protruded like toothpicks.

"Sorry," Sara said. "I'm used to seeing them. Sometimes I forget…"

He stuffed his hands into his sweatshirt pouch. "So tiny."

"Eighteen ounces of tiny."

Brie's nostrils flared. Her tiny chest caved.

"Is she in pain?"

Sara watched lines spike, dip, then stabilize on a monitor. "Symptoms of respiratory distress. They should resolve within the next few days."

"Can she move?"

"She doesn't have the strength yet, but her muscles twitch. She's too fragile to hold, but you can touch her."

"Won't I hurt her?"

"I'll show you."

"Don't wake her."

"I have to bundle her, so now's a good time."

Mirroring Sara's movements, Michael pushed his hands through the portholes.

"Because Gabriella's pain receptors aren't fully developed," Sara said, wrapping her inside a blanket like a burrito, "it's best to use firm, but gentle pressure." She took his hand and placed it on the crown of Brie's head.

Her hair was soft, skin moist. As if cradling a warm peach in his palm. Her lashless lids puffy, eyes oversized for her face. She lifted eyebrows. Small lines creased her forehead.

Sara smiled. "She feels your touch."

"When will she open her eyes?"

"Not for several weeks, but she can recognize your voice. The incubator amplifies sound, so speak softly, soothingly." Sara smoothed the folds of the blanket and removed her arms from the incubator. "I'll give you a few minutes."

"But what if—"

"I'll be around the corner." She checked the numbers flashing on the screen, dimmed the lights, then left.

He sat on the edge of a chair. "Hey, little girl," he whispered, "Remember me? I held onto you every night when you were cocooned inside your mother. We weren't supposed to meet for another 115 days. Ready or not, here you are."

He cleared his throat. "You're probably wondering where mommy is. To be honest, I'm not sure. About anything, anymore. Except this. She loves you more than fish love to swim, more than birds love to fly, more than the stars love to shine. If she could move earth and sky to hold you, she would. But she can't. You're stuck with me." Her eyes shifted under closed lids toward the sound of his voice. "Raw deal, I know."

He rested his forehead against the smooth plastic of the incubator. "I'm sorry I left you. But I promise, I'll stay by your side, fight with you. And every day," he said, stroking his thumb over her forehead, "I'll tell you about your mom, and you'll know how special she was."

3:00 p.m.

The NICU team revolved around Michael and Brie with precision. At least a dozen times, alarms buzzed or pinged. Before panic could take root, Sara would appear, check the monitors, adjust tubes and wires, and reassure him everything was fine.

Preoccupied with the rhythmic sounds and blinking numbers on the monitors, Michael didn't notice Colin until he settled into the chair on the other side of Brie's incubator. The stubble shaved, color in his cheeks restored.

Colin stared at the quilt-covered incubator with unfocused eyes. "When Anna was six," he said, rubbing a scar on the back of his hand, "she made a picture for me. I thanked her, then told her pink wasn't a rainbow color, unicorns were fabrications, and she should shade the grass in one direction. A perfect teachable moment. Or so I thought.

"On my way to bed, light spilled from the crack underneath Anna's bedroom door. She'd fallen asleep in her clothes. I removed her shoes, tucked her in, and kissed her goodnight. It wasn't until I switched off the light that I noticed the crumpled strips of paper and broken crayons in the trash can beneath her writing desk.

"It took two hours to flatten out the pieces, tape them together. Took a hell of a lot longer to repair the damage I'd done to her faith in me.

"Fatherhood," he said, examining the scar he'd been rubbing, "is a lesson on how utterly imperfect you are." He shook his head and then looked at Michael. "You need a break? I can stand in for you."

"Thanks," he replied, "I'm good."

5:00 p.m.

Michael opened his eyes. Must have dozed off because Mac sat in the chair Colin had occupied. Dressed in priestly garb, he looked uncomfortable, like a nightcrawler on a fishing hook.

"I hate this thing," he said, sliding his index finger under the snug-fitting Roman collar. "Feels like a choke chain."

"Why are you wearing it?"

"Grace asked me to baptize Gabriella."

"Why?"

"Catholics believe infants must be baptized to cleanse them of original sin and make them members of the Church."

"Why *now*?"

"Canon law states that any infant in danger of death should be baptized without delay. You can understand why Grace and Colin—"

"Because your God is going to condemn her to some hellish limbo if she dies without being baptized?"

Mac twisted his neck and tugged his collar. "Limbo is a theological theory, one which is not embraced officially by the entire Church or formally taught as a doctrine."

"Well, *Father*," Michael said, pinning Mac with his gaze, "what do you believe will happen to Brie if she dies without being baptized?"

"The Church tells us to entrust them to the mercy of God and pray for their salvation."

"That's not what I asked."

Mac squirmed in his chair. "I cannot baptize her without your consent."

119

"Then you won't be baptizing her."

"Jesus said, 'Let the children come to me, do not hinder them.' They should not be denied the gift of holy baptism."

"So now it's my fault Brie's going to hell?"

Mac dropped his gaze. "Anna would have wanted—"

"Anna's not here, is she?"

Several alarms sounded. Sara arrived within seconds, checking lines and monitors, concern etched on her face. This time, she offered no reassurances.

Icy pins pricked his heels. Michael leapt to his feet. "What's happening? What's wrong?"

Dr. Webber appeared and spoke in a swift string of words and acronyms, none of which Michael understood. Two nurses wheeled the incubator out of Brie's pod and rushed her down the hall in rehearsed chaos.

Mac grabbed the crook of Michael's elbow, stopping him in his tracks. As Brie disappeared from sight, Michael got the sense that once again, he'd failed.

Chapter 14
6:00 p.m.

Brie's pod, too tiny to pace, had Michael counting beats from the neighboring monitor.

Mac offered him a paper cone of water, then sank into a chair. Michael's mouth was cotton, throat sandpaper, but even the thought of soothing liquid roiled his gut.

"Sorry. I was out of line."

"You're worried about Brie." Mac detached his Roman collar, wound it around his hand. "Thing is, I don't have all the answers. And often question the ones I have."

"I can't lose her, Mac. She's the only thing left. Of Anna."

Mac nodded. "Grace is making a list of people to contact about Anna's passing. Anyone you want me to call? Someone from the station?"

Oh, god. Jane. He pressed the palms of his hands into his eyelids to stop the tears. "Jane Bishop. She'll tell the others."

"Any relatives?"

"Brie's my only family."

"But you're not the only family Gabriella has." He stood, fastened the collar around his neck, set a hand on Michael's shoulder. "Find a way to resolve your differences. For Brie."

Mac glanced down the hall. A grin emerged from within his beard.

Dr. Webber rolled Brie's incubator into the pod.

Michael stood. Relief gushed like a deluge through floodgates. "What happened?"

"As a fetus develops," Dr. Webber said, checking the leads to Brie's chest, "a blood vessel connects the two major arteries of the heart. Usually, this vessel closes after birth. But in some babies, it remains open, allowing oxygen-rich blood from the aorta to mix with oxygen-poor blood from the pulmonary artery. This strains the heart and increases blood pressure. *Patent ductus arteriosis.* PDA for short."

He glanced at the changing numbers on Brie's monitor and continued. "Since Gabriella is too small for cardiac catheterization, we closed the opening with a medication called Indomethacin." He wrapped Brie inside a snuggle-up and cupped his hand over her head. "You gave us quite the scare, little one."

She crinkled her nose.

"That's Anna's expression," Michael said. "When something stinks."

Dr. Webber chuckled. "Probably smells the onion from my burger."

Sara closed Brie's incubator, sheltered it from overhead lights with a heart-covered quilt, then handed Michael a pink swaddling blanket.

"What's this for?"

"Sleep with it against your skin. We'll wrap Gabriella in it tomorrow. In a few weeks, when you hold her, she'll know your scent."

Hold her? Michael eased back into the chair before the icy pricks took hold.

8:00 p.m.

With no windows in the NICU, night slipped in unnoticed. If it wasn't Grace in the chair across from Michael, it was Colin. Neither spoke. They all stared at the heart-covered quilt as if it had the power to keep the life hidden beneath alive.

Perplexed by the tangle of wires and machines sustaining Brie's life, Michael, with Sara's help, deciphered their signals and lines. The two electrodes attached to Brie's chest and the one on her abdomen detected heart activity, displayed it as a wavelength on the cardiopulmonary monitor. The system measured her respiratory rate and her oxygen saturation through a probe attached to her hand. Blood pressure was monitored through the artery in her umbilicus. Any time the number dropped below or rose above normal, an alarm would sound. A nurse would appear, check wires and leads, and then reassure him all was fine. Knowing that most alarms were false set Michael's mind at ease, but didn't stop his heart from jumping at the blare.

The hospital had private rooms for parents. At 9:00, Mac arrived with Michael's toiletry bag and a suitcase. While Mac and Colin kept vigil, Michael showered, changed clothes, and then sat in the cafeteria, hunched over a plate of wilted lettuce and tasteless spaghetti, too exhausted to lift a fork.

123

Grace appeared, inspected the fixture hovering over Brie's incubator, casting her in a blue light.

"Brie developed jaundice overnight," Michael said. "Dr. Webber started phototherapy. The light helps break down excess bilirubin."

"How long will she need phototherapy?"

"A few days."

She squared her shoulders and faced him. "We need to talk."

"About?"

"Colin and I finalized Aine's funeral arrangements. Visitation is from two to eight tomorrow at McKay's Funeral Home in Oak Park." She paused. "At five on Saturday, Father Mulcahy will lead mass at Divine Child, and then perform Rite of Committal at Mt. Hope Cemetery."

"*This* Saturday?"

"The church was available."

He glared at her. "Is this your idea of a joke?"

She crossed her arms, battle-ready. "You put me in charge."

He pushed to his feet, stood inches from her. "You're holding a funeral in the church Anna and I were to wed? Burying her on the day she was to become my wife?"

She didn't flinch. Not even a blink.

Sara sailed in, dispersing tension like a cool breeze on a humid day. She hummed while she checked Brie's IV's and monitors. "Everything looks good," she said, turning to face them. Her smile faded. "Something wrong?"

Michael stepped back.

Grace dropped her arms to her sides and tugged down her sleeves. "I've got things to attend to."

November 25th, 1995
2:00 p.m.

While Brie was sleeping, Michael changed into jeans, a long-sleeved Henley, then tugged on a windbreaker and exited the front doors of the hospital. The outside world felt surreal, his perspective distorted. As if he'd walked into a sensory fog. Muffled sounds, muted colors, blunted smells.

Once he gained his bearings, he ambled along the sidewalk. Church bells chimed three o'clock. Cloud shadows swept across his path. People rushed past as if he were standing still. Everything moved forward. Except him.

He settled onto a bench in the hospital courtyard under a naked oak. The brisk November winds cleared his head, flushed his lungs of hospital.

Mac, wearing a dark suit and tie, sat next to him, hair damp, beard glistening. The scent of birch and cedar mixed with a hint of vanilla. Two nurses in green scrubs walked by, glanced at Mac, giggled like flirtatious teenagers.

"I'm not going," Michael said.

"Okay."

"You're not going to try to talk me into it?"

"Nope."

"You think I should go."

"Not my decision."

Michael peered into the sun. "Give me one good reason I should."

125

Mac leaned forward, rubbed his hands together, but remained silent.

"You're supposed to say it's the right thing to do."

"Am I?"

"Brie..."

"I'll stay with her."

"I don't have anything to wear."

Mac raised his brow. "Something wrong with what you've got on?" He held up the keys to his Jeep. "If you leave now, you'll make it on time."

Michael swiped the keys, took a few steps, hesitated.

"Parking garage, level three."

5:00 p.m.

The lot at Divine Child was packed. Michael parked the Jeep in the last row beneath the shadow of the towering steeple, rushed toward the entrance before he could change his mind.

The massive oak door closed behind him with a thud. People mingling in the narthex turned their heads, glared at him as if he'd sinned. He stuffed his hands in his coat pockets and, gaze downward, shuffled past.

The air in the nave felt stifling. A somber rendition of "Amazing Grace" played through the pipe organ. The congregation stared in unison as he walked up the aisle, passing judgments as if mints. He focused on the closed casket cascaded in red roses.

He hesitated near the front row. Grace glanced with indifference, Colin, affirmation. The bench creaked as Michael sat to Colin's left.

While Father Mulcahy droned on about Christ's victory over sin and death, Michael studied his surroundings. The pews were spaced like rows of obedient soldiers. Life-sized statues of saints glared dutifully from their lofty pedestals. Stained glass trapped sunlight, muting all but the altar. The smell of bitter incense, pungent lilies, and unwavering conformity lingered.

He felt alone in a crowd who believed it was God's will Anna died. Lost in a sea of blind faith. He should be at the hospital, guarding the only hope of keeping Anna alive.

Afterward, he stood in the biting wind at Anna's grave. Endured The Rite of Committal, then joined Colin and Grace to accept condolences.

"We're sorry for your loss." *As if he'd misplaced Anna.*

"It was part of His plan." *But not part of mine.*

"God called her home." *Her home was with me.*

"She's in a better place." *Better than with her husband and child?*

While planning his escape, Jane approached. She hugged him so earnestly, his protective shell fractured. Grief threatened tears.

Jane pulled away, squeezed his hand. "I'm here. Anything you need. Anytime." She handed him a pink peony. "Anna's favorite."

"Where'd you get it?"

"Rita. Grows them in her greenhouse." She rendered a weak smile. "Harvey's in the car. He's not sure what to say."

"Tell him I understand."

"I'll come visit in a few days." She hugged him and walked away.

The line of people thinned, the crowd dispersed. Headed back to their homes, lives, families.

Time doesn't stop to grieve.

He wandered over to Anna's grave, let the peony slip from his hand. The heavy bloom bounced and nestled at the heart of her casket.

Had it been five days? Felt more like five lifetimes.

December 5th, 1995
2:00 p.m.

Jane hugged Michael and sat across from him in the break room. "You look —"

"Like shit."

"Exhausted. You've lost weight. When did you last eat?"

"The cafeteria food is…"

She pulled a Dagwood's Deli sandwich from her satchel. "Pastrami on Rye. Mustard."

His mouth watered, but his stomach lurched.

"Eat," she said. "You'll feel better."

He took a bite, and then another when his stomach didn't reject the first. "Thanks," he said, swallowing a third.

Jane placed a Coke on the table. "How's Brie?"

"Recovering from pneumonia."

"Good news."

"Yesterday, they discovered brain bleeds. Today, she's struggling to maintain an adequate heart rate." He scrubbed his face and then rested his arms on the table. "One step forward, two back."

"She's a fighter, Michael."

He stared at his empty hands. "She's so fragile. So helpless."

She set her hand on his. "And though she be but little, she is fierce."

"A Midsummer Night's Dream." Michael managed a smile. "Anna loved that play."

"When was the last time you slept?"

"Last night. A few hours."

"My place is ten minutes away. Guest bedroom's waiting."

"Brie. I can't…"

She squeezed his hand. "She's in expert care."

"There's a constant stream of doctors, interns, specialists, examining her. Hard to keep them all straight." He cracked open the Coke and sipped. "How's Rita?"

"Good."

"Six months?"

"Longest relationship I've had since…"

"Stacey."

Jane rummaged her satchel and placed a manila envelope in front of him.

"What's this?"

"A gift for Brie."

Michael opened the envelope, pulled out a picture of Anna cupping the curve of her stomach and a typed quote. *Sometimes the smallest things take up the most room in your heart. – Winnie the Pooh.*

Jane handed him a container of pushpins. "Andrea at the front desk told me there's a corkboard above Brie's pod. Fill it with love."

December 11th, 1995
11:00 a.m.

Now twenty-five weeks, Brie's vitals stable, a gastroenterologist inserted a PICC line, a soft plastic tube that ran from a vein in her leg to one near her heart to deliver antibiotics and nutrients. Last week, she'd recovered from pneumonia, but then developed sepsis. Trapped in a never-ending battle, she seemed determined to win.

***

"If Gabriella survives, what about health insurance?"

The question was posed by Sam Cummings, the social worker assigned to Brie's case.

Michael scanned the gray December sky from Sam's office window and then turned to face him.

Grace sat on the couch, fiddling with her silk scarf. She, too, waited for his answer.

Sam tapped a pen against the folder on his desk. "Anna's COBRA only covers part of Brie's expenses and expires after eighteen months. Premiums and deductibles will be steep."

"I'll sell the farm."

Sam glanced at Grace, then back at Michael. "Has Dr. Webber discussed the possible long-term effects of Brie's premature birth?"

A conversation not easily forgotten. Cerebral palsy, mental retardation, brain damage. An endless list.

"Yes," Grace responded, twisting her scarf. "But nothing like that will happen to Gabriella."

"She'll need occupational, speech, and physical therapy," Sam said. "Neurologists, ophthalmologists, early intervention specialists. We can discuss financial options—"

"I'll get a job that'll provide health insurance."

"There will be childcare expenses," he added.

"I can watch Gabriella while Michael's working."

Sam thrummed his fingers against his desk. "You should consider a Grandparent Power of Attorney. It's a legal document giving a grandparent authority to make medical decisions in the event a parent is unable to do so."

"Of course," Grace replied, ironing the scarf in her lap. "It's what Anna would want. I'll look into it."

Michael turned toward the window. Freezing rain pelted the pane. Wind twisted the branches of a willow in the courtyard. His exhale fogged glass. "Fine."

4:00 p.m.

Michael returned to the farm for the first time since his disastrous affair with Jack Daniels. Grace agreed to watch over Brie until he returned. Mac had collected the mail and fed the birds, but there were things Michael needed to take care of. Things he'd put off.

Sleet morphed into drizzly rain, and a gray ceiling of clouds hung over the farm. The bare branches of the maples disappeared into haze. The hardwood floors popped and cracked like an old man's knees as Michael entered the kitchen. He warmed a can of tomato soup, grabbed a spoon, sat at his desk.

He shuffled through sympathy cards, junk mail, bills, then opened the most recent edition of the *Tribune* and scoured help-wanted ads. Finding nothing of interest, he called and left a message for Shannon, then talked to Katie Adams about putting the farm on the market. He leafed through Anna's scrapbook and removed a few pictures to tack to Brie's corkboard.

In the laundry room, he filled a bucket with hot soapy water and another with rags, a scrub brush, baking soda, and white vinegar.

He set the buckets in the upstairs hall and opened the nursery door. Anna's hand-painted sheep frolicked on pastel pink walls. White eyelet curtains hung in the window, picture books lined a shelf, and a curly-coated lamb occupied the rocking chair. He wound the mobile hanging over the white-washed crib and watched chickens and ducks dance to "An Irish Lullaby." Humming the last too-la-loo-ra-loo, he stepped out, closed the door.

Steeling his nerves, he entered their bedroom. Faint lilac mingled with fresh memories. Anna's pillow bunched as if cradling her head. Sheets twisted and tangled. The comforter lay in a crumpled heap on the floor. Anna's terrycloth robe draped the chair. Her flowy skirt hung from the closet hook. *Sense and Sensibility* overturned on the nightstand.

He steadied his breathing, dunked a rag into the bucket of soapy water, and soaked Anna's bloody handprints from the windowpane. Next, he sprinkled baking soda over the dried puddle of blood on the hardwood floor and poured vinegar over it. It bubbled and foamed. He dropped to his knees and scrubbed the mixture into a paste. After mopping the runny red mess, a heart-shaped stain branded the hardwood like a metaphor.

He stripped, stepped into the shower, and cranked the hot water. Leaning back against the tile, he sank to the floor and set his demons free.

Chapter 15
December 24th, 1995
7:00 p.m.

For the most part, Michael had ignored the other parents in the NICU. A horse with blinders, his focus was Brie. Occasionally, he'd catch a sympathetic look. A weary glance. A dropped gaze that couldn't hide the darkest thoughts. *If God takes yours, He might spare mine.*

He'd seen empty incubators that had, just hours before, been filled with life. Heard the painful silence that echoed through the NICU after a frenzy of activity. Smelled fear drifting through vents like smoke before fire. They'd all learned to avert their eyes. Stare at shoes.

As days morphed into weeks, and Michael and Brie became veterans in the NICU, gazes became nods; glances, smiles.

When he'd returned from the break room after dinner, and no one would look at him, he knew.

He rushed past the nurses' station and into Brie's pod. Her incubator — gone.

He swung around, almost knocking Sara over. "Brie," he gasped.

"I was looking for you," she said.

"Where is she?"

"Brie developed a temperature and bloody stools. Dr. Webber ordered X-rays. He's consulting with the pediatric gastroenterologist on call."

"Is it serious?"

"They're evaluating Brie for necrotizing enterocolitis, a digestive condition where bacteria causes inflammation and infection, damaging the intestines. It's common in preemies."

"So she's going to be okay."

"It could lead to a perforation, allowing fluid to leak into the abdomen."

"But they can fix it."

"Every procedure carries risk. Especially in micro-preemies."

He eased into the chair before the icy-pin pricks in his calves could take him down.

Sara set her hand on his forearm. "It'll take a couple hours. Let's get some fresh air."

Something snagged her attention. The lines around her mouth and brow deepened.

Dr. Webber shuffled toward them. He removed his mask, revealing a grin. "Brie's fine. The nurses will bring her back in a few minutes."

Michael rubbed his thighs, forcing blood to circulate.

Dr. Webber smoothed his goatee. "Dr. Cooper confirmed my suspicions that Brie had developed necrotizing enterocolitis, which we refer to as NEC. We suctioned the gas and fluids from her stomach and intestines, relieving the swelling and discomfort. The x-rays showed no signs of perforation."

"What caused it?" Michael asked.

"There are many causes of NEC, but in Brie's case, I suspect reduced oxygen and blood flow to the intestines. We've started antibiotic therapy, adjusted oxygen levels, and fluids. She's responding well."

Michael raked his fingers through his hair and blew out a breath.

Dr. Webber squeezed Michael's shoulder. "One day at a time."

December 26th, 1995
2:00 p.m.

Michael was singing "An Irish Lullaby" to Brie when Grace arrived, wearing jeans and one of Anna's "Healing Hearts" T-shirts. Her porcelain skin appeared dull. Gray roots had sprouted.

"Colin sang that song to Aine after he tucked her in," she said, studying the collage of pictures Michael had pinned to the corkboard. She fixed her gaze on a photo of a five-year-old Anna clutching a beagle puppy. "He spoiled her." She moved on to a series of photo booth snapshots of Anna and Colin. "They were inseparable. Links in a chain."

For the first time since he'd known Grace, her voice wavered, an edge of remorse in its tone.

"I was with Aine when she bought this," she said, flipping the pages of *Guess How Much I Love You*. "We were arguing over baby names. Seems trivial now." She set the book down, turned to face him. "You look tired, Michael. Go home. Get some sleep."

"Soon," he said. Still not ready for the haunting silence; the painful memories.

"How's the job search?"

"Couple leads." He lied. No prospects and Shannon hadn't returned his call. "Applied for COBRA."

"Did you sign the Grandparent Power of Attorney my lawyer drafted?"

"Yesterday."

"And the farm?"

"On the market."

"You should buy a place near us. It'll be more convenient for you when I take care of Gabriella."

Brie balled her fists and scrunched her face.

"You'll need to buy a new car. Something safer. With a back seat. Sell that sports car of yours."

He rubbed the back of his neck. How could he part with Stella? The memories of his dad?

"Gabriella's five weeks, Michael. She needs to be baptized." She paused, and then added, "It's what Aine would have wanted."

She fingered the picture of Anna cradling her belly curve. "Wish I could turn back time, start over, do things…differently. But I can't," she said, looking at Brie, "Can I?"

4:00 p.m.

Mac collapsed into the empty chair. He dropped his head, massaged his nape.

"Everything okay?" Michael asked.

"Sally refuses to let me see Henry. Thinks he won't bond with Ed if I'm in the picture."

"What can you do?"

"Pray." He leaned back. "Passed Grace on my way in."

"She thinks I should go home."

"She's right. It's been five weeks." He smiled at Brie. "She's in expert hands."

"But I…"

Mac passed him a business card. *Georgia Collins. Grief Counselor.*

"She's expecting your call."

Michael pocketed the card. "Grace keeps hounding me about baptizing Brie."

"You should. Keep the peace." He raised an eyebrow. "Brie's not the only one who's going to need Colin and Grace. Compromise, Michael. What can it hurt?"

Brie sank her fingers into the curly coat of her lamb, screwed her eyelids tight, and then yielded to slumber.

Michael glanced at Mac. "Would you be Brie's godfather?"

"I thought Grace and Colin—"

"It's a compromise."

He chuckled. "I'd be honored."

January 1996

The morning Brie turned twenty-eight weeks, Dr. Adams, Brie's pulmonary specialist, satisfied with her respiratory markers, removed her from the ventilator. As they pulled the endotracheal tube, Michael expected to hear Brie's first cries, but the most she could muster was a raspy mew. "Give it time," Dr. Adams said. "As her lungs develop and the irritation in her throat resolves, her cry will strengthen."

He fitted Brie with a CPAP that provided a continuous flow of oxygen and kept the air sacs in her lungs open. Two hoses attached to a binasal cannula were held in place by straps wrapped around a cotton beanie. The cumbersome contraption overtook Brie's head.

With Brie successfully off the ventilator, Dr. Weber switched her to an orogastric feeding tube and consulted with her nutritionist about adjusting her formula. "Once her baseline measurements for oxygen, respiration, heart rate, and color are stable," he said, "I'll request a consult for a speech-language pathologist to assess her readiness for oral feeding."

"Then she'll be able to bottle feed?"

"It's a bit more complicated. First, we must determine if she's physiologically ready. Oral feeding will place significant demands on her little system. If we move too fast, push her too hard, she could shut down, increasing the possibilities of developing complications such as oral aversions and aspiration pneumonia." He set his hand on Michael's shoulder. "Safety is our primary goal. If we're patient, and follow Brie's cues, she'll show us what she can do and what feels safe." He smiled at Brie. "Every step forward is a victory."

Two days later, Brie's pediatric ophthalmologist diagnosed her with Stage Three retinopathy of prematurity, an abnormal growth of blood vessels in the retina. She'd need laser surgery, but he seemed confident that she would have no permanent vision damage.

Sunday, January 7th, Grace, Colin, and Michael crowded around Brie's incubator while Mac baptized Gabriella O'Leary Russo into the Catholic faith.

***

The following Tuesday, on his way home, Michael stopped at St. Columba. He parked Stella next to Mac's Jeep in the church lot and wandered down the path to his cottage. A thin plume of smoke spiraled from the chimney, drifted toward the starry sky. The house was dark, the door ajar.

138

He pushed it open. An orange glow emanated from the living room. The smell of sugar maple wafted.

"Mac?"

"In here."

Mac was sitting on the floor, gazing into the fire, a delicate strand of rosary beads wrapped around his massive hands. On the coffee table, beer bottles like bowling pins. Michael settled next to him.

Without averting his gaze from the dancing flames, Mac asked, "Why aren't you at the hospital?"

"Had my first appointment with Georgia Collins. She convinced me it was time to go home." He gestured toward the beer bottles. "Want to talk?"

"Sally moved in with Ed." He white-knuckled the rosary beads. "Not having Henry across the street…"

"Makes it harder to protect him."

Mac pried the cap off a Coors, handed Michael the bottle. Opened another, tipped a swig.

"The day Anna…" Michael swallowed the word with a mouthful of beer. "She had intended to see Sally. Try to talk her out of taking Ed back."

Flames flickered, casting Mac's face in a warm glow. Sadness tempered his eyes. The same sorrow Michael had seen the day they'd met.

Michael stripped the label from the bottle, wadded it into a ball, and tossed it into the fire. "From what you tell me about Ed, he won't stay sober long."

"One can only pray," he said, then drained the last of his beer.

Michael arrived home around midnight to a dark, quiet house. He flipped on lights, dialed heat, ambled up the stairs. He paused at the threshold. Nudged the door. The ghost of Anna's handprints frost-etched on the windowpane. Her flowy skirt, hanging from the closet door, quivered. The heart-shaped bloodstain in the hardwood pulsed. He grabbed a blanket, headed downstairs. Crashed on the couch.

***

At thirty weeks, Dr. Adams began alternating Brie's CPAP with a nasal cannula. While on the cannula, Brie experienced apnea—she'd stop breathing, and her heart rate would drop. Frightening, but Michael found rubbing Brie's back would stimulate breathing. Dr. Adams assured him the apnea would resolve in a few weeks.

Brie's speech-language pathologist began pre-feeding work. Her initial focus was getting Brie to tolerate touch to face and mouth area. "Once Brie develops stronger non-nutritive sucking and adequate suck-swallow-breathe coordination," she said, tapping Brie's chin, "we'll begin oral trials by bottle with a slow-flow nipple. The whole process will take weeks."

"Weeks?"

"It's a marathon, not a sprint," she replied, smiling at Brie. "Slow and steady wins the race."

Noon that day, Sara wheeled Brie's incubator into a private nursing room. She angled the blinds to block the afternoon sun while Michael eased into the recliner.

"You'll want to take off your shirt," she said.

"What?" He leaned forward, causing the chair to snap up. "Why?"

"Skin-to-skin contact bonds child to parent. It's called kangaroo care."

"Kangaroo what?" he said, wrestling out of his Cubs jersey.

"She closed the door, muffling the noise from the NICU. "Don't chicken out now."

"No. It's just…I'm afraid I might break her."

She laid Brie on his chest, adjusted the mask protecting Brie's eyes, and then disappeared from his line of vision. Brie wrapped her fingers around Michael's thumb and squeezed.

Time stilled, and the world stopped. His emotions converged, his brain fogged, and speech became impossible. The moment so unique and inexplicable, it transcended reason.

He closed his eyes, reveled in the scent of vanilla and oatmeal, the warmth of Brie's breath, the united heartbeats of father and daughter. He imagined Anna curling into his side, tucking her head under his chin, and placing her hand over his.

A sounding alarm pulled him from reverie. Anna disappeared. The clock ticked. Time moved.

Sara adjusted Brie's oxygen line and silenced the beeping. If she'd noticed his tears, she didn't let on. "I'll dim the lights and remove her mask," she said. "See if she'll open her eyes."

Once Sara settled into her chair, Michael asked, "Why did you decide to be a neonatal nurse?"

"Other than I thrive on chaos?" She paused as if choosing her words carefully. "Every day is a question mark. When I walk through the doors of the NICU each morning, I have no idea what my day holds. I like the challenge."

"Safe answer."

"Usually works. How come you're not buying it?"

"Anna ran a foundation for victims of domestic abuse. When she talked about work, you could hear the passion, see the determination on her face. You have that."

She set her heels on the edge of the rocking chair and hugged her legs. "Seven years ago, I gave birth to my son,

Elliot, at twenty-four weeks. Two days later, he caught pneumonia. Never got to hold him."

"Sorry. Shouldn't have pried."

"His death shattered me but made me stronger. By supporting others, I eventually recovered." She rocked back in the chair. "It's not easy. There are days I'm so frustrated, I say things. Nights, I get so angry, I want to quit. Times I'm resentful of the parents holding their child."

"I've never seen that side."

"I'm adept at hiding my horns."

Brie squirmed and let out a mew. "Think we woke her."

Sara studied Brie's face. "She's opening her eyes."

Brie's eyelashes fluttered, revealing dark blue irises. "Oh, god. Anna," he mumbled, and began to weep.

February 1996

The morning Brie turned thirty-four weeks, Dr. Webber called Michael into his office. He was pleased with Brie's progress and seemed cautiously optimistic. Even though Brie had yet to cry, an endoscopy revealed no vocal cord damage. She was completely off the CPAP and could breathe without supplemental oxygen for extended periods. Her apnea had disappeared. She'd adjusted well to the OG-tube, and her gut appeared to be tolerating formula feeds. Her pre-feeding therapy was progressing, and he'd expected to start oral feeding trials in a few days. For the first time since Anna died, Michael felt his world inch forward.

That afternoon, Harvey stopped by.

"With all those beautiful genes, she's going to be a heartbreaker," he said, waving fingers at Brie through her incubator. "You'll have to fight the boys off with a bat."

"Plenty of time to practice my swing."

"You need backup, you can count on Uncle Harvey. Played tee-ball when I was five." He unzipped his jacket, exposing his "The Snowstorm Was White on Time" T-shirt.

Michael stretched his legs, leaned back in the chair. "So, what's new in the weather business?"

"February in Chicago. Frickin' cold. And gray. Never changes. Happy Valentine's Day, by the way."

"And you decided to celebrate it with me. I'm honored, my friend."

He plopped into the chair. "How'd things go with Shannon?"

"Didn't roll out the red carpet, but didn't slam the door in my face. Sent me to see Chuck Simon."

"The editorial director? Why?"

"There's an opening for an assignment editor. Someone to develop story ideas and assign reporters."

"Bullshit. You're way overqualified for that." His raised voice earned a stern look from the nurse. "Sorry," he mouthed.

"Couldn't turn it down. Bills piling up. Need the insurance for Brie." Michael leaned forward. "I sold Stella to a collector in North Shore."

"What? Why?"

"Needed something safer for Brie."

"Have to protect the munchkin."

"Precious cargo."

"What are you driving?"

"Bought Hank's '71 F-100 Supercab. Has a back seat. Calls her 'Old Faithful.'

"Let's hope she is."

Sara came to check Brie's pulse ox monitors. "Ready for some kangaroo care?"

Harvey raised a brow. "Kangaroo what?"

"Care," Michael replied. "Skin-on-skin contact. Improves heart and respiratory rates and regulates breathing and body temperature." He wasn't sure Harvey heard since he was too busy watching Sara. Michael cleared his throat. "Harvey, this is Sara, Brie's neonatal nurse."

Sara unhooked Brie from her monitors and then scooped her up. "We girls are going to use the powder room."

Harvey's gaze trailed after Sara. "She married?"

On March 4th, Michael started as assignment editor for *The Chicago Nightly News* and an altered visitation schedule with Brie. If he wasn't with Brie, either Grace or Colin was. Mac, Harvey, and Jane visited on weekends.

At thirty-seven weeks, Brie experienced another setback when cow's milk fortifier was added to her formula to increase caloric intake. Within a few days, she showed signs of an allergic reaction. Her nutritionist switched her to a specialized formula for infants with protein sensitivities.

For the next month, several attempts were made to start oral feeding trials. Even after weeks of pre-feeding therapy, Brie refused to nurse from a bottle. She didn't have the strength or endurance to maintain feeding for more than a few minutes. Dr. Shaw, her gastroenterologist, diagnosed her with gastroesophageal reflux disease, or GERD. "Although there were drugs," she said, "time and patience were the best medicine."

Brie struggled to gain weight. On April 1st, Dr. Shaw inserted a gastrostomy tube through Brie's abdominal wall for long-term feeding. This G-tube would remain in place until Brie could maintain nutrition and hydration orally. "Which could take a year," she'd warned Michael. "Possibly longer."

By forty-five weeks, Brie was able to breathe on her own; however, she would have to continue oxygen therapy for several months. Her body temperature remained stable, and she'd reached her goal weight of five pounds. She frowned, yawned, fussed, and squirmed. Her GERD had subsided and, for the most part, she tolerated bottle feeds. She was offered three ounces of formula every four hours. What she didn't drink, Michael fed through the G-tube.

To the doctors and staff at Lakeview, Brie was the poster child for the advancement of medical technology and medicine. The press nicknamed her The Million Dollar Baby. Grace and Colin called her a miracle. But to Michael, Brie was simply an extraordinary child who'd inherited Anna's drive and determination and a hefty dose of his own stubbornness.

PART III

Chapter 16

On May 3rd, one hundred and sixty-five days from birth, Brie was released from Lakeview. Tucked into her car seat in the back of Old Faithful, Brie slept all the way to the farm.

The moment they arrived, Brie came to life. Color filled her pale cheeks, her deep blue irises brightened. Dark ringlets escaped the sides of her soft pink beanie, and tiny fingers poked from her cotton white cuffs. Her first full smile played on her lips. Michael grinned so hard, his cheeks hurt.

Grace offered to spend the week, help Brie acclimate. Michael declined. Twenty-three weeks in the NICU had prepared him. And, selfishly, he was tired of sharing her.

Although Brie had yet to find her voice, he could read her gestures and facial expressions. She'd rub her eyes when tired, suck her bottom lip when hungry, blush and frown apologetically when she needed changing or had gas.

While Brie spent the afternoon napping, Michael sorted endless stacks of bills. Even if he got asking price for the farm, it wouldn't cover a quarter of Brie's hospital expenses. His health insurance hadn't kicked in, and Anna's COBRA premiums were steep.

Next, he calendared all of Brie's upcoming appointments. The hospital had scheduled her occupational and physical therapy sessions three months out. She'd continue to see the speech pathologist and a registered dietician. On Tuesday afternoon, she'd have her first visit with Dr. Eply, a pediatrician Dr. Webber highly recommended.

He made a copy of the calendar for Grace and uttered a silent gratitude. He could not do this without her.

That evening, Michael settled into the rocking chair next to Brie. She seemed enthralled with the chickens and ducks dancing overhead. After she fell asleep, he sprawled out in bed. Anna's ghost haunted every corner of the room. He dragged his mattress into the nursery and collapsed. Listening to Brie's rhythmic breathing, he drifted off.

***

The following morning, he tucked Brie inside a sling, carried her against his chest, and hiked the farm. The pink peonies Jane and Rita planted last fall were blooming. In the field, Bumblebees buzzed the yellow petals of Black-eyed Susans. Meadowlarks chirped flute-like from fence posts. Butterflies flitted over the patch of lavender, and the sweet scent of lilac wafted.

They approached the barn. The turkey poked his head out, then clucked and hobbled toward the fence. Brie, who'd been sleeping contentedly, wiggled and squirmed at the peculiar sound. Her face exploded with joy, her eyes went wide, her mouth formed an O, and she cooed. So softly, he thought he'd imagined it. But she scrunched up her face, tightened her fists, and cooed again; this time with such force, she startled herself. For the first time, she giggled. And for what seemed like a span of years, Michael laughed again.

He rubbed his nose against hers and then smiled at the sky. "You were right, Anna. She loves the farm."

***

"Didn't you host *Wake Up, Chicago!?*" asked a fresh-faced college intern, one of three crowding Michael's cubicle.

"Thought you looked familiar," said the second. "Didn't they call you the 'Face of Chicago'?"

"That was years ago, right?" asked the third.

"Decades," he muttered. His phone rang.

"I don't know what she wants," Grace said, her voice cracking. "I've changed, fed, and rocked her, but she keeps squirming like a tipped-over turtle."

He'd dropped Brie off at Colin and Grace's an hour ago, happy and content. But he'd learned how quickly her mood could change.

"Put her on," he said.

"She's not even six months. She can't—"

"Hold the receiver to her ear."

The interns gawked as though he were speaking to Bill Clinton. He swiveled his chair around, then crooned. "Over in Killarney, many years ago. My mother sang a song to me, in tones so soft and low. Just a simple little ditty. In her good old Irish way."

Grace whisper-shouted. "It's magic, Michael. Keep singing."

151

"Too-ra-loo-ra-loo-ral. Too-ra-loo-ra-li. Too-ra-loo-ra-loo-ral. That's an Irish lullaby."

Grace hung up. He swiveled back to three gaping mouths. Channeling Shannon, he yelled, "What the hell are you still doing here? Go scrounge up a story."

They fled his office. Bees evacuating a burning hive.

"What's so funny, Mikey?" Harvey walked into his cubicle wearing a "What Kind of Underwear Do Clouds Wear? Thunderwear" T-shirt.

"Life, my friend. What brings you to steerage?"

Harvey scanned above the cubicle, his head like a periscope, and then sank into a chair. "I need advice."

"About?"

"You know the new intern? The leggy brunette?" He scooched until his knees hit Michael's desk. "I think she's got the hots for me. Keeps asking about my equipment."

"Maybe she's just interested in weather forecasting."

"You know women. They speak in code."

"I've been out of the loop a while. How can I help?"

"Should I ask her out?"

"My advice? Don't. Even the President of the United States isn't stupid enough to get involved with an intern."

"Thanks, Dear Abby. Speaking of which, how's the writing bit?"

He pulled off his glasses and rubbed his eyes. "Between work and Brie, hard to find time."

"Any offers on your place?"

"Guy wanting to start an ostrich farm. Claims they're the health food of the future. Katie says he's offered asking price. But Brie's so enthralled with the farm, I've decided not to sell."

"Thought you needed money."

He slipped his glasses on. "Looking into other options."

***

Twenty minutes after Harvey left, claustrophobia set in. He choked on dregs from the bottom of his coffee mug and emerged from his cubicle in search of fresh brew. Mac lumbered toward him; Henry at his side, jumping over purple carpet tiles.

A study in contrast: Mac's powerful build, dark hair, soulful brown eyes, next to Henry's slender frame, sandy blonde hair, wide-set blue eyes. If they shared similar quirks, as Mac claimed, they weren't evident.

Mac's beard could not contain his grin. "Hope we're not interrupting. The receptionist said it was okay—"

"Perfect timing. Needed a break."

Mac tucked in the belt on Henry's karate jacket. Henry lifted the binoculars hanging around his neck, placed them against his eyes, backwards, and peered at Michael.

"Master Luke." Michael bowed. "We meet again."

Mac held up a field guide. "Headed to Montrose Point to bird-watch. Thought we'd see how your weekend went with Brie."

"Anna was right. Brie loves the farm. She's babbling up a storm. Named the turkey 'Coo' and the rooster 'Goo'."

Henry tugged Mac's flannel shirt and pointed to the wall of windows overlooking Chestnut Street.

"Ask Mr. Russo."

Gaze downward, Henry signed the question.

"After you, young Skywalker."

Henry ran to the window—purple squares be damned—pressed hands and forehead against the glass, stared down thirty stories.

"He's getting tall," Michael said.

"He'll turn six on the twenty-first. Hard to believe."

"Sally have a change of heart?"

"Not exactly," he said, with a mischievous glance.

Henry scoped the skyline as if searching for Imperial Starfighters. Mac stood next to him, as if he too were scouting enemy ships.

"Sally doesn't know Henry's with you, does she?"

"Ed took Sally to visit relatives in Alabama for the week. Charlie's home for summer break and offered to watch Henry." He squatted next to Henry, tied his shoes. "Charlie came down with the flu, so I'm pinch-hitting."

"What about the shop?"

"Charlie's running the business while she and Ed are gone. In exchange, Sally's letting Charlie live at the shop rent-free. Ed told Charlie if it worked out, he'd take Sally out of town more often."

"Allowing you more time with Henry."

He stood, smiling.

"Ed's still sober?"

"Wears a six-month sobriety medallion around his neck like a badge of honor."

"You've seen him?"

"Came to confession last week. Asked me to pray for him. Part of the twelve-step process."

Michael stepped to the window, scanned the congested street below. Ant-sized people scurrying toward yellow taxis, white CTA buses, red double-decker trolleys. "Maybe his relatives will push him over the edge."

Henry swung his binoculared gaze between Mac and Michael.

"We'll let you get back to work."

"Glad you stopped by."

Mac nodded and led Henry, jumping purple carpet tiles, toward the exit.

***

August stifled Chicago like a bug under a magnifying glass. Buildings wavered in walls of heat. Sidewalks melted shoes.

On the last Saturday of the month, a breeze blew in off the lake, making the heat bearable. Michael, accompanied by Colin and Grace, strolled Brie through the Lincoln Park Zoo. While Grace pushed Brie toward the Farm-in-the-Zoo exhibit, Colin and Michael walked the edge of the pond.

Mallards splashed the tranquil water near the bridge. Cattails bowed to red-winged blackbirds. A blue heron stalked the shallows.

In the distance, a bird wailed. Wildlife stilled. Colin paused, craned his neck in search of the mysterious fowl. When the shrills subsided, the chatter of blackbirds restored the pond's serenity.

Colin swatted a mosquito and caught up with Michael. "How'd your appointment with the pediatrician go?"

"Dr. Eply is encouraged with Brie's progress."

"What'd she say about Brie not crying?"

"When Brie finds something to cry about, she'll let the whole world know."

155

Turtles sunbathed along reedy banks. Bumblebees buzzed tufts of lavender, and dragonflies hovered clustered lily pads. A redheaded toddler squealed and waddled toward the water's edge. "Look, Daddy," she said, pointing at a sailboating swan. Her father swung her onto his shoulders.

"I remember when Anna called me Daddy for the first time," Colin said. "Banged her head on the corner of the coffee table. Lifted her arms, sobbed, 'Daddy', then let out a heart-wrenching cry that sounded like—"

The mysterious wailing echoed again, an extended siren that sliced humidity and skimmed the pond. Blackbirds took flight, turtles dove, dragonflies darted.

Colin shook his head. "That is not a bird."

"It's Brie," they voiced in unison.

Michael hurdled fences, dodged strollers, found Grace at the sheep pen, clutching a bawling Brie. Brie's slick cheeks glowed red. Unfurling her tiny fists, she reached for him. He pulled her into his arms. She buried her face into his chest, dampened his shirt. He turned to Grace. "What happened?"

"One minute she was babbling at the sheep and the next, screaming at the top of her lungs."

"It's the heat," Colin said, coming up behind, huffing, wiping sweat with a handkerchief. "I told you it was too hot."

Brie fisted Michael's shirt and rubbed her face against it. "Baa," she sobbed. "Baa-baa-baa."

Michael searched the stroller. "Where's Baa?"

Grace scanned the surrounding area. "She must have dropped him. That's why she's upset. Colin, help me look."

Michael crouched and pointed to the sheep gathered near the fence. "Look, Brie. Baa."

She sucked in a shaky breath and turned toward the sheep. Uncontrollable sobs escalated into high-pitched wails. He bounced her in his arms. "Shhh." He kissed her forehead. "It's okay. We'll find Baa."

People gawked. "Sorry," he said, sheepishly. "She lost her stuffed lamb."

Clutching Brie, he searched the greenbelt back to the pond. Grace's voice resonated over Brie's hiccupy sobs. "I've got him," she said, waving the lamb. She rushed forward and handed Baa to Brie. She tucked Baa underneath her chin and rested her head against Michael's chest.

Colin appeared, pushing the stroller. "We've had enough heat. Let's head home."

"Baa," Brie babbled.

Colin chuckled. "Doc was right. She damn sure had something she wanted to tell the world."

Chapter 17

On November 21st, Brie's first birthday, Michael woke before the sun and stood at Brie's window, surveying the farm in predawn gray. After a starry night, a thick frost iced the barn roof.

He and Grace agreed to celebrate March 17th, Brie's original due date, rather than her actual date, separating Brie's birth from Anna's death.

After leaving Brie with Grace, he drove through the open wrought-iron gates of the cemetery, pulled into a parking space, and turned off the engine. He stared at the ivy climbing the crumbling mausoleum stones and wondered why he'd come.

He hadn't been to the cemetery since Anna's funeral. Didn't need some physical reminder she'd died or a place to visit to feel close to her. Maybe he'd come out of a sense of duty. Perhaps driven by guilt. Or both.

Colin came every Saturday. He had a stone bench installed at the foot of Anna's grave. Grace made sure the grounds were properly maintained, headstone polished, flowers delivered.

Michael grabbed the bouquet of peonies he'd ordered from Rita's, walked through rows of glossy headstones and shiny white crosses. The air was crisp, the sky icy blue. Frosted grass crunched beneath his shoes, leaving a trail of footprints.

Grace had spared no expense. The towering Celtic cross, carved of black marble and etched with Irish symbols, blocked the early morning sun and cast Anna's grave in shadow. Engraved in the stone base:

Aine Grace O'Leary
Beloved Mother — Cherished Daughter
July 11, 1959 — November 21, 1995

He sat on the granite bench and waited. For what?

A starling landed atop the black cross and eyed him.

He pulled a picture of Brie from his pocket. "It's amazing how much she reminds me of you. Your hair, your eyes, your determination." He choked back tears. "Your smile."

He squinted into sunlight pouring through the spaces of the cross. "This would be easier if I had an ounce of your faith."

Curled oak leaves tumbled across the ice-glazed grass, skittered on the asphalt path.

"You'd be proud of Brie. How strong she is, how hard she's fought, how brave. She'll be talking soon. What do I tell her when she asks about you?"

A brisk wind stung cheeks, stole moisture from eyes. Frigid air seeped through the wool fabric of pants.

He stood, walked to the headstone. "No need to worry. About Brie and me. I've got this. We'll be okay."

The starling bobbed its head, spread its wings, and took flight toward the sun.

He set the peonies and Brie's picture at the base of the cross and ran his fingertips over her name. "Thank you, Anna. For Brie."

***

That night, Brie couldn't sleep. Michael moved the couch in front of the picture window. They stared at frozen stars while eating Cheerios straight from the box.

"Want to hear about the night I fell in love with your mother?"

She nodded, stuffing Cheerios in her mouth.

"It was on a night like tonight. We were parked in Grandma's driveway —"

"Paaa?" she asked.

"Yes, Grandpa's too. We were having this fight about…I can't remember. I'm sure it had something to do with me not acting my age," he said, knocking over a tower of Cheerios with a flick of his finger. "She was so mad, I thought her hair might catch fire. But she was so amazingly beautiful, I couldn't stop smiling — which made her even madder. Then, before she burst into flames, 'I'll Stand by You' played on the radio. She stopped yelling, and in unison we said, 'Best song ever.'"

Brie stopped chewing and frowned.

"What? You don't believe me?" He loaded the *Last of the Independents* CD into the Sony player, hit track seven, then snagged the picture of him and Anna off his desk before plopping onto the couch.

Brie crawled into his lap and took the photo out of his hand. She pointed to his image and said, "Aah?"

"Yes, that's me. Daddy." He patted his hand against his chest. "Dad-dee."

Confusion played on her face.

He tapped his finger against her heart. "Brie." Then tapped his chest. "Dad-dee."

She pointed at herself. "Bee." Then pointed at him. "Aah." The corners of her mouth formed a triumphant smile.

He chuckled. "Close enough…for now."

She twirled a curl of her hair around her index finger and studied Anna's face. "Mah?"

"Yes." He kissed the top of her head. "Mommy."

She nuzzled her face against his chest and fell asleep.

He wrapped the old quilt around them and stared at the black sky with its million pinpricks of light. "Best Song Ever," he whispered, as the last notes faded.

***

March 17th fell on a Monday. Since Michael had to work, Grace hosted Brie's birthday party.

He left the station at 5:30, pulled into their driveway at 6:00. Colin stood in the doorway, shoulders hunched, hands thrust in pockets. A sharp "NO!" rang from the kitchen. Colin shrugged. "Brie's learned her first real word."

"No! No! No!"

Michael shouldered past Colin, rushed into the kitchen. Grace was on her hands and knees, mopping baby food; Brie, in her highchair, fists tight. When Brie saw him, she lifted her arms and flapped her fingers like wings. He lifted her out of her chair. She wrapped her legs around his waist and pointed at Grace. "No!"

161

"What's going on?"

Grace gestured toward the open jar of baby food on the counter. "I tried something new."

"Beef stew?" He held the jar up to his nose and winced. "Did you taste it?"

"I tried the chicken and rice. It wasn't bad." She pushed to her feet and tossed the sponge into the sink. "She needs protein, Michael."

"Her pediatric dietician said it takes time to adjust to new textures and flavors."

She picked up a jar of turkey with gravy and stared into the pale brown puree. "Aine used to love this."

"Grace." He shifted Brie to his other hip. "She's not Anna."

"Apparently not," she mumbled.

"What's this?" he asked, pulling a chunk of yellow goo from Grace's hair.

"Scrambled eggs. She threw them in my face."

He laughed. And for the first time since Anna's death, Grace cracked a smile.

"Go clean up," he said. "I'll take care of this mess."

She pulled off her apron, folded it over a chair, and looked at him. "She said her first real word, Michael."

"That she did," he said, trying to hide his disappointment.

He tidied the kitchen, spot-cleaned the baby food smeared on Brie's dress, the yellow one he'd bought for her party. Grace waltzed in, primped and polished, retrieved a two-tiered cake from the fridge, placed it on the counter.

"Isn't she a bit young to be getting married?"

"She'll only be one once," she said, pulling Brie from his arms. "Look, Gabriella. A princess cake."

A knock stole his retort.

"Get that," Grace commanded as she left the room. "Princess Gabriella needs to change before her subjects arrive."

"What's wrong with what she's got on?" he called out, heading into the living room. "And stop calling her princess!" He yanked open the door.

"Bad timing?" Mac asked.

"Only if you're Prince Charming."

Henry shadowed Mac through the door. "Charlie's home on spring break. She volunteered to sit Henry so Ed could take Sally to Alabama. Celebrate sixteen months of sobriety."

"Where's Charlie?"

Mac shrugged. "Sore throat?"

Gaze cast down, Henry held up a box wrapped in Star Wars paper.

"Thank you, Master Luke. I'll make sure Leia gets this."

Mac removed Henry's coat, then tucked him into a quiet corner of the living room with his X-wing fighter while Michael greeted Jane and Harvey.

"For Brie," Harvey said, handing Michael a gift bag.

Jane set a yellow gift box on the coffee table and hugged Michael. "How are you?"

"Brie keeps me busy."

"Has she taken her first steps?"

"Not on her own."

Colin popped the champagne, filled several flutes, passed them around. "Where's the birthday girl?"

"Ta-da!" Grace announced from the top of the stairs.

Heads turned in unison. Brie, dressed in a pink taffeta gown, white tights, and ballet slippers, smiled shyly at them from Grace's arms. A crystal tiara pinned back her curls, and a purple "Princess" sash hung across her chest.

Grace cleared her throat. "Colin."

"Oh, right." He held up his champagne flute. "All hail Princess Gabriella."

"Good god," Michael mumbled as Grace descended the stairs, waving her hand like a princess on parade.

Mac chuckled. "Compromise."

Jane curtsied. Mac and Harvey bowed. Colin snapped pictures with his new color digital camera. They sang Happy Birthday. Brie blew out the candle, and Grace cut the cake.

Once they'd finished eating, Grace breezed through the room. "Time to open gifts." She clapped, crisp and sharp. "Places, everyone."

"Is she for real?" Harvey whispered.

Michael scooped up Brie and sat on the floor in front of the couch.

Grace placed the presents next to Brie.

Michael helped Brie open Harvey's first.

"It's a picture book about food raining from the sky," he said. "A classic."

Brie pulled the tissue paper out of Jane's gift box. Michael held up Oshkosh overalls and a "Farm Girl" T-shirt. Grace rolled her eyes and downed the rest of her champagne.

Charlie bought her a Goth Girl beanie and Mac fuzzy hooded pajamas with sheep ears. "Baa!" Brie squealed. Everyone laughed.

"This is from daddy," Michael said, setting his present at her feet. She ripped off the wrapping paper. Her eyes went wide, her mouth formed an 'O'. Michael opened the box. The pieces of the Lego Duplo farm set tumbled to the floor. Brie picked up the cow and studied it as if it were about to moo.

Colin emerged from the hall carrying a dollhouse he could barely lift. He set the pink plastic monstrosity in the center of the room and opened it.

Cow clutched in hand, Brie crawled to the dollhouse. She stood and babbled a muddled string of sounds.

"I knew she'd love it," Grace exclaimed.

On unsteady feet, Brie turned, stared at her legs as if willing them to move. Michael held his breath, worried his exhale might knock her over.

Grace sank to her knees, held out her arms. "Come to Nana, Princess."

Brie searched each face, took a step, and tumbled.

A collective gasp filled the room. Mac set his hand on Michael's shoulder. "Leave her be."

Brie wobbled to her feet and, showing fierce determination, tottered toward Michael but took a detour from his outstretched hands and headed for the corner. She held out the cow to Henry. "Bee," she said, pointing to her heart.

Henry took the cow. She sat next to him and babbled like a brook. He listened intently as if he understood, then showed Brie how his fighter flew.

Mac shook his head, disbelief etched on his brow. "For years I've tried to get him to play with other children."

"Brie's probably less intimidating," Michael said, pushing up and onto the couch next to Jane.

"Maybe," Mac replied, a hint of skepticism laced in his voice.

Jane leaned into Michael. "Life is about to get quite complicated, Dad."

Chapter 18

Over the summer, Brie's arms and legs sprouted. At eighteen months, she was thirty-two inches of insatiable curiosity and twenty-two pounds of limitless energy, a combination that left Michael exhausted. She seemed determined to run before she'd perfected her walk. Her legs weren't as agile as her mind, and she would often trip, leading to a few bruised knees, a bloody lip, and the discovery of a new sound, "OW."

Dr. Eply diagnosed Brie with a flexible form of metatarsus adductus and prescribed orthopedic shoes for developing muscles. She soon discovered the shoes hindered mobility. She'd hide them under her crib, between couch cushions, or with the dirty laundry.

Michael learned several valuable lessons before Brie turned two: mayonnaise removes crayon from walls, peanut butter sticks to any surface, retrieving a rubber ducky from the gooseneck of a toilet isn't easy, and you can leave the house a half-hour early but still arrive a half-hour late. Life with a toddler was never simple, often messy, and forever unpredictable.

By twenty-four months, Brie could only produce a dozen meaningful sounds, including 'no'. She'd passed tests that eliminated hearing loss or receptive language issues. The speech pathologist could not rule out Apraxia of speech; however, she could find no physical defects, no errors or sound distortions, both hallmarks of the disorder. Dr. Eply referred Michael to Dr. Paul Dorian, a developmental psychologist.

***

The Friday after Brie's second birthday, Michael and Grace sat in overstuffed chairs and spoke with Dr. Dorian while Brie played with her Lego Farm.

Dr. Dorian crossed his legs and cupped his knee. "I can unequivocally state that Brie has no mental disorders or signs of autism."

"Why then," Grace inquired, "won't she talk?"

"Brie seems so focused on exploring her world, she has no time for talk, especially since her language is not developed enough to express her thoughts. Einstein didn't speak until age four."

Grace sat straight, shoulders squared. "Brie's gifted?"

"It's too early to test her IQ, but her receptive language and nonverbal communication skills are highly developed, and she has an uncanny ability to understand complex emotions. She's a remarkable little girl." He leaned forward, picked up Brie's Lego pig. She reached up and touched his cheek. He winked at her, handed back the pig, and settled into his chair. "Have you heard of emotional intelligence?"

They both shook their heads.

"EQ is the ability to understand and interpret emotions of others and use this knowledge to guide one's own thinking and actions."

"So Brie is emotionally gifted, not intellectually gifted?" Michael asked.

"They can work in tandem. Individuals with high EQs have advanced cognitive abilities. Think of emotional intelligence as the glue that binds heart and mind."

"Can we get her to talk?" Grace asked.

"In time," he said, watching Brie place her pig inside the barn. "Brie's not yet using words, but she's communicating. We just need to learn how to listen."

***

Saturday, the late afternoon sun dissolved clouds and melted snow. Michael zipped Brie into her puffy jacket, pulled on her muck boots. Waiting for Mac and Henry, Michael raked sodden leaves, and Brie picked up soggy twigs.

Last fall, Ed inherited a cabin on Hidden Lake from his uncle. Charlie returned home from college every weekend to take care of Henry and run the shop so Ed could drag Sally to the cabin. Ed's infatuation with hunting had morphed into an obsession with fishing.

On days Mac had Henry, he'd bring him to play with Brie. The six-year age gap didn't appear an issue. Neither talked, but somehow communicated.

Henry ran down the path wearing an inside-out sweatshirt and sneakers without socks. A flop of sandy-brown hair hid his broad forehead and wide-set eyes. A gangly seven-year-old, he still didn't resemble Mac.

Henry showed Brie his new R2-D2 action figure. They disappeared into the barn.

169

Mac approached, contemplation etching his brow. "Problem?"

"Ed came to see me yesterday," he said, unearthing a rock with his boot. "Wants to join the parish. Thinks church will help him be a more attentive husband. A better father."

"He's catholic?"

"Baptized in the Catholic faith. I have no grounds to deny him."

"The guy's a psychopath, Mac."

He picked up the dull rock he'd toed loose, turned it over, exposing bands of pink and gray that sparkled in sunlight. "Maybe he's changed."

"What?"

"He's twenty-eight months sober. Hasn't hit Sally —
"

"That you know of. Even so, what about the way he treats Henry?"

He wiped dirt off the rock. "Maybe I can help him understand Henry. Accept his mannerisms."

"You can't be serious."

"I cannot pray for someone to fail." Mac fisted the rock, hurled it into the meadow, rousing a flock of starlings. Birds swooped overhead, then settled into weathered stalks. He looked at Michael with a smooth, resigned brow. "How'd Brie's appointment go?"

"Doc said to be patient." Michael pulled off his gloves, pushed them into his coat pockets. "Said Brie has the ability to perceive how others feel."

"Emotional intelligence?" He hummed his agreement. "Makes sense."

In the barn, Brie had climbed the rungs of Coo's stall. Henry stood next to her, arms folded on the rail. She pointed at the turkey and let out a string of nonsensical sounds. Coo jumped, landed next to Brie, purred, and tucked his head beneath her chin. Henry stared at Brie as if she'd performed a magic trick.

Mac chuckled. "Never gets old." He glanced around the barn. "Where's Goo?"

"Over here," Michael said, leading him to Old Faithful.

Michael leaned against the truck bed. The rooster, hunkered in the corner beneath a pile of straw, stared through cloudy eyes. "Have to chase him out every morning before I leave for work."

Henry tugged on Mac's flannel shirt. They exchanged hand signals. Acting as interpreter, Brie babbled a few lines at Michael, and then marched through the door with Henry, Coo hobbling behind.

"What was that about?" Michael asked.

"Apparently, the Death Star looms on the horizon. Luke and Leia are going to alert the Rebel Alliance."

Outside, Henry and Brie sat back-to-back atop the picnic table. Brie, with Coo as copilot, flew the fighter jet while Henry shot at the pale moon, translucent in the cobalt sky.

Standing in front of the barn, Mac gripped Michael's shoulder. "Looks like our kids are saving the world."

***

Winter gave way to spring. In the fields, farmers cultivated land and optimism. April rains commingled damp, loamy soil and cow manure. May sprouted rows of sun-seekers that thrived in June heat. By July, corn stalks swayed to summer breezes and soy plants blanketed in a sea of emerald green.

Torrential downpours hammered the farm for three days, but on the Fourth of July, the sun broke through stubborn clouds. Since Sally and Ed were at the cabin for the holiday, Mac and Charlie had Henry for the week. Michael called Mac to come for a barbecue.

"We'll be there around four."

Jane and Rita had plans, but Harvey didn't.

"Need me to pick up anything?" Harvey asked.

"Come at two. We'll grocery shop."

Brie and Michael were in the backyard when Harvey arrived. He set a case of Bud and a Pringles can on the picnic table. "Shouldn't you be wearing a tutu?"

"Couldn't find one my size," Michael replied, leaping at the bubble hovering over his head.

Brie dunked her wand, pursed her lips, and blew another batch.

"Shouldn't Brie be chasing the bubbles?"

"It's part of her speech therapy." A breeze blew the next one out of his reach. "She won't blow them unless I try to catch them."

"You're not very good at it."

"Not as easy as you think."

"Cause you're not doing it right." Harvey positioned himself next to Michael, flipped his Cubs cap around, and rubbed his hands. "Okay, Brie. Let 'em rip."

A dozen bubbles floated their way. Michael snagged three before Harvey popped his first.

Brie writhed in a fit of giggles.

"You're not playing fair," Harvey said, smashing one between his hands.

"Whaddaya mean?"

"There's rules."

"What rules?" Michael leapt and caught a double bubble. "That counts as two."

"You're in my space," Harvey said, elbowing Michael before snagging the bubble floating between them.

"Hey, that was mine. Brie! We need more..."

She'd abandoned her wand to examine something furry, sitting on its haunches, whiskers twitching as it wriggled its nose at her.

Harvey panted. "Is that—"

Michael scooped Brie onto his back. The mouse stared as if he'd stolen its cheese, then flicked its tail and scurried underneath the porch.

Harvey wiped the sweat from his forehead. "Looks like Mickey's found a home."

"If Grace finds out, she'll lose it."

Brie slid off his back and pointed to the hole. "Mu-mu-mu-ow!" she squeaked.

Michael crouched, eye level. "M-ou-se," he said. "But it's a secret mouse. Don't tell anyone you saw it, okay?"

She pressed her index finger against her lips.

"That's right. Mum's the word."

"Mu-mu-mu-mouse," she squealed.

Harvey chuckled. "At least the speech therapy thing's working."

"Let's go grab groceries for the barbecue. And a trap for Mickey."

***

Michael settled Brie into the kiddie seat of the grocery cart and sent Harvey to pick out veggies while he gathered other items on his list.

"She's adorable."

173

Michael stopped thumping watermelons. A tall brunette in yoga pants and a tight T-shirt, reminding him to "Just Breathe" bent over and smiled at Brie. "All those curls."

"Not so adorable when they're all tangled," he replied, averting his gaze from her cleavage to her baby pink toenails.

"Her eyes are so blue. And those freckles."

A summer of sun freckled Brie's face. "So much like her mother."

He looked up. The woman was gone, and in her place stood Harvey, balancing a plump tomato in each hand. "She's a chick magnet," he said, gesturing to Brie.

"Got everything but the steaks," Michael said. "I'll head to the meat department. You check out. I'll meet you at the truck."

"Leave the munchkin with me," Harvey replied, commandeering the cart.

Michael pulled Brie from her perch and anchored her to his hip. "Not on your life."

A half-dozen people stood in line at the meat counter. Michael pulled number sixty-seven from the ticket dispenser. Sixty-one glowed on the display.

He studied his options through the glass. Butch, the 300-pound bald man with the blood-smeared apron, hollered, "Sixty-two." Brie squirmed. He didn't blame her. The guy was intimidating, even without his cleaver.

Sixty-two, an elderly lady with bony fingers, insisted Butch trim any visible fat from her roast. Sixty-three disappeared. "Must've chickened out," Michael muttered to sixty-six. Sixty-four made Butch explain the different cuts of beef, and then chose a salmon fillet. By the time Butch called sixty-five, Brie was wiggling, a worm on a hook. Michael set her down. She grabbed his wrist and tugged.

"A few more minutes."

"Nooo," she whined. She backed up and pulled with all her might. When he didn't budge, she latched onto his forearm and lifted her feet, as if all her weight would change his mind. That didn't work, so she held her breath. Her face turned beet red. Those in line watched and waited. Should have left her with Harvey.

"Sixty-seven," Butch yelled, slapping a price sticker on the white paper wrapped around sixty-six's pork roast.

"Your name really, Butch?" Michael asked, handing him his ticket.

Butch set his massive hands on the counter and crooked his eyebrow. "Do I look like someone who'd lie?"

"Ah...no. How fresh is your sirloin?"

Butch smiled, revealing a gold-capped incisor. "Hacked it off the carcass today. Fresh enough?"

No one could hear Michael's answer, because Brie blew like a geyser. Let out a high-pitched wail, punctuated with a molecule-splitting scream, and didn't let up until they exited the store.

He buckled Brie into her car seat, handed her Baa, jumped into Old Faithful.

"Where's the steak?" Harvey asked.

"They ran out," he said, driving out of the lot.

"Why didn't you get chicken?"

"Didn't have any."

"Hamburger? Sausage? Hot dogs?"

Michael turned onto Pine.

"What're we gonna grill?"

Michael felt a thud under his front tire and a thump in the steering wheel. Brie fussed and then fell silent.

He pulled over, slowed to a stop, and then glanced in the rearview mirror. A mound of brown feathers lay in the middle of the road.

"Shit," he mumbled.

Harvey looked over his shoulder. "Now we got something to grill."

Michael opened the door. "Keep an eye on Brie."

"Oh, sure," he yelled out the window. "Now that we're in the middle of nowhere, you trust me to watch her."

Michael retrieved the shovel from the truck bed and headed to the duck. She was dead. "Sorry," he muttered. He scooped her up and placed her near an evergreen at the side of the road.

Six ducklings, each no bigger than his fist, cowered beneath the low-hanging spruce branches. Muddy water swirled in the culvert that separated the road from a cornfield.

He returned to the truck bed, dumped his tools from the Duckwall apple crate.

Harvey stuck his head out the window. "What're you doing?"

"Not sure."

He approached the tree. The ducklings panicked and swam to the other side of the culvert. The distance across was probably about eighteen feet. He lifted his face and squinted into the sun.

When he was a senior at Adams High, Michael held the school record for the long jump—twenty feet, one inch—for exactly two minutes. Stevie Spinnerman, with his spindly legs, beat him by a quarter inch. Not only did

Stevie steal the first-place trophy, but his track scholarship to MSU.

Michael backed up to the edge of the road and took off running. "Screw you, Stevie Spinnerman," he screamed, propelling across the great divide.

The water was only two feet deep, and apparently, a soaked man with his face in mud didn't intimidate ducklings. They cackled, zoomed past Michael, and raced to the other side.

Harvey stood at the edge of the culvert. "Oh, for a video camera."

"When you're finished laughing," Michael said, wringing water from his T-shirt, "help me catch those little buggers."

"Brie's got that covered."

Brie stood in the grass, surrounded by ducklings.

***

They pulled up the drive, Michael's drenched underwear suctioned to his skin, dried mud on his face. Mac slid off the hood of his Jeep and walked toward Michael. Harvey helped Brie out of her car seat and headed to the house for soap and a towel.

Brie vaulted into Mac's arms. He hoisted her above his head, and Brie stretched her arms like wings. He spun in circles and then set her on her feet. She giggled, stumbling dizzily.

"Where's Henry?" Michael asked, hauling the apple crate out of Old Faithful.

"Coming with Charlie." He studied Michael's face. "New beauty treatment?"

"Long story."

"I've got time," he replied, as they followed Brie down the path.

Michael set the crate on the ground.

"Kack!" Brie explained.

"I can see that," Mac said. "Where'd you get them?"

"That's part of the story," Michael said, stripping to his underwear. While hosing off, Michael told Mac about hitting the duck. Harvey joined in, spinning the story with detail.

"What am I supposed to do with six orphaned ducklings?" he asked, wrapping a towel around his waist.

"It appears," Mac replied, "they're no longer orphans."

Brie had pulled the ducklings out of the crate and herded them onto the grass.

Henry raced down the hill, Charlie close behind.

She sat on the edge of the picnic table, popped open the Pringles can, and shoved a few into her mouth. "I see you guys found some chicks for the party."

Brie ran around flapping her arms. All six ducklings, chests extended, chased her. Henry tailed them, his X-wing fighter soaring. Coo poked his head from the barn; Goo watched from the loft.

Brie babbled something to Michael and then resumed her motherly duties.

Charlie tossed the empty Pringles can into the oil drum. "So where's the food?"

***

Hank came that night with duck feed and mealworms. Told Michael to add brewer's yeast and supplement their diet with fruits and veggies. They set up a brooding area in the corner of the barn with a heating lamp and then filled Brie's Kiddie pool and made a ramp.

"How long before they're old enough to fly away?" Michael asked Hank as he climbed into his Dodge Ram.

"About eight weeks," he replied. "Doesn't mean they will."

"They might stay? For how long?"

"Fifteen years or so."

Chapter 19

The first Sunday in October arrived wet and chilly. Brie and Michael fed the birds (including the ducklings, who'd taken up permanent residency), made pancakes, and then settled in the living room.

Michael dumped Brie's bucket of farm animals and divvied them up. "Trade you two chickens for a cow," he said, lining up his pieces.

She clutched her Guernsey and shook her head.

"Okay, two chickens and a goat. Final offer."

The doorbell rang. Michael pushed to his feet.

"I know exactly how many horses I have," he called out, "so don't be stealing—"

"Michael." Grace stepped into the entry, stared at the water-stained ceiling, tugged off her gloves. "Where's my granddaughter?"

He swung the door shut. "To what do we owe the honor of your company?"

She slid off her trench coat and handed it to him. "I'm taking Brie to church."

"You should have called and asked."

"You would've said no."

"Your insight is impeccable." He trailed her into the living room and tossed her coat over his office chair. "Your presence doesn't change my answer."

Brie ran to Grace. "Nanna!"

"There's my princess!" Grace picked her up and surveyed the room: farm pieces littering the floor, blankets piled from last night's fort-building contest, syrupy breakfast plates on the coffee table. "Nanna's going to take you to church. Would you like that?"

Brie clapped and squealed, "Urch!"

Grace flashed a victorious smile and marched up the stairs, Brie's arms wrapped around her neck.

"She doesn't even know what church is," Michael said, following.

"Whose fault is that?"

Brie peeked around Grace's shoulder and held out the stallion hiding in her hand.

"Horse thief," he muttered.

She giggled as Grace carried her into her room.

Grace set Brie on her feet and rifled her dresser. "Nothing but T-shirts and overalls?" She stripped off Brie's nightgown and gawked at the yellowing bruises on Brie's knees. "Michael!"

"She tripped on the radiator pipe by the back door."

Grace pursed her lips as if stifling a retort. She tugged a long-sleeved shirt over Brie's head and buttoned her into overalls. "We'll go shopping tomorrow," she said, wiping the syrup off Brie's cheek with her thumb. "You'll need some big girl dresses now that you'll be going to church."

"Urch!" Brie shouted, jumping on his mattress. "Urch!"

"CH-urch," Grace corrected. "CH-urch."

"She's too young to understand the concept of God."

Grace retrieved the brush from the changing table and worked on Brie's hair. "Church isn't just about God. It's about family, community, belonging. Besides, it's what Aine would have wanted." She picked up Brie and maneuvered the stairs.

"How long are you going to play that card?" he shouted from the top of the steps.

"Until you consider what's best for Brie."

"Meaning?"

"Do you really think a dilapidated house in the middle of nowhere is the best place to raise a child?"

"Brie loves the farm."

"She spends too much time in that barn with those filthy birds. She needs to be around kids her own age. Maybe then she'll talk."

"Wait." He ran down the steps. "You're blaming me for Brie's speech delay?"

Silence answered his question.

Brie twisted in Grace's arms and pointed at Michael. "Urch."

"No, Bee," he replied. "Grandma's taking you."

Grace walked to the door. Brie's chin quivered. She was in a full-blown wail by the time Grace zipped her coat. "Michael," she pleaded.

He threw his hands in the air. "Fine. But we're going to Mac's urch."

"But Colin's expecting—"

"If you're going to manipulate me, it'll be on my terms."

"I suggest you change. We're leaving in fifteen minutes."

Michael had witnessed many peculiar things, but what he saw when he entered St. Columba deserved top spot. In the nave, scattered among the parishioners, was a menagerie.

Susan Archer's 200-pound Great Dane, Baby, eyed the five-pound Siamese across the aisle. Don Thompson petted a pygmy goat; Ted Williams a potbelly pig. George and Doris Brown held onto a pair of hens, and their son, Kenny, coddled a teacup poodle.

Brie's giggle echoed through the vestibule, and heads, both human and animal, turned.

"Have we entered Noah's Ark?" Michael said.

"It's the blessing of the animals," Fran Dixon whisper-shouted behind them. "A ceremony that celebrates St. Francis' love for all living things."

He slid into a pew next to Scott Dawson, who had a parrot perched on his shoulder.

Betty Carson, at the end of their row with a chicken in her lap, smiled a toothy hello. Michael nodded, then inclined his head toward Grace. "I thought Catholics bless animals before eating them."

"We should have gone to Divine Child," she said, handing over Brie, who'd become as restless as the caged canary on Bea Davis's lap.

From the pulpit, Mac raised his hands. "Today, we honor St. Francis of Assisi, a humble man who loved all living things. He envisioned a compassionate world. One without selfishness or greed. Without violence toward our fellow man or God's creatures."

Sam Dillon's rooster crowed, and the congregation laughed.

Mac stepped forward, hands in the front pockets of his khaki pants. "While taking a journey with his brethren, St. Francis happened upon a meadow with birds of every kind—larks, doves, crows, jackdaws, swallows. He stopped to preach, telling the birds they owed God thanks and should sing his praises. 'For He has given you the sky so you can fly freely and a coat made of feathers so you can stay warm.'"

Mac continued, but Brie's constant wiggling and giggling kept Michael from catching the import of Mac's preaching.

When Hank lumbered up the aisle with a 300-pound calf, Brie squirmed from Michael's lap and scampered toward Mac.

"Brie," Michael called.

"Let her come," Mac said as Brie maneuvered the steps. "For Isaiah claimed, 'The wolf will live with the lamb, the leopard with the goat, the calf and the lion and the yearling together.'" He stopped, smiled, and looked down at Brie. "And a little child will lead them.'"

Brie babbled nonsensical words. Mac smiled as though he understood, then hoisted her into his arms. "We gather to celebrate a most treasured gift from God. We bless our pets during the Feast of St. Francis to acknowledge how animals enrich our lives. We thank God for the companionship of our pets, their loyalty, and their lessons of laughter, love, and forgiveness."

The organ played, and the congregation filed out. Grace took Brie outside to release her wiggles. Michael waited until Mac greeted his last parishioner, then joined him on the front porch. The sun's rays, having breached the clouds, glistened wet grass.

"Enjoy the service?" Mac asked.

"Not what I expected."

"Which was?"

"Droning of scriptures, hymns, responses."

"Maybe next time."

"Won't be a next time. I was coerced." Brie tromped across the lawn with Don Thompson's goat. "Why do you bless animals if they don't have souls?"

"To impart God's grace and protection upon them."

"Wasn't asking for a rote Catholic answer."

Mac squinted into the sun. "Your question assumes we don't believe animals have souls."

"You believe they do?"

"It isn't a question of belief, Michael. I can't prove animals have souls any more than I can prove there is a God."

"But you have faith."

"You're catching on."

***

The week before Christmas, as Brie and Michael worked on their to-do list, a truck lumbered up the drive. Michael dumped a clean load of towels over Brie's head. "I expect those folded when I get back," he said, then walked to the door.

A stocky man wearing a red baseball cap flipped papers on a clipboard. "You Michael Russo?"

"Who's asking?"

"Alvin," he said, pointing to the name embroidered on his jacket. "Got a delivery. Canopy bed." He stuck his thumb and forefinger in his mouth, whistled sharply, and then waved his arms as if a marshaller at O'Hare.

185

"Who ordered it?" Michael asked over the truck's backup beeper.

"Uptight lady in a black suit. Tracie…Stacie…Gracie…somethin' like that. Gave us an extra hundred bucks if we'd deliver and assemble today." He inspected the door frame. "Haveta remove the door. Pop the pins outta the hinges. I'll get my hammer."

"Take it back."

"No can do," Alvin said, tapping on the red block letters stamped across the receipt. "Final Sale. No refunds."

The driver, a lanky guy in a green jumpsuit, leaped out of the truck, rolled open the rear door.

"Where you want this thing?" Alvin asked.

Alvin followed Michael into Brie's bedroom. "You're gonna have to move everything out of here," Alvin said, eyeing Michael's mattress. "I'll get Simon to help. He's bringing in the bedding. Bunch of pink frilly stuff."

For the next two hours, Alvin and Simon, under Brie's supervision, assembled a queen-sized princess canopy bed inside her tiny room.

Alvin handed Michael the paperwork. "Hope you ain't moving anytime soon."

Brie chose her bedtime book, *Guess How Much I Love You*, and then crawled under her fairytale pink comforter. Michael settled next to her and opened the cover. She stared at his mouth while he read, as though he spoke great truths.

"Daa-daa," he said. "Daa-daa."

She hooked her index finger on his lower teeth and pushed down.

"Daa," he repeated, as she peered down his throat. "Daa."

"Aa-aa-aa," she said.

Michael exaggerated the placement of his tongue on the roof of his mouth. "Daa. Daa."

The phone rang. He handed Brie the book and ran into his bedroom.

"Michael."

"Gracie."

"Did you get Brie's Christmas present?"

"If you're referring to the pair of cowgirl boots you promised her, then no, we didn't."

She sighed. "It was time, Michael."

He cradled the receiver between shoulder and ear, wandered into the hall. "It was my decision to make."

"Does she like it?"

Brie had fallen asleep, her hair splayed across her princess pillow. "Unfortunately."

After Grace hung up, Michael tucked Brie in, returned to his room, and crawled into bed. The boiler kicked on, pipes knocked, valves hissed, radiators hummed.

Anna smiled from her picture on the nightstand.

"She's growing up. Way too fast."

Brie shuffled into the room, climbed onto the bed, and hunkered against his chest. He wrapped the quilt around them and fell asleep holding onto the most precious gift life had given him.

***

Christmas Eve arrived, and with it, a mountain of snow. Whiteness blanketed field and meadow, hill and valley, oak and maple. Brie traipsed through the house in her winter coat and boots until Michael caved. They fed the birds and set out for a moonlit trek.

Breath clouds hung in the chilly air. A great horned owl circled the edge of the woods and dove through the tops of snow-covered pines. Moon shadows stretched like skyscrapers.

Brie marched into drifts that pulled her feet from her boots. She climbed onto Michael's back, and they continued. A gust blew icy crystals. Brie's breath warmed his nape.

He trudged through the valley bordering the forest preserve. Brie pointed toward the trees and said, "Gog!"

A shaggy dog tumbled down the slope like a slinky and landed at Michael's feet, a ball of fur and snow. Pathetic looking. Eyes too large. Ears stuck out as though glued on.

"Gog!" Brie squealed.

It wagged its scruffy tail and wiggled its scrawny body.

"Where did you come from?"

The dog sat, chest out, lips in a smile, exposing crooked teeth. Brie's giggle launched the dog into body spasms.

"Bee. Gog."

"No, not Bee's dog. Probably lost. Sure, his people are out looking for him." Who was he kidding? Most likely dumped on the roadside like trash. He turned homeward. Thankfully, the dog didn't follow.

"Gog," Brie repeated over and over until her voice became a cross between a cry and a plea. He slowed, stopped, whistled into darkness. The dog barked in return, barreled through the snowdrifts, and fell in step behind them.

Michael made a bed of straw in the barn. Coo and Goo studied the dog, then hunkered into their nests. The dog trembled. Balls of snow clung to matted fur. Brie and

Michael fetched a bucket of warm water from the laundry room and soaked his legs. While Michael toweled him, the mutt cocked his head and quirked his eyebrows as if deep in thought.

"Don't be getting any ideas. It's just for a night or two." The mutt circled in the bed of straw and curled into a ball. "See you in the morning," he said, then rolled the barn door closed.

Michael kissed Brie goodnight, slipped into bed, and cracked open a book on organic farming, research for an article in progress. A few chapters in, a muffled bark sounded. He walked to the window, drew up the shade. Light flooded the backyard, illuminated the barn, and glinted off a fresh layer of powder. The dog had tripped the motion sensor and was now dancing with a frenzy in the yard below. How'd he escape?

His bark became loud and frantic. "All right," Michael said, yanking on his robe. "I'm coming."

At the bottom of the steps, a faint odor hung. Smelled similar to rotten—

Oh, god. Covering his nose with his forearm, he bolted into the kitchen, cranked shut the valve on the gas pipe connected to the Wedgewood. He swung the back door open, sucked in the night, and then ran upstairs.

Brie stood in her doorway, Baa dangling from her hand. Michael dropped to his knees and held her until his heart stopped pounding.

"Tay?" she asked.

He kissed the top of her head. "Am now."

Brie tucked into bed, he rechecked the gas value. Cold air had swept the residual odor from the house. He found an old ratty quilt, arranged it in the corner of the laundry room, stood at the backdoor and whistled. The dog loped into the house, bunched up the blanket, sank into it. He tucked his nose beneath the folds and stared at Michael, eyebrows twitching.

"Sleep tight," he whispered, shutting the door.

***

The next morning, Michael rolled out of bed before Goo woke Brie and headed downstairs to put Santa gifts under the tree. He opened the laundry room door. No dog. Escaped again?

He searched the first floor and then climbed the stairs. Brie was sound asleep, her face buried in a mound of messy curls. The crooked-tooth mutt lay at her feet, grinning.

Michael leaned against the door frame. "Either you're Houdini, or my daughter has learned to open doors."

***

Three hours later, Brie and Michael stood on Grace and Colin's porch. Brie stared up at the Celtic cross. He squeezed her mittened hand and knocked. "Let me do the talking."

Grace opened the door. Houdini slipped past her and trotted inside.

She slapped her hand against her chest. "What on Earth?"

"Gog!" Brie blurted, then clapped her hand over her mouth and looked at Michael wide-eyed.

"I know what it is," Grace huffed. "What's it doing in my house?"

Michael looked over her shoulder. "Licking himself in Colin's chair."

"Get it out!"

"Okay." He whistled. Houdini scampered out of the house and followed Brie and Michael down the walk.

"Wait!" Grace called, panic rippling her voice. "Where are you going?"

He buckled Brie into her car seat. "If Houdini isn't welcome, we're going home."

"Houdini?" Grace scoffed.

"Gog!" Brie shouted.

He looked at Grace, shrugged. "We're having a bit of a disagreement about what to call him."

"Fine!" Grace relented. "But it's not allowed on my furniture."

"What'd I tell you?" He ruffled up Brie's curls. "Got to play the game."

After dinner, while Grace and Michael washed dishes, Colin and Brie assembled her deluxe barnyard playset on the living room floor. Houdini observed the action from the comfort of Colin's chair, head between paws.

Grace poured coffee into china cups and then sat across from Michael at the kitchen table. "What if it's got some disease?"

"Hank examined Houdini this morning. Said he's healthy."

"You're not keeping it."

"Why not?" He shoveled sugar into his cup, waited for her to swallow the bait.

She didn't nibble. Swirled the cream in her coffee with a dainty teaspoon and said, "It's a homely dog."

"That homely dog saved our lives."

Grace listened to Michael's story without interrupting. She set her cup on the gold-rimmed saucer. "That house isn't safe, Michael."

"It's just a leaky valve. I'll replace it."

"The boiler's a ticking time bomb."

"Had it inspected last month. It's fine."

She rotated her cup like hands on a clock. "There's a darling little ranch for sale in the neighborhood."

"We're not moving."

"You'd be closer to work, and Brie could start preschool at Divine Child next year."

"Don't go there."

"If it's about the money, Colin and I—"

He pounded his fist on the table. Cups rattled.

Brie bolted into the kitchen in a fit of laughter.

"Whoa there, missy." Colin swept Brie off her feet. His gaze traveled from Michael to Grace. "Something wrong?"

Grace stole Brie from Colin and walked into the living room. "I've got another gift for you, princess." She retrieved a present from under the tree and sat with Brie on the couch.

Brie lifted the lid, stared into the box.

Grace pulled out pink leather cowgirl boots. "Aren't they cute?"

Brie crinkled her nose and pushed the box off her lap. "No!" She slid off the couch and marched to her farm set.

"What was that about?" Grace asked, watching Brie spread the barn animals around the plush carpet pasture.

"Not sure." Michael settled next to Brie. "You okay?"

She handed him a cow. "Ow."

"C-ow," he said.

Houdini stretched his neck across Michael's knee, looked at him with expressive eyes, as if trying to communicate. What, he did not know.

Chapter 20

The first week of April, winter loosened its grip on the farm. Longer days, warmer nights. Leaves burst from buds on sugar maples, crocuses bloomed in meadows, white clover sprouted over fields. Everything grew and blossomed right along with Brie.

Independence Day had arrived when Brie turned three on March 17th. She now resisted help getting dressed, eating, or using the potty. Although her speech development lagged, she had no problems telling Michael how she felt, what to do, or where to go. She continued to babble as if all verbal communication failed due to his inability to listen. Whenever Michael voiced frustration, Colin would laugh. "Welcome to my world."

Easter morning, Goo broadcasted the risen sun. Brie flew down the stairs in a blur of auburn curls and denim overalls, Gog at her heels. When Michael entered the kitchen, she was pouring soy milk over Cheerios. White waves sloshed, tossing toasted O's like rafts in a storm. She climbed onto a stool and shoveled cereal while Gog vacuumed spillage.

The previous evening, Hank called. Lucy, his pregnant ewe, was lambing, and thought Brie might enjoy the miracle of birth. Michael thought she was too young to witness such an event, but told Hank they'd swing by to see the newborns before Grace picked Brie up for mass.

When he'd tucked Brie into bed, he mentioned visiting Hank's lamb. But now, by the looks of her tangled hair and sleepy eyes, she appeared to have been counting sheep all night.

He poured coffee and leaned against the counter.

Brie stopped chewing and glanced up through her sweep of lashes.

He hid his grin behind his mug. "Why in such a hurry?"

She smiled like a chipmunk, Cheerios stuffed in her cheeks.

Michael couldn't suppress his laugh. "All right. Let me finish my coffee first."

He wrestled Brie's hair into pigtails and then drove to Hank's. Michael lifted Brie out of her car seat. The moment her feet touched the ground, she tore off.

Hank emerged from his house and watched Brie disappear through the barn door. "She's growing up."

"Overnight, it seems."

"Drove by your place the other day," Hank said as they walked toward the barn. "The deer were thick as ticks on a dog. You feedin' em?"

"Wildflower's sprouting in the meadow."

Hank stopped to greet Millie. Michael wandered past three inquisitive goats, a probing pink snout, and a couple curious chickens. In addition to the retired dairy cows, Hank had acquired several other abused or neglected farm animals over his years as county vet. He'd found Lucy at a livestock auction last February, left for dead on top of a carcass heap. Didn't know she was pregnant till he got her home.

Lucy was in the last stall, cleaning her two nursing lambs. Brie sat huddled in the corner, an unmoving bundle of white woolly fur curled in her lap.

Michael crouched, lifted her chin. Tears pooled, clung to lashes. Her chin quivered. She pursed her lips together, unable to contain muffled sobs.

The pain in her eyes gutted him. He cupped her hot cheek and smudged tears with his thumb. How do you explain death to a three-year-old? As he searched for words, the ball of wool began to wiggle and twist. It raised his tiny pink nose, blinked, and stared up at Brie with its bright blue eyes.

"Well, I'll be." Hank leaned against the stall and chuckled. "Never thought that runt would make it through the night. Was so weak, she wouldn't even suckle."

Brie set the lamb between Lucy's front legs. The ewe nuzzled the lamb and licked Brie's wet cheeks.

"That's peculiar," Hank said, glancing around the barn. "It's a beautiful spring morning, yet all the animals are inside." He chuckled. "Looks like a nativity scene."

***

Home less than ten minutes, the knock startled him.

Grace breezed through the entryway wearing a straight black dress and a wide-brimmed hat.

"You're early."

She skirted around scattered farm pieces. "Where's Gabriella?"

"In her room. She insists on dressing herself now." He stared at the ostrich plumes on her hat. "Taking Brie to mass or the Kentucky Derby?"

"It's Easter," she said, as if it answered his question. "You laid out the dress I had made for her. The one with the white bodice embroidered in silk flowers?"

"You do realize Mac's church isn't the fashion capital of the Midwest."

"A girl always needs to look her best," she replied, eyeing the crumbling plaster over the brim of her hat, "even in the midst of ruins." She pulled off her black satin gloves and folded them over her clutch. "While we're waiting for Gabriella, we need to discuss preschool."

"That's five months away."

"We must apply now. Divine Child only accepts thirty preschool students, the cream of the crop. Since Colin and I are long-standing members of the parish, I don't know how they could refuse Gabriella."

"Maybe because she's not ready."

"She's a bright little girl who should be interacting with kids instead of those filthy birds." She flipped her hand toward the back window. "I've discussed Brie's speech delay with Sister Mary Agatha. She assured me it would not interfere with her admissions testing."

"Testing? *For preschool?*"

"It's just a formality, but it wouldn't hurt to hire a tutor."

"You can't be serious."

"Admission to Divine Child Preschool guarantees a spot in their award-winning elementary school program. Sister Mary-Margaret has an excellent reputation for preparing young minds."

"*Sister?*"

"The nuns run the preschool program. They'll provide the structure and discipline Gabriella needs."

"Then Brie won't be attending."

"Why in heaven's name not?"

"I won't have Brie brainwashed by a bunch of religious nut jobs in habits."

Grace fired a mile-long glare.

"I'm her father. I'll decide when and where she'll attend preschool."

"If Aine were here…"

"Nanna!" Brie stood at the top of the stairs wearing her cowgirl underpants. Her hair was a mix of chaos and confusion, and there was toothpaste smeared across her face.

The hard lines on Grace's face melted. "Why, Princess Gabriella," she said, ascending the stairs. "You're too grown up to be running around the house half-naked. Where is your ball gown?" She scooped Brie up and carried her into her bedroom. Michael followed.

Discarded on the floor, in a crumpled mess, was the dress. Grace picked it up and frowned, then turned the dress inside right and tugged it over Brie's head.

Brie squirmed and fussed.

"Hold still," Grace said, guiding Brie's left arm through the sleeve.

Brie fisted the bodice in both hands and tried to pull it back over her head. "Nooo," she whined.

"Michael! Help me."

"Looks like she doesn't want to play princess today."

"She'll love the dress as soon as she sees herself in—"

Grace froze. "Michael. Her eyes. They're red and puffy." She took the dress off Brie. The skin on her neck and shoulders was blotchy. "She's having an allergic reaction."

"To what?" He placed his hand on Brie's forehead, cold and clammy.

Grace fingered the neckline of the dress. "The bodice contains wool."

"She's allergic to wool?"

"Or has a sensitivity to it," she replied, examining the rash on Brie's back.

"Brie played with Hank's lambs this morning. If she were allergic to wool, wouldn't she have had a reaction then?"

Brie lay on her side, clutched Baa against her chest, swiped her eyes. Gog jumped on the bed and stretched his neck across her legs.

"I'll call Dr. Eply." He sat next to Brie, tucked a coil of hair behind her ear. "She's staying home today."

Grace walked to the door, hesitated. "About our earlier discussion." She turned and held her head high, her face shadowed by the floppy brim of her hat. "I only want what's best for Gabriella."

"So do I," he said to Anna's picture after Grace had left. "Just not sure what that is."

***

Twenty minutes after giving Brie the Benadryl prescribed by Dr. Eply, Michael piggybacked her to the barn. As they walked through the doors, her eyes had cleared, she stopped fussing, the rash faded. "Stuff works fast," he mumbled, setting her down.

While Brie schooled the ducks on proper wing formation, Michael set to work on Old Faithful, finishing the tune-up he'd started yesterday.

Mac's shadow entered the barn before he did. Brie ran to him, arms wide. He picked her up and flashed his eye-brightening smile. She threaded her fingers into his beard and giggled.

Over the last few months, Mac and Brie had perfected the art of wordless conversations. Feeling a twinge of jealousy, as if an outsider, Michael rummaged through the Duckwall apple crate for his socket wrench, then shimmied underneath Old Faithful. Using all his might, he wrenched the oil pan nut.

Mac's boots appeared. "Brie missed church."

"I'll make sure," he replied, through strained voice and clenched teeth, "she says three Hail Marys before she goes to bed. Damn it!"

"Something wrong?"

He crawled out and threw the wrench at the crate. "Nothing a hammer couldn't fix."

Mac handed Michael a rag. Waited.

Michael leaned against the truck, wiped the oil from his hands. "Grace wants to enroll Brie in preschool at Divine Child."

"Excellent idea."

"Whose side are you on?"

"Brie's. It'll be good for her social-emotional development."

"Agreed. That's not the problem." He rubbed the back of his neck. "She's only three, Mac."

"You don't think she's ready?"

"Don't think I'm ready. What if the kids make fun of the way she talks? Or her shoes?"

"Teach her to stand up for herself. Great opportunity to build her confidence and self-esteem."

"Hate when you're right."

"Don't worry, Michael," he replied. "She'll always need her old man."

Michael tossed the rag into the crate. "What'd Brie miss this morning?"

"Ed brought Sally to church."

"You mean dragged her. Thought they were headed to the cabin."

"Ed wanted to attend Easter mass before they left."

"Must have been awkward."

"Not as awkward as the conversation afterward. Ed approached, arm snaked around Sally's neck. Said he'd asked Sally to marry him. Wanted me to perform the ceremony. By the look on Sally's face, I don't think he'd consulted her."

"What'd you say?"

"Nothing. Sally got flustered, claimed she hadn't accepted his proposal yet, stormed down the steps, Ed chasing."

Michael picked up the socket wrench and slid beneath Old Faithful, determined to remove the stubborn nut. "Brie had an allergic reaction to the wool in her dress. Gave her Benadryl. Perked up when we came to visit the birds." He banged on the oil pan with his fist, then threaded the socket wrench onto the nut and tugged. The nut turned.

He emerged from underneath the truck. Brie stood on top of a haystack and babbled to Coo and the ducklings. Gog lay at her feet and listened intently. Goo perched on the truck bed, head cocked. Mac stared at Brie.

"Mac?"

He shook his head as though coming out of a spell. "Sorry. You were saying?"

"Brie's spending too much time watching you preach."

He chuckled. "Maybe."

***

Michael tucked Brie in for the night and then lay in bed listening to rain batter windows. Lightning flashed. He counted. Made it to five before Brie's feet hit the floor; reached ten before she burst through the doorway, leapt on the bed, and crawled beneath the covers. She nestled into the crook of his neck and curled into his side. Minty breath, lilac hair. He kissed the top of her head and smiled. Still needed her old man.

***

Michael took three days off at the end of May to work on his writing. Most of his salary went toward the home equity loan he'd secured for Brie's medical expenses. If he sold his exposé on global warming, he'd make house repairs.

Saturday morning, he parked Brie in front of the TV, turned on *Sesame Street,* and settled at his desk to revise his work.

After fifteen minutes of rewriting the opening paragraph, Brie climbed onto his lap. She played on the keyboard until the screen filled with a jumble of letters, numbers, and symbols, then ran to the window and said, "Baa."

Last week, Hank had gifted the lamb to Brie since, he claimed, she'd raised him from the dead. It was hard enough keeping Brie away from the barn before Baa. Now darn near impossible.

"In a few minutes," he said.

He'd revised and deleted a paragraph twice before the banging started. "Brie." He pulled her away from the window. "Don't pound on the glass. It'll break."

She pointed toward the barn. "Baa." Gog pressed his nose against the pane and barked.

"Let me finish, then we'll go." He placed her toy workbench on the floor and gave her the mallet. "Bang on this."

Ten minutes of banging left his head pounding.

"Brie!" He grabbed the mallet and put it on the coffee table. She stared at her empty hand. Her bottom lip trembled. He retrieved "The Farmer Says, See and Say" from underneath the couch and pulled the cord. The electronic voice chimed, "The cow says moo." She took it from his hands and examined the yellow plastic case as if trying to figure out how the cow got trapped inside, and then pulled the cord. "Here is a duck—quack-quack-quack."

While struggling to finalize his last paragraph, the banging started. "Brie!" He snatched the mallet before she could hit the "See and Say" again, and then handed her a box of Cheerios. She shook it, opened the top. "We'll go to the barn soon," he said, ruffling up her curls.

He brought the article to a close and pushed away from the desk. "There," he said, turning his attention to Bric. "Now—"

Either she was hiding beneath a mountain of Cheerios, or she'd vanished. Gog's muffled barks sounded from the backyard.

Michael bolted through the barn doors. Looked up. Brie stood at the top of the ladder, left foot on the highest rung, right on the loft floor. Images of Meg falling from the tree flashed. Icy pins pricked his heels.

She placed her left foot next to her right, wobbled a bit, found her balance, and then stood up straight. "Coo," she said, pointing. She turned with a triumphant smile.

A cloud shifted. Blinding sunlight poured through the loft. He heard Brie's piercing scream. Flap of wings. Thud of dead weight.

Silence.

Chapter 21

Waiting for Dr. Peters, the ER resident at St. Joe's, to sign Brie's release forms, Michael called Mac. Told him what happened and inquired how to explain death to a toddler.

"Be honest. Stick to facts, avoid euphemisms, share feelings. Have Brie draw. Kids can express grief better through pictures than words. I'll bury Coo. Plan a memorial."

Michael rehearsed on the drive home, but now, at his desk with Brie in his lap staring up at him as if he'd swallowed her fat crayon, he had doubts.

"Brie. We need to talk. About Coo." *Be honest, just facts, no euphemisms.* "He died, and we won't see him again."

"I'm sad," he added when he realized he forgot to share his feelings.

She splayed her fingers over his heart.

"Father Mac will help us say goodbye. Would you like to draw a picture of Coo?"

She picked up a brown crayon and drew a lopsided football.

Mac walked up the path, hands stuffed in his pockets, head hung. Michael scooched out from underneath Brie, stepped onto the porch, and closed the screen behind him. "Buried?"

Mac lifted his face, nodded.

Michael sat on the stoop and scrubbed his face. "Don't mention this to Grace."

Mac scuffed the bottom of his boot on the step. "How's Brie?"

"Don't think she understands what happened. Not sure I do." Michael pinched the bridge of his nose. "She fell twelve feet, Mac, and there's not a scratch on her. Dr. Peters said it was a miracle she didn't break bones. Or worse." A stiff wind bent the meadow grass and rotated the rusty windmill blades. "Doesn't make sense. Coo was in the loft when Brie screamed. How'd he wind up underneath her?"

"Miracles happen." He searched the cloudless sky. "I'll wait at the gravesite until Brie's ready."

Brie pushed the screen door open and offered Michael her picture. The lopsided football had spouted rectangular wings, a circular head, a triangular beak, and was winging across a blue sky. Hanging from its body, two perfectly formed legs. He kissed her forehead, then together, with Gog at their heels, walked through the meadow toward Mac.

At Mac's feet was a cross made of twigs and twine. Stones bordered the mound perimeter. A sprig of lilac lay atop. Mac stood on one side; Brie, Gog, and Michael, on the other.

Mac raised his arms. "Let us pray."

Brie steepled her fingers, bowed her head. Gog sank to the ground, crossed his paws, and rested his chin on his legs. Michael waited for Mac to speak, but it seemed Mac was at a loss. Brie elbowed Michael and held up her clasped hands. "Oh," Michael whispered, then intertwined his fingers and lowered his gaze.

"Dear Father. We come before you this day to celebrate Coo, who brought joy to our lives. We're grateful to you for entrusting us with his care. And now, with heavy hearts, we pray he finds comfort in your arms. Amen." Mac lowered his arms and winked at Brie. "Let us share fond memories and thoughts of Coo."

Brie picked up her foot, balanced like a crane, lifted her face skyward. She cooed, flapped her arms, and then folded them against her body. She stared up at Michael, unblinking. Mac kicked dirt with the toe of his boot, waited. Gog lifted his nose and gave Michael his crooked, toothy smile. Apparently, it was his turn.

"Coo was a turkey."

Mac raised his brow and tapped the back of his hand with his finger.

"Coo was smart. Most farmed turkeys can barely walk, but Coo could fly. He only had one leg but could dance. He was only twelve pounds but knew how to stand his ground." He knelt in front of Brie, held her gaze. "Coo made you smile when you were sad and laugh when you were mad. He was a brave turkey who loved you. And for that, I'll be forever grateful."

***

In June, Charlie graduated from UIC with a Bachelor of Architecture and would return in the fall for her master's. Mac was as proud as any father. Their arrangement with Henry, while Ed and Sally were away, would continue. An added bonus.

Henry turned nine in June. His obsession with birds escalated. He'd amassed dozens of books and could identify any bird by sound. Sally tolerated his fixation, but Mac encouraged it. Brie and Michael often spent Saturday afternoons hiking local parks and bird sanctuaries with Henry and Mac.

Over the summer, Grace enrolled Brie in dance. She could hop like a frog, leap like a deer, and waddle like a duck in a frilly pink tutu and white ballet shoes. After dance, she'd attend swimming lessons and learn how to dolphin kick and dog paddle. On the days she didn't have dance and swim, Grace took her to yoga to practice cat stretches, downward dogs, and tree poses; then art class, where she became an expert at drawing tadpole people.

Grace and Michael had compromised about preschool. Brie would start in the fall, but without testing or nuns.

Michael found a public school close to Grace and Colin's that offered half-day Pre-K classes. She would receive speech, occupational, and physical therapy three times a week.

A week before school began, he and Grace met with Mrs. Thomas, the principal at Jefferson Elementary; Ms. Sterns, the preschool teacher; and Mr. Bell, the speech pathologist, to finalize Brie's Individualized Educational Plan. Grace drilled them until satisfied they would challenge Brie academically.

***

On the first day of school, Grace and Michael stared out Old Faithful's windshield at the three-story, red brick building. "It looks a lot bigger than I remember," he said.

A jolting bell split the silence. The doors on a dozen buses flung open simultaneously. A river of students flowed beneath the *Welcome Back* banner and pooled around the front door.

Several older kids mocked a chubby girl wearing a pleated skirt and pigtails. A brutish boy with a butch cut shoved a scrawny kid into a thicket of thorns. The burble of voices crescendoed into shouts and laughter.

Behind Grace, belted into her car seat, Brie clung to Baa. Images of her tiny and helpless in the NICU surfaced.

"Maybe," he said, dislodging his tongue from his throat, "we should wait until the next bell."

"Can't be tardy on her first day," Grace said, but made no move.

The front doors opened and swallowed the kids. Grace lifted Brie out of the truck, straightened the hem of her white cotton dress, folded the top of her frilly anklets, and tied her saddle shoes.

Michael slipped her farm animal backpack over her yellow sweater and tucked Baa into the side pocket. "Ready?"

Brie folded her lower lip underneath her top one and nodded. She walked toward the entrance hand-in-hand between him and Grace. Wide-eyed, she absorbed her surroundings: flag snapping in the wind, chalk drawings on concrete, a starling watching from the gutter.

"Remember what Ms. Sterns told us," Grace whispered. "Keep it short, walk away, don't look back."

Michael's shoes squeaked across the newly waxed entry tiles. Hundreds of paper doves fluttered overhead. Bold patterns and primary colors popped off bulletin boards. The smell of wet clay and wood pulp mingled near the art room. Laughter echoed from the bathroom.

At the end of the hall, Ms. Sterns stood outside her door, lips etched in a smile. "Hello, Brie. Welcome to our classroom," she said, as though Brie were deaf.

Brie latched onto Michael's leg and buried her face in his khakis. He crouched, tightened the ribbon around her ponytail. "You're going to love school. You get to paint animals with your fingers and build barns in the sandbox. And maybe," he said, lifting her chin, "Ms. Sterns will introduce you to Skittles, the class hamster."

Brie craned her neck, peeked into the room of kids running around tables and jumping over building blocks. She stepped between his legs and fisted the pocket of his shirt. It felt as if she were squeezing his heart.

He pulled Baa out of her backpack. "Baa's nervous. If you're brave, he will be too."

Brie unfurled her fingers, clutched Baa, and looked at Michael through Anna's eyes. "Tay?" she asked.

"Yep," he replied, allowing the lie to slip between his teeth.

Brie took Ms. Sterns' hand and disappeared into chaos.

"Michael. Slow down."

He picked up his pace and bolted through the front doors. The brisk wind dried his eyes and stung his throat. He jumped into the truck and leaned against the steering wheel.

Grace settled into the passenger seat. They sat in silence before she spoke. "She's going to be fine, Michael."

"I know." Gusts romped over the deserted playground, swings jumped, chains twisted, clanged. Leaves tumbled across dewy grass and snagged against the chain-link fence. Sand swirled the sandbox.

Grace glanced at her watch. "What are you doing for the next three hours?"

"Watching grass grow."

She pulled off her shoes, leaned back, and closed her eyes. "Let me know when it's recess."

***

Around ten-thirty, the preschoolers ran out of the building toward the play structures. Michael folded his newspaper and pulled off his glasses.

"Where's Gabriella?" Grace whispered, as if in church.

A swatch of yellow peaked around a moving mountain of gray. "Next to the redhead in the Bulls sweatshirt."

"What's she doing?"

"Following him."

"Why isn't she playing with the girls?"

"No idea. I'm not—"

A rap on the side window startled him. A barrel-chested man, wearing a blue shirt and tie, hooked his thumbs inside his duty belt.

"Great," Michael mumbled and unrolled his window. "Morning, officer."

"First day of school?" He glanced at the playground. "Which one's yours?"

Grace leaned forward and beamed. "In the yellow sweater. My granddaughter."

"Cute." The officer set his palm against the door frame and shifted his bulk. "I'll need your ID. Sorry, but you can't be too careful these days."

"Understandable," Michael said, handing over his driver's license.

"You look familiar, Mr. Russo."

"Hosted *Wake Up, Chicago!* a few years back."

He took off his hat and scratched his balding head. "Was never into those entertainment shows." He looked at Grace. "License?"

"Is that necessary, officer?" Grace asked, fishing it out of her purse.

"'Fraid it is, Ma'am." He studied her license. "You related to Colin O'Leary, the county circuit judge?"

"He's my husband."

The officer cracked a smile, exposing perfect teeth. "Well, it's an honor to meet you, Mrs. O'Leary," he said, handing Grace her license. "Colin's highly respected by the CPD. One of the finest." He waved at Principal Thomas, standing at the entrance with her arms crossed, and then addressed Michael. "Next time you spy on your daughter, you'll want to let school personnel know. They tend to get a bit nervous in these types of situations."

***

Grace and Michael sipped coffee at Starbucks before returning to pick up Brie at noon. They got stuck at the end of the carpool pickup line.

"What a mess," Grace said, as they eased into the congested parking lot.

"They need a traffic cop," Michael said, combing the lot for an empty spot.

By the time they arrived, Brie's classroom was empty except for Ms. Sterns, on her hands and knees, searching under her desk.

Grace faked a cough. Ms. Sterns hit her head on the desk. "Mr. Russo. Mrs. O'Leary," she said, pushing to her feet. "Brie's in Principal Thomas's office." She smoothed her hair and straightened her blouse. "There's been an incident."

Chapter 22

"What kind of incident?" Grace demanded.

Ms. Sterns glanced at her phone. "We tried to call, but—"

"Is she okay?"

"Brie's fine." She smiled nervously and fumbled around her desk. "I'll take you to her."

They followed down the hall. Grace whisper-shouted, "I told you we should have enrolled her at Divine Child."

Mrs. Thomas stood. "Mr. Russo, Mrs. O'Leary." Her gaze traveled to the corner. Brie sat on a beanbag chair, hugging her backpack—dress hemline ripped, saddle shoes grass-stained, knees covered in Hello Kitty band aids.

Grace framed Brie's face with her hands. "Oh, Princess. Are you okay?"

Brie pursed her lips and looked at the floor.

"What happened?" Michael asked.

Mrs. Thomas gestured toward two chairs. "Brie and another student had a playground disagreement."

"What student?" Grace asked.

"We're not allowed to release the boy's name."

"But he's being punished?" Grace said. "For what he did?"

Mrs. Thomas tapped a pen against her blotter. "According to the boy, Brie attacked him."

"Gabriella isn't capable of such a thing."

"Did he say why she attacked him?" Michael asked.

"He was throwing rocks at a bird. Brie shoved him. They fell."

Michael turned his head toward Brie. "Is that true?"

Her chin quivered, tears pooled. She clutched her backpack.

"I'm sorry, Mrs. Thomas," Michael said. "I'll make sure Brie understands what she did was wrong and apologizes."

***

Michael opened the front door. Brie raced up the steps, bolted into her room, and slammed the door. He draped his blazer over his desk chair, shuffled through the mail, checked the answering machine, and then climbed the stairs.

"Brie." He rapped the door with his knuckle. "I'm coming in."

Brie's dress lay crumpled, backpack abandoned, shoes discarded. She sat on the edge of the mattress, toes peeking out of jeans, hands shoved into sweatshirt pouch.

He straightened Anna's picture, searched her face for advice.

He settled next to Brie. "Rough day, huh?"

Tears.

He unbuttoned his collar, loosened his tie. "I have days like that."

She sniffled.

"What that boy did, throwing rocks at the bird, was wrong. But shoving him was wrong, too. You can't change someone's behavior by force. You have to convince them what they're doing is wrong. Might not make sense to you now, but you'll understand soon enough."

She dried her cheeks with her sleeve.

"You'll have to apologize." He glanced at the pouch of her sweatshirt. "And take Skittles back."

She peeked at him through wet eyelashes.

"Maybe, if it's okay with Mrs. Sterns, we can buy Skittles a friend."

An Anna smile melted wet eyes.

***

Autumn lingered then fled on wings of ice. Brisk north winds stripped fall color from oaks and maples, left them all knuckles and joints. Days later, winter bombed the landscape in cascades of white.

Brie took to preschool like a duckling to water. She'd written an apology to Tommy. Drew a picture of them in the sandbox, a black bird with green and blue speckled wings flying overhead. With Michael's help, she wrote "sorry" at the bottom and hand-delivered it with her favorite Lego cow.

During parent/teacher conferences, Ms. Sterns said Brie and Tommy had become inseparable. And that Skittle's new friend, Lollipop, had birthed three bundles of fluff.

Holidays approaching, work slowed. Michael took several days off for home projects. He rented a sander to strip the hardwood floors and bought a bucket of patching plaster, three gallons of paint, and a new light fixture for the entryway.

Since Sally refused to leave Henry at Christmastime, Mac headed to Florida for the week. He'd be home New Year's, the day Ed and Sally would head to the cabin.

On Christmas Eve morning, Brie and Michael untangled lights and wrapped gifts they'd bought at the East Haven Holiday Flea Market. Brie found a horseshoe belt buckle for Colin and pig earrings for Grace. She picked out a barnwood bird house for Mac, a wooden duck whistle for Henry, gothic red nail polish for Charlie, matching cow mugs for Jane and Rita, and a T-shirt for Harvey—'What Do You Call It When It Rains Chickens and Ducks? Fowl Weather.'

They stopped at Harold's Feed Store and purchased a plastic pool for the ducks, a heated water bowl for Goo, a mineral block for Baa, and a new paw print collar for Gog.

With the house in project mode, they hung strands of clear lights from the barn loft. All they needed now was a Christmas tree.

After lunch, Michael gave Gog a buzz cut, locked him in the warm barn, and then bundled Brie in winter gear.

They trekked toward the pine forest. Gray clouds swept the horizon. Snowflakes swirled. Deep powder muffled the crunch of boots. Pine limbs sagged, glinting whiteness. Brie trudged at Michael's heels, imitating his stride.

In a clearing, a seven-foot blue spruce grew. Michael sat Brie on the trunk of a fallen oak. "Stay put while I cut down the tree. We'll brush the snow off together before we drag it home. Okay?"

She nodded, and he set to work. The first axe whack sent an avalanche raining. Brie's giggle echoed the clearing. He dusted off his shoulders. "Think that was funny?" She covered her mouth with her mitten. He chuckled and continued his assault.

Halfway through, his shoulders ached, hands throbbed. Arctic air spanked his cheeks. Sweat prickled his neck. The snowfall intensified, pelted his eyes, blurring his vision. He dropped the axe, threw his weight against the spruce. "Maybe," he said, turning toward Brie, "I should have picked a smaller —"

She was gone. He scanned the clearing, cupped his hands. "Brie!" His shout ricocheted the woods and faded to deafening silence.

His thoughts raced with his pulse — Brie — alone — lost. Blinded by blizzard, nightfall approaching. Helplessness weighed like snow sagging spruce branches.

He turned circles, shouted, "Brie! Brie!" What if she's hurt? Or unconscious? Meg screaming his name pierced his thoughts. Images of her dead body flashed. He shook his head to clear it. Then he saw boot prints filling up with snow.

He followed. Deep tracks where she'd jumped over a fallen tree. Farther apart where she'd marched. Closer together where she'd run. He entered a forest of jack pine so thick with tangled branches, the ground was snowless. He'd lost all traces of Brie.

Panic propelled him. He crashed through the woods. Twigs snapped. Branches clawed. Visions of the dead baby from his dream haunted. Heart hammering, he slowed to a stop. Sucked in cold air, laced with the smell of wet bark and damp moss. He spun. Which way? Trees blurred.

A starling landed on a low-hanging branch, cocked its head, shrieked, and then took flight. Abandoning sanity, he barreled through the trees after it.

The starling led him out of the pine forest and up a snow-covered hill overlooking a frigid meadow. He surveyed the open space and spotted an enormous buck, lying on its side, chest heaving. It grunted and clawed the earth with its front feet and lifted its massive rack. Moisture from ragged breathing vaporized. The fork of its left antler shot off, leaving jagged edges. The buck pulled its bulk up with front legs, staggered. Blood-stained snow. Stretching its neck, it bellowed. Snow fell off antlers like powdered sugar. It tottered toward—

"BRIE!" Michael called. She walked toward the buck with an outstretched hand. Nothing he could do. Even if he could fly, he'd never reach her. Both buck and Brie ignored his screams.

The buck lowered its nose, nuzzled Brie, and licked her fingers. She placed her hand against the side of its face. They stood motionless, figurines in a snow globe. Then, with a flash of white tail, it bounded away.

Brie collapsed to her knees, vomited.

"Oh, god." He slipped on ice, tumbled the steep decline. Disregarding piercing side pain, he rushed toward Brie. He pushed hair from red, swollen cheeks and set his hand on her forehead. She was burning up.

He hoisted her into his arms, trudged the deeps, headed home. Snow assaulted, swirling all directions. Fat flakes clung to Brie's eyelashes, melted on her cheeks. Her body convulsed. He tightened his hold, willed his feet faster.

The wind muffled Gog's frantic barks. He could just make out the silhouette of the barn. A warm glow emanated from windows, a beacon of light.

Repositioning Brie, he rolled the door open. A gust battered his back and swept through the loft. The strands of Christmas lights flickered and swung. Baa paced her stall. The ducks poked their heads between slats. Gog placed his front paws on Michael's thigh and reached his nose toward Brie. "Not now," Michael said, kneeing him away.

He opened the back door and settled Brie into her car seat. "Bee." He yanked off her hat. "Can you hear me?"

Gog barked, circling the truck. Brie scrunched up her face. "Gog," she whined.

"Don't worry, Bee," Michael said, fastening her belt. "You're going to be fine."

He opened his door. Gog leapt in, hunkered into the driver's seat. "Get out!" Michael yelled. Gog jumped over the seat, wedged himself next to Brie. Michael fumbled the glovebox for keys.

Goo winged down and landed on the hood. He craned his neck and blasted an earsplitting crow.

"Move, you stupid bird!" Michael turned the key. The engine responded with a yeeh-hee-hee, and then fell silent. He closed his eyes, tried again. The engine repeated its mocking laugh. He slammed the steering wheel. "God damn it!"

Gog lay his head on Brie's lap. She curled her fingers into his coat, her face still slick with sweat, but her cheeks no longer beets. He took a deep breath, tried the key again. The engine roared. Goo flew into the loft. Michael shifted into four-wheel and plowed snow.

Chapter 23

Michael, with Brie on his lap, awaited blood work results. Two hours after the incident, she showed no signs of ever being sick.

Reluctantly, he'd called Grace upon arrival. "Brie developed a fever. I rushed her to St. Joe's, but she's—"

"We're on our way." She hung up.

Brie stuck a tongue depressor in Michael's mouth, peered down his throat. "Aa-aa-aa," he said.

"Aa-aa-aa," she mimicked.

"Da-aa-aa," he said, exaggerating his tongue.

She tapped hers against the back of her teeth. "Aa-aa-aa—Nanna!"

"Princess!" Grace swept Brie into her arms. "You okay?"

Brie stuck out her tongue and said, "Aa-aa-aa."

"You look perfectly fine."

"Where's Colin?"

"Coming from the courthouse." She tucked in Brie's undershirt, straightened her sweater. "What happened?"

Michael dismissed the lie forming in his mind. "We'd found a Christmas tree in the woods. While I was chopping, Brie disappeared."

She blinked several times. "A child doesn't just disappear."

He focused on the melted snow puddling his boots. "I wasn't watching."

"She's not even four, Michael," she snapped. "Why would you take your eyes off her?"

Dr. Peters, the resident who'd examined Brie after her fall from the loft, strode in. "There's our little miracle," he said, apparently oblivious to the tension.

Brie stuck out her tongue. "Aa-aa-aa."

"What beautiful tonsils," he said. "Saw Brie's name on the patient intake board. Hard to believe it's been seven months since the accident. Most kids would not survive a fall from that height."

An oppressive silence. Waves of anger radiated off Grace. Dr. Peters' gaze shifted between Grace and Michael. He gave Michael a fleeting smile and rushed out.

"Survive a *fall?*"

His boots felt too tight, his feet swollen. "She fell from the loft."

She sucked in an oxygen-depleting breath. "You didn't tell me."

"Because I knew this is how you'd react."

"That farm is no place to raise a child."

"So you've mentioned, repeatedly."

She opened her mouth, but said nothing, as if reconsidering her retort.

He loosened his boot laces. "How long do test results take?"

"I'm running an ER, Mr. Russo, not a fast-food restaurant." A heavy-set man with a cane limped into the room. "Dr. Cohn, attending." He pulled a red pen from his pocket, flipped open Brie's chart. "According to the account you've provided my resident, your daughter suffered a seizure."

"Brie has epilepsy?"

He raised an eyebrow at Michael's intrusion and clicked his pen in rapid succession. "Since you've indicated there's no history of family epilepsy, we'll explore other possibilities." He clicked and flipped the page. "Has Brie been exposed to any infectious diseases?"

Grace sat next to Michael and shook her head.

"Other than her fall from the loft, any head trauma?"

"No," they said in unison.

"Could she have ingested poison, like d-CON or Seven Dust?"

"I store chemicals out of her reach," Michael replied.

"What about prescription medications or illegal drugs?"

Michael flexed his fingers and then fisted them.

Grace set her hand on Michael's forearm. "I'm sure your staff has already asked Michael these questions."

"You'd be amazed what people forget." He scrawled something, then set Brie's chart on the counter. "Since Brie had a fever and vomited before she convulsed, my diagnosis is febrile seizure."

"Febrile seizure?" Michael asked.

"Seizure from infection and high fever. However, since Brie no longer has a fever," he said, punctuating his words with a click of his pen, "and her blood work shows no signs of infection, I'll release her. Make an appointment with her pediatrician tomorrow."

"Thank you," Grace said. "We will."

Dr. Cohen slipped his pen into his pocket and grabbed his cane. "A nurse will review the discharge instructions." He struggled to his feet and left.

Grace anchored Brie to her hip, perused the medical instruments on the counter. "That cute ranch down the street from us hasn't sold. We can drive by after Gabriella's appointment tomorrow. Three-bedroom, big yard. Lots of space to play."

"She loves the farm."

"A young couple just moved into the house next door. They have a girl Gabriella's age."

"Brie has Henry."

"That autistic boy?" She turned to face him. "The one who doesn't speak?"

Sweat trickled between his toes. Brie fussed. Grace bounced her. "She'll be safe. There'll be no reason to worry—"

"We're not moving."

"When are you going to make decisions on what's best for Brie?"

"Drop it, Grace."

"That pigsty is making her sick. Probably mold growing throughout that old house."

"Enough!"

"If it's about the money…" She shifted a whiny Brie. "Colin and I are willing to cosign the loan."

The wool in his socks ignited. He leapt to his feet. "Mind your own—" He looked at Brie, swallowed his next words.

"What's wrong with you two?" Colin stood in the doorway, consternation creasing his forehead. "Heard you bickering all the way down the hall." He pulled a pouty Brie from Grace's arms.

"Sorry, Bee," Michael said, rubbing her back.

She burrowed her face into Colin's neck.

Michael shouldered past Grace. "I'll check on the discharge papers."

***

January 1st, Mac and Michael stood on the back porch watching Brie and Henry tromp fresh snow. Gog snapped at fat falling flakes. Baa frolicked drifts.

He told Mac what had transpired Christmas Eve. "Febrile seizure? Never heard of such a thing."

"Usually triggered by a high fever from a viral infection."

"An infection?"

"Grace insists she caught it from house mold, but Dr. Eply dismissed her theory. Had an inspector come out, in case. All his tests came back negative." Goo poked his head out the barn door. A snowflake landed on his beak. He shook his feathers and retreated. "Hank examined the animals. Said they're healthy."

"What about the buck?"

"Dr. Eply said an infection couldn't develop that quickly."

He scratched his beard. "She reached up and touched him?"

"He could have killed her, Mac." A gust swirled a snow tornado around Brie. Jagged icicles dropped from the barn overhang—daggers piercing snow. "Maybe Grace is right." Michael kicked his boot heel into ice along the path. "Maybe this isn't the best place to raise a child."

"Danger exists everywhere, Michael. Fear resides only in the mind."

"How am I supposed to protect her?"

"Faith."

"In your God?"

"No, Michael. In yourself."

***

Winter held the farm firmly in its grasp until late March. Crocuses poked through snow patches, promising spring. April exploded yellow buds on frail willows. May warmed wind, lengthened days, infused lilac.

Now four, Brie constantly challenged boundaries. Step her toe across a line, smile, and bat lashes. So Anna. About killed Michael.

She no longer wore orthopedic shoes, but when in a hurry, would trip. If she had a fear of falling, it didn't show or slow her down.

She still struggled with speech, but her non-verbal communication, receptive and written language, matched her peers. She could string together two-word phrases, but articulating seemed a hassle. In Brie's world, Michael's inability to understand her was his incompetence.

Mac stopped by the evening of April 15th. Michael had just finished spooning homemade chili into bowls. Brie took one look, pushed her bowl off the table, and stormed outside.

Michael scooped up the mess. "What am I doing wrong, Mac?"

They watched Brie through the window. Fists clenched, she paced the muddy path in her yellow muck boots. Gog, sitting at attention, looked at Brie as though she were commander-in-chief. She stopped in front of him to have an arm-flailing discussion. He barked his support, and she continued her march.

"Might help," Michael said, "if we spoke the same language."

"What if you could? Not with words, but ASL."

"You mean the way you communicate with Henry?" The ducks emerged from the barn, waddled behind Brie as if joining her revolt. "Could you teach us?"

"Absolutely."

"When can we start?"

He smiled at Brie, who'd recruited Baa to her protest. "No time like the present."

***

Ms. Sterns had scheduled a field trip to the local dairy two days before summer vacation. Michael volunteered to chaperone. Brie woke him up the morning of, dressed in pink overalls and muck boots. Her hair wrestled into a ponytail, their stomachs full of peanut butter toast, they headed to school.

The yellow school bus jounced into the pothole-ridden parking lot. Brie pointed at the old red barn and signed "cow". The ASL sessions with Mac were paying off.

Michael mimicked her sign, "Cow." She rolled her eyes, took his hand, pressed his index finger in, and pulled his thumb out. Apparently satisfied she'd corrected his error, she bounced off the green vinyl seat and followed classmates off the bus.

Farmer Phil welcomed the class to the dairy and motioned to follow. They traipsed toward an enormous rectangular building at the top of a hill. Mrs. Sterns walked alongside Farmer Phil, her charges marching behind like obedient soldiers. Michael brought up the rear, herding

227

stragglers. Brie, who waddled like a duck instead, stopped abruptly and spun around.

Michael crouched. "What's wrong?"

She clapped her hands over her ears and shook her head. Her eyes flashed fear.

He watched the last kid disappear inside the metal structure. Worried Ms. Stern would think he was shirking his duty, he grabbed Brie's hand and tugged her toward the door. "Maybe they'll let you milk a cow."

A concrete walkway separated two rows of cows, their heads locked inside metal bars. They grazed mindlessly while droning machines pumped milk from swollen udders. Workers, wearing heavy plastic aprons and sanitary gloves, methodically checked an array of tubes, hoses, and cylinders.

Michael, Brie in tow, rushed to catch up. Cows lifted their heads and watched through somber eyes. Brie was clutched to Michael's leg, eyes squeezed shut. The cows, now agitated and restless, twisted their necks in the shackling bars. They bellowed and stomped hooves. The kids panicked, causing chaos. Brie escaped Michael's grasp. Bolted for the door. He chased after her, dodging workers herding frightened children outside.

He tented his eyes and scanned the parking lot. Brie raced toward a domed metal shed.

He shouted. She stumbled. Slammed against the ground. Scrambled back up, sprinted as if on fire. He called, begged her to stop, but she squeezed through the crack in the door.

He grabbed the handle, flung open the door. Sunlight flooded the windowless shed. Hay dust hung thick. Swarms of flies, buzzing in irritation, escaped into shadows. The stench of fermented hay and urine-soaked straw stung his eyes and throat.

Brie stood on the dirt path between two rows of narrow wooden crates. Inside each, a calf tethered by a neck rope. They stared at Brie as if a ghost—her ashen skin, pale lips, dulled blue eyes. Was she breathing? His throat tightened around her name.

"Brie."

A calf stretched its neck through slats. Brie reached out, touched its nose. She screamed, her voice ricocheting metal walls. Her voice faltered. She fell, her body limp and lifeless.

Chapter 24

Michael held Brie's hand while Ryan, an ER nurse, placed her in a fetal position. Her lids flashed open, exposing flecks of fear. Michael rested his latex-gloved hand against her head, brushed his thumb across her hot, swollen cheek, and hoped the surgical mask concealed his anxiety. "It's okay, Bee. Daddy's here."

Upon arriving at Providence, Michael had provided Brie's medical history, called Grace, then Mac.

During the fifteen-minute wait for the ambulance, Brie suffered three seizures. The paramedics stabilized her, but she fell in and out of lucidity as they transported her to the ER. The attending physician, Dr. Patel, injected penicillin, acetaminophen, and prepped for a spinal tap.

Ryan anchored Brie to the bed as Dr. Patel inserted a needle into her lower back. Michael cradled her head. He swallowed helplessness and waited. Tears pooled, slid down her cheeks. Her chin quivered. With pursed lips, she held her breath. "Breathe, Bee," he said, "Breathe." She sucked short bursts through her nose, sobbed on exhale. "Good girl. Almost done."

Dr. Patel patched the insertion site. Ryan rolled Brie onto her back and checked IV lines.

Michael set his fingers on Brie's tear-stained cheek. "Why is she still burning?"

"Takes a few minutes for the acetaminophen to enter her system," Ryan said. "I'll put a cooling blanket beneath her."

Grace entered, panic-stricken.

"Brie's grandmother," Michael said in introduction. "Grace O'Leary."

Dr. Patel acknowledged Grace with a curt nod. "We should have the results of Brie's spinal in seventy-two hours."

"Dr. Patel thinks Brie has meningitis," Michael said, shifting Brie while Ryan positioned the cooling blanket.

Grace placed a hand against her throat. "Isn't that serious?"

"Could be," Dr. Patel replied. "We've probably caught it in time."

"But meningitis? How?" Grace asked.

"Depends on type. Bacterial is spread through body fluids, viral by an enterovirus. Fungal from soil contaminated with bird droppings."

"Could she have been infected at the dairy?" Michael asked.

"Although the symptoms can develop quickly, incubation requires two to ten days. It's most likely been brewing for a while." She wrote on Brie's chart, flipped it closed, slipped her pen into her lab coat pocket. "Once we pinpoint type, we'll work on identifying source. Anyone who visits Brie wears gloves and mask."

Thirty minutes later, Brie's temperature had not subsided. Sweat slicked her hair, soaked her cotton gown. Grace dabbed Brie's forehead with a cold washcloth.

Brie moaned "ow" several times and then cried herself into a fitful sleep.

Grace's heels clicked across the tile floor. She tugged off her mask and motioned for Michael. "Is this what it's going to take?" she whispered in harsh tones. "Brie's fighting for her life because you insist on raising her on that farm."

"You're blaming me?"

"You and those filthy birds."

Michael scoffed. "As always, jumping to conclusions."

"Fine! We'll wait. But if the test results confirm she got it from the farm?"

Brie cried, "Gog," and fell back to sleep.

"Then I'll do what's best for Brie."

Mac appeared, his expression a mix of relief and concern. He headed toward Brie.

"Mac." Michael caught his arm. "You have to wear a mask and gloves."

Mac shrugged Michael off and sat on the edge of the bed. Framing Brie's face in his hands, he recited a prayer. Grace signed the cross and bowed her head. Mac uttered amen and backed away.

Brie stirred, lashes fluttered. Blue eyes deepened, cheeks lightened. Grace set her gloved hand against Brie's forehead. "Fever's down." Through her mask, she kissed the back of Brie's hand. "Welcome back, Princess."

Michael cupped Brie's cheek. "Hey, Bee."

Brie didn't smile until her gaze traveled over his shoulder.

Michael turned toward Mac, whose face was ashen, lips pale. He slid his trembling hands into his pockets and stumbled past Ryan, who'd just entered.

"Looks like our patient is feeling better," said Ryan. He placed a thermometer in Brie's mouth and checked her IV. "The acetaminophen kicked in," he said. "Her temperature's normal."

Grace rambled about buying Sleeping Beauty pajamas for Brie. Fragments of Mac's prayer played in Michael's mind. *Where there is doubt, faith; where there is despair, hope.*

"Michael." Grace's voice snapped like a rubber band. "Have you heard anything I've said?"

"Can you stay with Brie? I need to talk to Mac."

She tucked the sheet under Brie's arms and smoothed her blanket. "Not going anywhere."

Michael kissed Brie's head, removed mask and gloves, and headed to the reception desk. "Chapel?" he asked the admitting nurse.

"Second floor, turn right, end of hall."

Michael slipped into the hushed room. Sunlight sifted through stained glass and cast kaleidoscope patterns on hardwood. Mac knelt in the shadow of the altar, hands tented.

"You should be with Brie," he said, without turning.

"I believe," Michael replied, trying to hide the resentment in his voice, "she needs you more than me." He climbed the stairs, dusted the edge of the lectern with his fingers, and rubbed his thumb across fingertips. "Anna used to recite The Prayer of St. Francis every night. Said it restored her faith. Gave her hope." Michael scrutinized the iron cross mounted above him, then turned to Mac. "It wasn't your prayers or your God who healed Brie, was it Father Francis?"

Silence.

"I saw what you did," Michael said.

"Don't believe everything you see."

"You've spent five years trying to convince me to believe in things I cannot see, and now you want me to doubt when I do? Show me your hands, Mac."

Mac peeled open his hands. Even in shadow, Michael could see Mac's fingertips were red and inflamed; his palms swollen and raw.

"Are you some kind of healer?"

Mac flexed his fingers, winced. "If I am, I'm not a very good one."

"Yet you were able to take away Brie's fever. Care to explain?"

"It can wait. We need to talk."

"About?"

"Brie's gift."

Mac studied Michael's face as if waiting for his expression to change.

"Gift?" Michael said, without inflection. "What gift?"

"Her ability to perceive emotions."

"That's not a gift. It's her intelligence."

Mac shifted, settled onto the step. "What if Brie can sense the emotions of animals? Would that be a gift?"

"She's just a little girl who has a soft spot—"

"What if she knew what they were feeling? Fear, sadness, anger, loneliness."

"How is that possible?" Michael asked, his voice laced with skepticism.

"She listens with her heart, not her ears. Think how attuned she is to our thoughts and feelings. Maybe her emotional intelligence extends to animals."

"Even if there were a shred of truth to your claims, how is that connected to Brie getting sick?"

"I have a theory." He paused, as if choosing his words wisely. "What if Brie's gift goes beyond understanding? What if she feels their emotional pain and somehow," he said, examining his blistered fingertips, "Absorbs it? The pain then manifests as infection."

"That's ludicrous."

"Then why did she get sick immediately after touching the wounded buck? Or the calf torn away from its mother?"

"Coincidence."

"You sure?"

Michael lifted his face toward the stained-glass skylights. A thousand pins of light. A stabbing pain exploded like buckshot in his brain. He squeezed his lids, fisted his hands. "Can you hear what you're saying?" His voice echoed through the chapel. "Do you honestly think I'd believe such…absurdity."

Mac stared at his hands.

"I'm done listening to your nonsense. Stay away from my daughter. I don't want you anywhere near her." He stormed from the chapel.

Anger curbed, nerves calmed, Michael stepped into Brie's room. Mac's words would not settle. They swirled around his mind. Leaves in an updraft.

Brie was propped in bed wearing a surgical mask, blue eyes peeking through dark lashes. She'd plugged a stethoscope into her ears, listening to her heart.

"Dr. Patel checked on Brie," Grace said, weaving her fingers through Brie's tangled curls. "Fever's gone, but they'll continue to monitor her until they get test results."

He adjusted his mask and sat on the side of the bed. Brie, stethoscope in ears, crawled into his lap and placed it against his chest. She took deep breaths through her nose, mask undulating like an accordion.

Grace rummaged her purse and then dumped the contents onto the bed. "It's here somewhere." She pushed aside Brie's princess sunglasses, a container of wet wipes, a deck of Old Maid cards, sorted through broken crayons, Barbie shoes, and barrettes. "Here it is." She held up an elastic hair band as if a diamond.

Michael muffled a laugh.

A blush colored the alabaster skin on Grace's forehead. She shrugged. "Amazing how a child has the power to change us."

Brie held her breath like a yoga instructor and looked at Michael with eyes full of wonder.

"Daddy's heartbeat," he said.

She stared at the stethoscope diaphragm, then scrambled off his lap and headed toward the pile Grace had dumped on the bed.

While she searched through the junk, Grace lassoed Brie's hair into a ponytail. Mac's words swirled again. *She understands their thoughts…knows what's in their hearts…absorbs their pain —*

"Ow!" Brie cried. She'd found her Lego cow and clutched it.

"It's a *cow*," Grace corrected. "She needs a new speech pathologist."

Balancing on her knees, Brie set the stethoscope against the cow. "Ow."

Everything stilled. The air current. Brie's IV drip. His pulse. Time.

Brie moved the stethoscope to her chest. "Ow." She'd mumbled through her mask, but it rang in Michael's head with the clarity of a church bell.

How many times had she tried to open his eyes? How long had she been trying to tell him?

Brie inserted the stethoscope buds into his ears and set the cow in his hands.

"Ow," he said, placing the stethoscope against the cow. "Ow."

She tugged off her mask and smiled.

He tugged off his and smiled back.

"Michael," Grace said. "You're not supposed to —"

"She doesn't have meningitis."

***

Two days later, Brie was released from the hospital, all tests negative. Grace appeared to have abandoned her attack on the farm. For now.

Michael tucked Brie into bed, left her under the care of Grace and the watchful eye of Gog, and drove into town.

He found Mac sitting on a bench in his garden, a monarch perched on a gauze-wrapped fingertip.

"Did you know," Mac said, "butterflies develop wings as caterpillars? A miracle waiting to unfold." The monarch batted its wings, launched skywards. "How's Brie?"

"Home." He settled next to Mac. "I apologize. I overreacted."

"Bad timing. I should have waited."

Michael planted forearms on thighs, rubbed his hands. "I have questions."

"Thought you might."

"Do you have Brie's gift?"

"Yes."

"That's how you were able to heal her? By absorbing her pain?"

"Emotional pain."

"How exactly does that work?"

Mac scratched his beard. "It's complicated."

"I'll keep an open mind," Michael said, smothering the sprouting seed of skepticism.

"Not sure where to start."

"Beginning's best."

He nodded. "I was born in a backwoods cabin in the Smoky Mountains. My mother claimed that when she went into labor, the birds flocked outside her window and sang joyful songs."

"Which is why she named you after St. Francis."

A smile played. "She was a devout Italian catholic."

"And your father?"

His smile faded. "A stubborn Irish mule who gambled everything away. I was three when he abandoned us. My mother and I moved to her parents' farm outside of Knoxville. Mom worked two jobs. Gran taught me cooking, Gramps barn restoration. Both fostered my fascination with birds."

A bright red cardinal landed on the arm of the bench, regarded Mac with a tilt of his tuft before taking flight to a nearby feeder. "By my eighth birthday, I'd discovered I could heal wounded birds. Not in a physical sense, but a spiritual one."

"Spiritual?"

"If their spirit was broken, I could heal their soul."

"Tell anyone?"

"Father James, our parish priest. He helped nurture my gift but warned not to tell a soul. Said people feared what they didn't understand. I heeded his advice until my final week of seminary, when I confided in my spiritual adviser, a man I'd come to trust. He asked me to prove why God felt me worthy to bestow such a gift, so I healed one of his pigeons that had lost its will to fly."

"How'd you know it'd lost its will?"

"Part of the gift. Like a sixth sense."

The cardinal retreated into a raspberry thicket.

"The following day, I was summoned to the dean's office. My adviser stood in the dean's shadow, with an expression that assured my mistake. As we took our designated seats, I prepared for interrogation. Instead, the dean informed me the bishop had a change of heart. I was no longer assigned to St. Peter's in Chicago but would shepherd a small parish in the rural town of East Haven."

"A clear indication they didn't believe your gift was from God."

"Or feared the ramifications."

A pair of chickadees landed on the edge of a birdbath. Mac continued. "For a year, I struggled. Should I leave the church? Seek a different profession? Then Ed, reeking like a brewery, staggered into church clutching a three-week-old Henry. Claimed all his kin, dating back to his great-great-granddaddy, had been baptized in the Catholic faith, and that he wasn't about to tempt fate by breaking tradition. He handed over Henry and told me to perform my duty. I looked at Henry, bundled in my arms. I had to protect him."

"So you stayed."

Mac nodded.

"That day, Henry climbed the water tower. You told me he'd developed some of your quirks."

The chickadees splashed about in the bath, flicking water.

"On his fifth birthday, we were at the park. Henry found a dove mourning the loss of its mate. He scooped up the listless bird, cradled it as if spun sugar. When he opened his hands, the dove cooed, then flew."

"He'd inherited your gift."

"With a slight variation. Whereas I find companionship and acceptance around them, Henry finds peace. They calm and comfort him."

"So when Brie encounters these emotionally wounded animals, she's trying to heal their souls?"

"Exactly."

"She takes their pain, and it makes her ill?" Michael shook his head, pushed from the bench, and paced. "That's not a gift. It's a curse. A curse that's going to wind up killing her. Take it back."

The chickadees took flight, sheltered in a birdhouse.

"Gifts from God cannot be returned."

"I won't allow it."

"Not your choice."

"We'll move to the city."

"You think it will be that easy? There are animals suffering everywhere."

"I'll rent an apartment. Away from animals."

"She'll seek them out. This gift," he said, rapping his knuckles against his chest, "is who Brie is. You cannot—"

"Control it?" An angry laugh emerged. "Watch me."

"Michael!" The command in Mac's voice jolted him. "You cannot outrun fear."

“You can’t expect me to do nothing while they make her sick.”

“They do not intend to harm her. The sickness is a side effect. We’ll teach her how to protect herself.”

“How?”

“I’ve got a plan,” he said, standing. “Meet me in the barn. Thirty minutes.”

“Mac,” he called as Mac strode toward his cottage.

He turned.

“What heals an animal’s soul?”

“Hope,” he replied, as if it was that simple. With a grin, he disappeared through his doorway.

Chapter 25

Back at the farm, Brie and Grace had fallen asleep in Brie's bed. Gog lifted his head off Brie's leg and regarded Michael with an expression conveying; Don't worry. I've got this.

He walked to the barn and waited for Mac. Baa dozed in the shade of a maple. Had Brie saved her? By some invisible spiritual force?

The ducks splashed in their pool. They'd clearly imprinted on Brie. Had they refused to migrate because of her?

Goo flapped his wings and settled into Old Faithful's cargo bed. According to Hank, the rooster had lived well beyond his life expectancy.

Michael had a sudden revelation. Coo had been in the loft the afternoon Brie was conceived. June 21st. Summer solstice. Brie spoke her first words to Coo. Was there a connection between them? Had he intended to save her when she fell from the loft?

Mac strode in, backpack over shoulder. Michael's thoughts scattered. "So what's the plan? How do we stop the animals from infecting Brie?"

"*We* can't." Mac unzipped the backpack.

"But you said—"

"You can't stop the waves, but you can learn to surf." He shoved a book into Michael's hands and tapped his bandaged finger on the cover, *Mindfulness Meditation for Everyday Life.*

"Meditation?"

"And Tai Chi."

"Teach her how to fight?"

"Fight the waves. Once she develops her *qi*, she'll be able to block the flow of negative energy."

"*Qi?*"

"Life force. It's what makes our hearts beat, trees grow, rivers run."

"Thought your God did that," Michael said, flipping through the book. "Isn't Tai Chi Taoist?"

"Although Tai Chi is a physical representation of Taoist ideas, it isn't a religion. It is a practice that draws on internal strength to combat external forces."

"This *qi* is what keeps you and Henry from getting sick?"

"Yes, however, the side effects Henry and I experienced before developing our *qi* weren't as debilitating as Brie's. Just flu-like symptoms. Absorbing the emotional pain of a duck isn't as toxic as that of a buck. And considering her violent reaction with the calf, we must consider the degree of trauma they're experiencing." He rifled through his backpack. "When she's ready, we'll test her in a controlled environment."

Mac unfolded an oversized Chicago map, nailed it to the wall, and circled several areas in green Sharpie. "Jelke Creek, Burnham, Jarvis, Montrose Point, McCormick. Bird sanctuaries we've visited. Brie didn't have any adverse effects, so they're safe zones." He exchanged the green Sharpie for a blue one and handed Michael the Chicago Area Yellow Pages. "We'll visit riskier places, like humane societies and shelters. Many of those animals have been abused, abandoned, neglected. After that—zoos, petting farms, circuses. Anywhere we might encounter emotionally wounded animals."

Mac marked locations, while Michael scoured the phonebook and studied the map. "What are those?" he asked, referencing the dozens of skull and crossbones symbols Mac had inked in red.

"No-go zones. Slaughterhouses, factory farms, research facilities."

"If Brie gets sick again?"

Mac drew a heart on the map over East Haven. "Get her to the barn. The animals will heal her."

"Heal?"

"They love her. Unconditionally. And that love has the power to heal." He leaned against a stall. "The seizures she had after touching the wounded buck. When did they stop?"

"When I entered the barn."

"She regained consciousness?"

"In the barn."

"And her fever subsided?"

"Before I made it to the hospital. That's why Gog wouldn't leave her side."

"What about the reaction to the wool in her dress?"

"It wasn't Benadryl that cured her rash. It was the animals."

Mac smiled.

"Why didn't you tell me?"

"Would you have believed me?"

"Probably not." He shook his head. "But you healed her in the hospital."

"Something I've never done." He looked down at his gauze-covered fingertips. "May not have the power to do it again."

A swallow regarded him from the loft. Why'd it take him so long to understand? He'd always felt there was something special about the barn. It held memories of Anna. Of Meg. Memories that helped him heal. And if it hadn't been for Mac, he'd have demolished it.

"Mac," he said. "Why did your God choose Brie?"

"A question I have no answer for."

***

By the end of June, they'd visited most of the blue sites. With Mac acting as spiritual guide, Brie handled exposure without side effects. Mac coached her through the encounter. She'd close eyes, bow head, press hands together at heart-center, and take deep breaths until Mac sensed danger had passed. In time, he claimed, protecting herself would become second nature.

July 2nd, brilliant sunshine, clear skies. Michael sat on a bench in Mac's garden, editing his article on agriculture's contribution to global warming, third in a series for publication in *Earth Talk Magazine*. Despite alarming statistics, the media continued to blame the automobile industry and completely ignored agriculture's contribution to methane emissions. Something Michael hoped to change.

Barefoot, wearing matching linen pants and jackets, Mac and Brie flowed through Tai Chi under the trellis. Henry usually practiced with them, but he'd gone to the cabin with Sally and Ed to celebrate the Fourth of July.

Mac and Brie were "taming the mane" when Mac's phone rang. He bowed to Brie and ran into the house.

Michael couldn't make out Mac's words, but his calm tenor voice escalated. Brie stopped abruptly. Birds shot skyward. He bolted from the house, face etched in panic. "That was Sally. Henry's missing."

Michael scooped up Brie. "I'll drive."

Mac directed Michael onto Route 47, and then explained what Sally had said. "Ed got drunk last night. Fought with her, then split. When she woke this morning, he hadn't returned. Henry was gone. Along with Ed's fishing boat." He raked his fingers through his hair. "Sally said Henry's been obsessed with the ducks. But he's terrified of water. Doesn't know how to swim."

Michael pushed Old Faithful to her limit. Sped along silent country roads for forty minutes until a sign for Hidden Lake Road appeared. He turned right, drove a mile, and then pulled into a dirt drive. No sign of Ed's truck.

A rustic log cabin sat atop a hill, surrounded by overgrown weeping willows. A police vehicle and a search and rescue unit had parked by the lake. Mac jumped out before Michael rolled to a stop.

Michael unbuckled Brie, carried her down the slope. No wind. Hints of catfish and stink bait. Globs of iridescent-green pine pollen floated. A slime-covered concrete seawall dammed stagnant water. Blue-green algae bloomed along the reedy western edge.

The lake veered sharply at the north end. Dilapidated cottages dotted the landscape. Boat docks cluttering the shoreline, filled with people watching.

An officer, brown vest—SHERIFF embroidered in yellow—stood like a sentry at one end of the T-shaped dock. Sally, clutching a faded pink robe against her slender frame, paced behind him.

Mac's bare feet pounded over worn planks until he reached Sally. She clung to him, cried hysterically.

Brie fidgeted. Michael moved her to his other hip and listened.

"We've got two divers and an EMT in a rescue boat around the bend," the sheriff said to Mac. "Found two life preservers and some fishing gear floating near the weeds." He glanced at Sally. "With no sign of Mr. Walters or his truck, we're assuming the boy launched the boat."

The sheriff strong-armed Mac away from the dock edge. "We've cleared boat traffic. Let us do our job."

Brie squirmed. He shifted her weight and scanned the sluggish water, the cold expanse, the murky depth. Bloated perch belly-up in duckweed.

Sally, sobbing, turned to Mac. "Ed started drinking. Halfway through a quart of Smirnoff, he got mean. Called Henry a dumb-fuck. I slapped him. He twisted my arm, shoved me against the wall."

"Henry, see this?"

"Ran. Heard his bedroom door slam." She tightened her robe. "Ed wouldn't let go. I told him Henry wasn't his son. He backed off. Laughed. Said, 'thank the fuck', then left." She swiped her nose with the back of her hand. "Found Henry in his closet, clutching his wooden duck whistle and one of your flannel shirts, rocking. I fell asleep on his bed. When I woke and couldn't find Henry or Ed's fishing boat, I called the sheriff." A fresh round of tears. "It's my fault."

Mac stared across the lake.

Sally rubbed her arms and sniffled. "Henry's your son."

Mac lifted his face skyward.

Brie wiggled and whined. "Henwe."

A voice boomed from the sheriff's walkie-talkie. "Sheriff?"

He unclipped it from his vest, pushed the button. "Here."

"We found a body."

"Alive?"

"Expired, sir."

The sheriff glanced at Mac. Pressed the button. "Is it the boy?"

Sally leaned into Mac. Michael pressed Brie's head against his chest. Counted heartbeats.

"White male. 6'1. Approximately 170 pounds. Fishing hat, vest, waders."

"Anything else?"

"A capsized boat in the reeds. Flannel shirt caught in the prop. Wooden duck whistle in the pocket."

Sally wailed.

The sheriff scanned the lake, replied. "Keep looking."

Brie grabbed Michael's cheeks, locked gazes. "Henwe."

She pointed. He turned toward the log cabin. The ramshackled house sat on level ground. A rickety deck extended outward. Worn lattice covered two feet of crawl space between warped wood and uneven ground. Two mallards pecked at the lattice. A dozen others circled, waddling and honking.

Michael carried Brie toward the house, set her on the edge of the deck, and squatted.

The bottom of Henry's bare feet. Bloodied.

Oh, god. He swept Brie up, hollered, "Mac!"

Mac, propelled by panic, charged up the slope, Sally following. He kicked in the lattice, wormed his way underneath.

Michael held Brie, his breath.

Mac scooted backward, inching out, clutching Henry against his chest. Cradling Henry's limp body, he sat on the deck, kissed his forehead, and recited the prayer of St. Francis.

Brie flailed against Michael's chest.

Mac fell silent. Stared at a patch of blue sky, then the bruises on Henry's body.

Sally dropped to her knees.

Mac's soulful tenor rose above her sobs. As he sang "Blackbird," dozens of mourning doves flocked to the willows.

Brie, kicking and squirming, escaped Michael's grasp and ran to Henry.

Brie prayered her hands, heart-center, then set them on Henry's cheeks. "Henwe." He didn't move. She closed her eyes, sucked in a deep breath.

Henry stirred. Coughed. "Bee," he moaned.

She smiled. Clapped. "Henwe."

"Oh, thank god!" Sally cried.

Brie placed her hand on Mac's cheek. "Tay?"

Mac grinned so wide, it's a wonder his face didn't break.

***

Brie sat next to Henry while the EMT examined him. Brie pointed at the ducks, made her quacking sound, kept Henry's focus on the birds while the woman poked and prodded.

The sheriff approached Mac, Michael, and Sally. "We found Ed's truck at a local pub. Bartender claimed Ed stumbled in drunk. Lost his keys. He offered to call a cab, but Ed walked away." The sheriff tucked his thumbs inside his belt. "Best guess is that Ed came home and decided to take Henry fishing. Henry refused. Ed forced him, causing the bruises. Henry squirmed free. Ran barefooted and cut his feet. Hid under the deck."

Sally followed the sheriff to the dock to identify Ed's body.

Mac shook his head. "Henry's an autistic child who can't express emotions, so he buries his feelings. Yet, somehow, Brie was able to find them. Heal the damage Ed caused."

"And used *qi* to protect herself."

"That she did."

They stood silent, watching Brie entertain Henry with duck antics.

"Mac," he said. "She can heal people."

Brie stopped flapping. Looked over. Smiled. Waved at Mac.

Mac grinned. Waved back. "She is a miracle."

"And then some."

***

Over the summer, while Mac worked with Brie, Michael researched the meat and dairy industry. He'd uncovered disturbing facts and, upon further investigation, found himself knee-deep in bullshit. And it wasn't coming from a cow's ass. He'd finished part one of his exposé, mailed it to several magazine editors he'd worked with, but kept running into resistance.

Mac resigned and opened a construction business. Charlie, still working toward her master's, designed houses for him to build. Sally and Mac signed a formal custody agreement and applied to correct Henry's birth certificate.

The gated community inside the barn was growing, a new resident almost weekly: a piglet who'd escaped from a truck bound for slaughter, two orphaned kittens Brie found in a storm drain, an abandoned goat.

"We'll need to build another barn," Michael said to Mac as two goslings waddled into the barn behind Brie.

***

On the first Sunday in September, Michael headed to the Hyatt Place Hotel in Hyde Park to meet with Alex, a feature editor for *Time*. Alex was in town and interested in discussing Michael's exposé on the meat and dairy industry.

Grace called Michael that morning. Colin had an angina attack, and she'd be nursing him at home. Mac and Henry had gone bird watching, so he took Brie to the meeting with Alex.

Traffic along I-90 was light. The sun beat down on Old Faithful's windshield and radiated off the hood. Eight o'clock and the temperature was already a balmy eighty degrees. Near 35th Street, red and blue flashed the horizon. A line of police cars blocked the expressway. He pulled over. A state trooper approached. Michael rolled down his window.

Sweat dotted the officer's upper lip, stained underarms. He removed his campaign hat and rested his forearms against window frame. "Expressways closed," he said, scratching his butch cut.

"What happened?"

"Overturned semi." He glanced at Brie, fussing in her booster seat. "Gonna be a while before we can open her up."

"Anyone hurt?"

"Driver's fine." He wiped his brow with his forearm. "The cargo, not so much."

"What's he hauling?"

"Chickens to slaughter." He chuckled. "Birds running loose all over the expressway. The ones that weren't crushed."

Brie balled her hands into tight fists, scrunched her eyelids.

"Is there a detour?"

"Pershing Road exit. Wentworth's closed. You'll have to take Halsted south until you hit Fifty-first Street. You can get back on the expressway from there." He rapped on the doorframe and then backed up. "Drive safe."

Michael checked on Brie. She'd closed her eyes, hands heart-center, practiced breathing.

He took a left on Halsted. Old Faithful stalled at Forty-first Street. He cranked the key several times. The engine turned over but wouldn't catch. "Well, shit."

He glanced around. An empty parking lot on his left, a vacant one-story red-brick building to his right. Up on the corner, a payphone. He rummaged the console for quarters, pulled Brie from her booster seat.

"Tough break," Alex said, through a mouthful.

"Can we reschedule for tomorrow?"

"Won't matter. We're not going to run the story."

"Why?"

"It's too hot."

Sweat beads trickled Michael's neck. Brie squirmed. "What do you mean, it's too hot?"

"You can't blame top government officials and a senior member of Congress of supporting abusive practices in the meat and dairy industry."

"They're not doing anything to stop it."

"If you continue to dig, you'll be blacklisted."

An errant cloud erased Michael's shadow. "NO 1 GIVES A FUK" etched above the phone. A stiff breeze batted a crumpled Big Mac wrapper down the street. Brie whined.

"Messing with the meat and dairy industry," Alex said, "is like taking on the NRA. You can't win unless you've got a bigger gun."

"People deserve the truth."

"Truth is, people don't want to know." He paused, spoke through another mouthful. "They're just animals, Mike. Let it go."

"I can't, Alex. I can't fail Brie. Not again."

"What? Look, Mike. Where are you? Least I can do is send a tow truck."

"I'm on South Halsted. Across from a vacant two-story building with a clock tower and a green spire. Looks like Independence Hall in Philly."

"The former Stock Yards National Bank?"

"Stock Yards?"

"You're at the gates of one of Chicago's most infamous historical sites. The meatpacking district. People came in droves to watch the slaughter of millions of animals for entertainment. It's how Chicago got the nickname 'hog butcher for the world.' Jesus, Mike. I can't believe you lived in Chicago and —"

The receiver slipped from his hand. Danced at the end of its lifeline.

Chapter 26

Michael pulled Brie's head from underneath his chin. Face beet red, hair sweaty-slick.

"Ow, ow, ow," Brie cried, punching her own forehead.

Michael turned a circle, searched for signs of life.

A rusted Buick turned off Root and puttered toward them. Michael bolted into the street, waved his arm. An old man, coke-bottle glasses, peered over the dashboard and then slammed the brakes. Michael jumped aside.

"Are you fucking insane?" the old man screamed, head out his window.

"My daughter's sick. Can you take me —"

"Get away from my car."

"Please." Michael hustled to the driver's side. "She needs a doctor. It's an emergency."

"Ain't taking you nowhere. You could be a hoodlum trying to swindle me. Rob me blind."

Michael grabbed the handle and yanked the door. Reached in, fisted the man's shirt.

"What the—"

"Sorry." He dragged the man onto the sidewalk. "No time to argue."

He hopped into the rolling car, set his foot on the brake. He laid Brie on the passenger seat, her forehead burning, cheeks slick. Bracing her with his arm, he floored the accelerator. Momentum slammed the door.

He drove two miles. Skidded to a stop at Garfield Blvd. Stores closed, buildings dark, intersection abandoned. Brie's sobs intensified. Where the hell is a hospital?

Sirens split the silence. Red lights reflected off glass windows. An ambulance sped west on Garfield. Michael peeled onto the boulevard and followed.

Within minutes, St. Mercy came into view. Trailing the ambulance, he pulled underneath the covered entrance. Scooped up Brie's limp body. Ran through the automated glass doors.

"Help!" he cried. "My daughter."

A stocky woman in navy scrubs hurried toward him and tried to take Brie.

Brie stirred, roped her arms around his neck, and cried, "No, No...No."

"It's okay, Bee. They're going to make you better."

Brie tightened her grip. The nurse managed to disentangle Brie, engulf her in fleshy arms. Brie squirmed against the nurse's hold, looked back. Red-faced, wide-eyed.

"No, Dad-dee! No!"

Her cries ricocheted. The nurse rushed toward steel doors.

Daddy. The word wrapped his heart. Squeezed. He closed his eyes, dropped his head.

"The barn, Michael." Mac's voice rang through his head. *"Get her to the barn."*

A horrifying scream scattered thoughts, shattered nerves.

A woman near the vending machine clasped her mouth. The receptionist slammed her palm against a red button on the wall. The doors opened. A hulky man in green scrubs and a young Asian woman in a lab coat rushed to the nurse, hovering over Brie, who lay on the floor, convulsing.

Michael's heart exploded. Adrenaline surged. He pushed the Asian doctor aside, shouldered the green hulk, shoved the nurse, and dropped to his knees.

"Oh, god. Brie!"

Bubbles of saliva on blue lips. Every muscle spasmed. Her eyes rolled back. He tried to scoop her up, but a hand grasped the crook of his elbow. Jerked him to his feet.

The green hulk positioned himself between Michael and Brie. "Step back, sir."

Michael sidestepped. "She needs me."

He grabbed Michael's bicep. "Let us do our job."

"But I can save her. I know how to heal her."

He tightened his grip, forced Michael backward.

Michael craned his neck but couldn't see past the hulk. Voices rang out.

"Time."

"Three minutes."

"Prep for diazepam. Get a gurney in here. STAT!"

Michael thrashed, broke free. The hulk lunged. Michael anchored his weight, swung. His fist found face bones. Blood spewed from the hulk's nose, splattered against stark white walls, dripped onto yellowing tiles. The hulk staggered backwards and fell.

Michael sprinted toward the doors that had swallowed Brie. Slammed his palms against the hard metal. Screamed Brie's name as if voice could move steel.

A thick arm snaked his neck, tightened around his throat, crushing his larynx. Dragged off his feet and hauled backwards, Michael dug fingernails into sinewy forearm.

The pressure released. He crumpled to the ground, gasped for air. Blood rushed to his head. "Brie." He crawled. "She needs—"

The sole of a boot pinned his fingers to tile. A brown polyester-clad security guard of significant bulk tapped her fingers against her belt. "Not on my watch."

"My daughter. I know how to heal her."

She folded her arms across her girth, raised a heavy brow. "You don't look like Jesus."

He slumped against the wall, dropped his head. Why didn't I take her to the barn? Mac. She needs Mac.

The security guard squatted and cuffed him. "You just won a pair of shiny new bracelets." She hauled him to his feet.

"I need to call someone."

"If you play nice, the CPD allows a call after you've been charged and fingerprinted."

"*Arrested?*"

"Familiar with the terms assault and battery? Or do I need to clarify?"

He read the name engraved on the polished-chrome tag pinned to her uniform. "Please, D. Knight."

"Dorothy."

"I need to call a friend, Mac. He'll watch my daughter until I can get this mess straightened out."

She turned her head, looked both ways as if crossing an intersection. "You pull any shit, you'll be wearing studded anklets that match those bracelets." She led him to a bank of payphones.

Michael patted his pockets. "You don't happen—"

"Do I look like the First National Bank to you?" She rolled her eyes and deposited a quarter into the phone.

Michael cradled the receiver in cuffed hands and held it to his ear. "Um…could you…" He gestured toward the dial.

She blew a heavy sigh through pursed lips. "Number?"

The phone rang a dozen times before Mac picked up. Michael explained what happened.

Mac said, "On my way."

Dorothy took the phone and set it in its cradle. "Appears Chicago's finest are busy this morning. Might be a while before someone comes to fetch you."

"You're stuck with me, huh?"

"Like gum on my shoe." She led him to an orange plastic chair bolted to the floor. "Might as well get comfy."

He collapsed into the hard molded seat, stared at the doors, willing them to open.

"Excuse me, Mr. Russo." A gray-haired woman with soft blue eyes, clutching a clipboard.

"Michael," I replied. "How's Brie?"

"I'm sure God is watching over her." She sat in the chair next to him, smoothed down the hem of her white scrub dress. "I'm Sister Adeline, a nurse at St. Mercy." A soft laugh escaped. "Yes, a nurse who's a sister. Or rather, a sister who's a nurse. A dying breed, I know. Need you to fill out some forms."

"And they sent you because they figured I wouldn't assault a nurse who's a sister. Or a sister who's a nurse."

She leaned toward him. "Or an old woman in a dress."

"Wouldn't bet on it," Dorothy murmured.

Michael wiped sweat on his Dockers and tried to melt the steel door with concentrated gaze.

"Michael." Sister Adeline set her cold, frail hand on his forearm. "Your name means God-like. Michael is the prince of archangels, defender of all that is pure. He intervenes to save lives and protect our loved ones."

"I thought Michael was the angel of death," Dorothy said. "Rips souls from dead bodies."

Sister Adeline turned a stern eye on Dorothy.

"What?" Dorothy shrugged her shoulders. "Saw it in some god-awful apocalyptic movie."

Sister Adeline pulled a silver necklace over her head and dropped it in Michael's hand. "Michael represents the spiritual warrior inside each of us. A warrior willing to stand for his beliefs."

He ran his finger over the winged messenger. "An angel bearing a sword?"

"A blade that slices through illusion and exposes truth. What's your daughter's name?"

"Brie, for Gabriella."

"God's special messenger."

A smile tugged. "That she is."

She folded his fingers over the charm, squeezed his fist with both hands. "Keep it. Fill out the paperwork. I'll check on Brie."

Michael slipped the chain over his head.

Dorothy rolled her eyes. "God-like my ass."

Michael completed and signed the paperwork.

A rickety voice echoed the waiting room. "That's him! Beat me up and stole my car."

The old man jabbed his crooked finger toward Michael from a wheelchair manned by an officer in duty blues.

Michael pinched the bridge of his nose, squeezed his eyelids.

Dorothy cleared her throat. "Something you need to tell me, St. Michael?"

The old man pushed his coke-bottle glasses over his nose bump. "Arrest him. Bastard tried to kill me."

The officer left the man with the receptionist and walked toward Michael.

"If I were your attorney," Dorothy said, through a tight-lipped smile, "I'd advise to keep your trap shut."

"Bradford," the officer said, introducing himself to Dorothy. "Was bringing Mr. Crag in when Central called. Said you had a pickup." He glanced at Michael's cuffs. "This the guy who thinks he's God?"

"Nah. Just having an identity crisis," she replied.

Bradford hooked his thumbs under his duty belt and gazed at Crag. "Looks like we can add auto theft to the assault and battery."

"My truck broke down. I had to—"

Dorothy stepped on Michael's foot.

"Let's go, buddy. I'll read Miranda on the way."

Michael stood, turned to Dorothy. "Do me a favor? Make sure Mac gets to see Brie? You can't miss him. Big bearded guy. Think Paul Bunyan."

***

Amos Wright, the attorney sent by Harvey after the phone call, sat in the interview room studying Michael's rap sheet. "You don't look the part," he said, scratching the back of his head like a dog after a flea. "Accosted an old man, stole his car, assaulted medical personnel, and punched an orderly in the face?"

"Sounds about right."

Amos tossed Michael's file into his briefcase, snapped it shut. "Well, you'll have plenty of time to mull it over."

"Wait…what?"

"Unless you know a judge who'll give up his Sunday afternoon nap to set bail, you're stuck till morning."

"Actually, I do."

***

The door to Michael's holding cell rolled open. Colin nodded to the officer, watched him walk away, and then sat on the bench next to Michael.

"Brie?"

Colin pressed his thumbs into the corners of his eyes, as if halting the flow of tears. "Grace is with her."

"Where I should be."

"Agreed. Which is why I'm here, instead of with Brie."

"You're going to get me out?"

"I'm going to catch hell from Grace, but I'll post your bail and drive you to the hospital. As a judge, I can't condone what you've done. As a father, I understand. You protect your child." He tugged at his wedding band. "I need to tell you something." He looked at Michael through eyes that hadn't slept in days. "Grace has an appointment with a lawyer. She's seeking full custody of Brie."

"Custody?" He shook his head. "She can't do that. Can she?"

"Probably not. But considering the number of times Brie's been hospitalized for accidents and weird illnesses, and now the arrest…" He rubbed his nape. "Watch your step, Michael. Make sure you're doing what's best for Brie."

***

"Even if I knew your daughter's condition, Mr. Russo," the ER receptionist replied, "I'm not qualified to discuss it with you. I'll let the doctor know you're here."

Colin set his hand on Michael's shoulder. "I'll grab us coffee."

In the three hours he'd been gone, the waiting room had filled. A pregnant woman rocked a sobbing child. Two teenagers sporting blood-spattered T-shirts lingered near the drinking fountain. A couple clung to each other as though their world had collapsed. Mac sat in a chair by the window, staring at his hands.

"I couldn't help her." He fisted his hands. White knuckles popped through stretched skin. "Not strong enough."

"How is she?"

"Not sure. Grace arrived. They wouldn't let me stay."

Michael sank into the seat next to Mac. "She was in so much pain, I forgot about the barn."

A stocky man, brush cut, USMC tattoo inked on his bicep, passed by, bouncing an infant in his arms.

"The stockyards, Mac. They weren't even on our radar."

"Michael Russo?" A lanky man with ruddy-red hair wearing a white coat stood before them, posture ridged, hand clutching wrist. The Asian doctor Michael had shoved, hung in his shadow.

Michael stood to meet his gaze. "Dr. Kelly."

"Wait." Mac got to his feet. "You know Brie's neurologist?"

"Duncan Kelly," Michael replied. "Anna's ex-fiancé."

Mac's brow furrowed. "The one…"

"He stole Anna from?" Duncan arched a brow. "Water under the bridge. I believe you've met Dr. Lee," he said, without moving. "She called me for a consult."

"Last I heard, you were head of neurology at Providence," Michael said.

"We've recently acquired St. Mercy's." He gestured toward the construction zone signs. "As you can tell, we're in the middle of renovations."

Colin walked up. "How's Brie?"

Duncan's gaze shifted from Mac to Colin, then Michael. "There's a private room in back." He nodded to an officer standing near a side door. "It would be in Michael's best interest if the two of you join us."

Chapter 27

They followed Duncan into a windowless office. The stench of cigarettes and Lysol bit Michael's throat. Fluorescent lights washed skin in muted yellow. Drab walls, dingy ceiling, faded linoleum.

Duncan settled into a worn leather chair, placed a folder on the steel desk, gestured Michael and Colin toward plastic chairs. Mac stood next to Michael, the officer behind Duncan.

A dead rose hung wilted in a crystal vase on the corner of the desk.

Duncan tapped his index finger against the folder. "As you witnessed, Brie had a seizure."

"Febrile seizure," Michael replied. "She's had them before."

"Many things cause seizures. Low blood sugar, infections, a drug overdose, accidental poisoning, brain tumors, epilepsy, or," he said, gaze rolling over Michael's hands, "a head trauma." He leaned forward, hands clasped. "We've done preliminary blood work and a lumbar puncture to rule out meningitis. I've ordered an EEG and an MRI to check for brain abnormalities."

"Can these seizures cause brain damage?" Colin asked.

"A single seizure lasting under thirty minutes, no."

Michael purged the breath he'd held. "So Brie's okay." Duncan pressed his lips into a thin line. "Your daughter suffered seven grand mal seizures within two hours, the first lasting forty-six minutes." He paused as if to punctuate severity. "Brie went into status epilepticus. She never regained consciousness between seizures."

"But you stopped them?" Michael asked, swallowing panic down his thickening throat.

"We administered anticonvulsants and found one that controlled frequency, severity, and duration. So yes, I've stopped them. For now." He opened the folder. "If they recur, I'm prepared to put Brie into a medically induced coma to mitigate harm to her brain. There are risks."

Michael shook his head. "She doesn't need more drugs. She needs—"

Mac set a firm hand on Michael's shoulder.

"You can't put her into a coma without consent," Colin said.

"Which I have." Duncan pushed a Medical Consent Form, signed by Grace, and a copy of the Grandparent Power of Attorney across the desk.

"But Michael's present, capable of making decisions for Brie," Colin said.

"Is he?" Duncan tapped his finger on the folder. "A Mr. Crag stated you assaulted him and stole his car. Said you jumped in front of his moving vehicle, endangering his life and that of your child. Furthermore, several of the staff heard you claim,"—he picked up a memo and read the words in a monotone voice— "she needs me. I know how to save her. I can heal her."

Mac squeezed Michael's shoulder. "I am sure Michael merely meant she needs him to pray for God's healing."

Duncan raised a brow. "The Grandparent Power of Attorney includes a clause for *non compos mentis*—if Michael is of unsound mind—"

"You can't prove that," Colin replied.

"Let me try." Duncan cleared his throat. "The orderly Michael punched has a deviated septum and an orbital blowout fracture. He's seeking legal advice. Our attorneys have advised to limit Michael's exposure to hospital staff."

"You can't keep me from my daughter."

"We've received a faxed copy of Brie's medical records. On three separate occasions, she was admitted to an ER while under your care. The first involved a potentially fatal fall. The others involved life-threatening infections, root cause undetermined."

"Are you accusing me—"

Duncan let the memo drop and picked up another paper. "Our attorneys have obtained an emergency order of protection on behalf of your daughter. It seems the medical staff is worried that in your current state, you might do more harm than good."

Colin shook his head. "That won't hold up in court."

"Feel free to challenge it."

"That could take days," Colin said.

"Brie doesn't have..." Michael shook his head. "I want Brie moved to Lakeview."

"I advise you to find a lawyer versed in *parens patriae*."

"What?" Michael asked.

"It's a doctrine," Colin said, "that gives states the right to intervene when it's believed the parents are not acting in the best interest of the child's well-being."

Duncan ironed his tie. "A social worker has been assigned to Brie's case and will investigate to determine Brie's best interest." He leaned forward, a smirk edging his thin lips. "The truth is, Michael, you never wanted Brie to begin with." He held up his hands like stop signs. "Anna's words, not mine."

Michael leapt from the chair, slammed his hands on the desk. The vase tipped. Water spilled over the edge and onto Duncan's lap.

"You pompous ass. I won't—"

The officer forced Michael back into the chair.

Duncan flicked water off his pants. "After you serve Mr. Russo, escort him off the premises."

***

Colin and Mac followed as the officer ushered Michael to Mac's Jeep. After a stern warning to Michael, he left.

"I can heal her?" Colin glanced between Mac and Michael. "Care to explain?"

Michael sat on a bench anchored to a parking lot median and scrubbed his face. "You wouldn't believe me."

"I'm not the one with faith issues."

Michael gave Mac a silent plea, but he simply nodded encouragement.

"Brie has a gift. She can feel the emotions of animals." He waited for the shadow of doubt to cross Colin's face, but his expression remained unchanged, so he forged ahead. "When an animal has a wounded soul, Brie absorbs their emotional pain. That pain manifests itself in

267

her body as an infection. Which is why she became so sick after she touched the buck and the calf."

"But you weren't near any animals this morning."

"My truck broke down at the Stock Yard gates."

"They stopped slaughtering animals there over twenty years ago."

"Brie sensed evil that still haunts the yards. The only way to heal her is to get her to the barn."

Lines deepened in Colin's forehead.

"It sounds crazy. But I've seen the animals heal her."

Colin shook his head, as if dismissing the idea outright.

"Knew you wouldn't believe me."

Colin leaned against the Jeep. "When Anna was five, I bought her a beagle puppy. Named her Rosie. Like Brie, Anna struggled with the R sound and called her Ozie. She loved that puppy. Rosie worshiped Anna.

"About six months later, Anna developed a fever. Gave her Tylenol and put her to bed, but she couldn't sleep. Fussed for hours. Pleaded to let Rosie sleep with her. Around midnight, I caved and let Rosie on the bed. She licked Anna's face, curled up on her pillow. Within minutes, Anna was sound asleep.

"An hour later, I checked. Still asleep, no fever, but Rosie lay lifeless at Anna's side."

Colin rubbed his palms together. "I buried Rosie behind the shed. The next morning, when Anna asked where she was, I took the coward's way out. Told her Rosie escaped from the yard. We searched for days. Of course, we'd never find her.

"Found out later, there'd been a listeria outbreak. The CDC had linked it to a vendor at the state fair, where I'd purchased a hot dog for Anna."

Colin interlaced his fingers. "Last week, when Brie and I were in the park, she picked wildflowers. When we got home, she took my hand and led me to where I'd buried Rosie thirty-five years ago. She set the flowers atop the unmarked grave, looked at me and said, 'Ozie.'"

"So you believe me?"

Colin stared at the hospital. "The only thing I believe in is my love for Brie. And right now, she's fighting for her life. I need to get back to her."

Michael watched Colin disappear into the ER entrance. "I need to get her out of there, Mac."

"How?"

A nun emerged. Wind billowed her veil. She secured her headpiece, ducked back into the hospital.

"Still got your priestly frock?"

"In the trunk? Why?"

"I've got a plan."

***

"That might get you in," Mac replied. "But getting out with Brie?"

Michael zipped into Mac's cassock. "Just tell me how to find her."

"The ER is shaped like a 'T'. Main entrance is at the bottom. Nurses' station is halfway up the stem. Brie's room is at the intersection, left side. There's an emergency exit at the top left of the 'T', the ambulance entrance at the top right." Mac secured his zucchetto to Michael's head. "I'll sneak in. Convince Grace and Colin to take a break while I watch Brie. Once I see you, I'll head out and pull the Jeep near the ambulance entrance. Wait for you there." He placed a chain with a small wooden cross around Michael's neck. "Part of the outfit. A calling card."

Michael bunched up the loose fabric of the cassock. "What am I doing, Mac?"

"Saving your daughter."

Michael headed toward the entrance, determination in his stride. A gust battered the cassock against legs, rippled grass. Maple leaves flipped in on themselves, tiny broken umbrellas. Clear sky, but the smell of rain.

He stepped onto the sidewalk, catching his foot on the cassock. He stumbled, caught himself before he fell. Turned to face Mac. "What if I fail?"

"Faith, Michael," he replied. "Faith."

Chapter 28

Michael lingered near a bank of payphones. After Grace and Colin walked out the front doors, he headed to the reception desk and waited behind an elderly woman whose head barely reached the counter.

"All I have is a cut," she said, holding up her fingertip. "Why can't someone just look at it?" The doe-eyed receptionist politely argued with the woman. Michael exhaled through pursed lips, checked his watch.

A kid in a Northwestern T-shirt behind him coughed as if hacking up a lung. A fussy toddler whined.

Michael wiped sweaty palms on Mac's cassock.

"I've been waiting two hours," the woman said. "I'm going to sue the hospital if I get sick."

The college kid coughed, the toddler bawled.

Michael worried the cross with his hand.

The receptionist's gaze shifted to Michael. He returned an expression of grace and empathy, gestured at the steel doors with steepled hands. She pressed the red button and continued with the irate woman.

Michael glided down the hall into a cacophony. A sharp antiseptic smell wrestled with a dull disinfectant odor. A fluorescent bulb buzzed and flickered. An orderly, wheeling an empty bed, hummed.

Behind the command center, a nurse with hair like steel wool peered up at Michael over half-moon frames. She removed her glasses and let them hang from a beaded chain. "Can I help you?"

Michael fingered the smooth edges of the wooden cross. "Gabriella Russo."

She drummed purple fingernails against a mound of files. "Credentials?"

"You look familiar." A doctor with wavy blonde hair and freckled cheeks approached. He tapped a folder against the counter and studied Michael's face. "Have I seen you before?"

"I'm the new chaplain."

"You look like that guy from the morning show my mom used to watch. Michael Roubay…Rabaut…something like that. You're like his doppelgänger, but older." He handed the folder to the steely nurse. "I need a history on this patient. Stat."

"First on my list, Dr. Howser," she mumbled as he turned away.

"Gabriella?" Michael asked.

She slid on her glasses and opened up the file. "Down the hall. Last door on the left."

Mac passed with a silent nod.

Brie lay in bed, eyes closed, no movement except the slight rise and fall of her chest. Her skin paled against the dark ringlets framing her face. At least a dozen wires snaked from a cap covering her head.

He studied the machines, then flipped off the alarms on the EEG and pulse oximeter machines, removed the cap.

Pulled off the surgical tape holding the IV lines to Brie's arm.

Footsteps sounded outside the door. He froze.

"The man who stole my cassock just walked around the corner to the left," Mac said, blocking the entrance to Brie's room. Mac stuck his head inside, a mixture of concern and panic etched on his face. "Hurry," he whispered, then disappeared from the doorway.

Michael removed the catheter from Brie's arm, bent her elbow, and placed it against her chest. "Hold on, Bee," he said, scooping her into his arms. "We're going home, to the barn."

Two hundred feet from the ambulance bay, sirens fractured the silence. He ducked into a supply closet. Voices rushed down the hall, then faded. He emerged from the closet and headed toward the emergency exit. One hundred feet away, the backside of a security guard appeared in the doorway. "Inform parking lot security," he said into his walky-talky. "Guy dressed as a priest."

Mac, at the nurses' station, turned his head. He slapped his hand against his chest. Staggered backwards into a cart of metal trays. Sent them clattering. The nurses scurried from behind the desk. Mac swayed, fell into a room.

Michael adjusted Brie's weight. Navigated the litter of trays. Rushed toward the steel doors.

In the waiting room, heads raised. People too sick, tired, or shocked to react to a priest carrying a child. The receptionist gawked while wrapping a Band-Aid around the elderly lady's finger.

The automatic door opened. A stream of cool air brushed Michael's heated cheeks. "Hold on, Bee," he whispered, feeling the force of everyone's stare.

A police car at the entrance, lights flashing.

Michael backed up, bolted for the entrance to the east wing. Broke through construction tape. Pushed open the door. Sprinted down a dimly lit corridor.

Caution tape and warning signs papered the walls. Wires like nooses hung from the ceiling. No directional arrows, no indicators. No idea where he was headed or what direction. He shifted Brie's weight, ran blind.

At the end of the corridor, an exit sign glowed red. He clutched Brie firmly to his chest, kicked the metal panic bar, and emerged into an expansive three-story atrium.

Afternoon sunlight streamed through the glass ceiling, darted between the branches of ornamental trees, and cast leafy patterns on the tile floor. Dozens of people lounged around tables throughout the café. Water cascaded the sides of a giant stone statue of the Virgin Mary, pooled at her feet.

A nurse hollered. Michael hid behind a marble pillar. After she passed, he stepped into the light. Edged toward the automatic sliding glass exit doors.

The doors slid open. A strong gust of wind blew through the atrium, scattered trash, rustled leaves. Particles of dirt embedded in his eyes, tiny shards of glass. Tears ran. He clutched Brie tighter, stepped forward.

A massive black cloud plunged the café into darkness. A chorus of gasps. Sunlight swept back, framed the silhouette of a lanky man with ruddy-red hair. Duncan.

He blocked Michael's path. "Going someplace?"

Michael turned a circle, searched for another exit. A crowd gathered. A security guard hovered. Duncan pressed forward.

Brie's arm fell from Michael's grasp. Her head lolled, bare feet dangled. Her body sagged between his arms. He slumped to the floor, pushed curls from her face, rocked her. "Wake up, Bee, please."

A loud thump from the front entry. Brie stiffened. A large black bird had slammed into the glass door and was thrashing about on the concrete. A rapid succession of birds crashed into the glass. Brie's body jerked as if hit by machine gun fire.

"Brie!" Grace raced down the steps of the atrium and dropped to her knees. "She's having a seizure," she shouted at Duncan. "Do something!"

Another gust blew open the doors. Dozens of birds swooped through the entrance and soared overhead. They circled the atrium and landed on tree branches. Brie stopped seizing, hung like a rag doll. Michael brushed his fingers over her ashen skin, her bloodless lips.

Duncan reached for Brie, and then jumped back. Swung his arms at a bird darting around his head.

Michael pushed to his feet, tightened his grip on Brie, staggered forward.

Grace caught the cassock hem in her hand. "Michael," she pleaded. "Give Brie to me."

Colin roped his arms around Grace and looked at Michael. "Go."

He wavered through the doorway, shuffled through dead birds riddling the concrete, belly up, exposing their emerald-feathered breasts and fragile broken necks.

Mac stood on the terrace in a crowd, staring at an enormous black cloud hovering above the hospital. Yet no lightning streaked, no thunder boomed, no rain fell. The dark cloud mushroomed and thinned, then folded back into itself.

"Mac. What—"

"Starlings. Thousands upon thousands."

"Why are they here?"

"They came for Brie."

The birds swirled, shifting into the shape of an hourglass, then banked and looped around the parking lot as if on a speeding rollercoaster. They completed a circuit, then veered into a hairpin turn and ascended in a massive wave that pulsated like a jellyfish.

The center of the cloud rippled in concentric circles and then whirled back together. The crowd on the terrace scattered like leaves. Mac smiled at Brie and backed away.

The birds cascaded from the sky and rushed at Michael. He tucked Brie's head into the crook of his neck, engulfed her in his arms, and closed his eyes.

Wind rushed from all directions. Battered the cassock against his legs. Ripped the zucchetto from his head. The clamor of screeching birds and howling wind echoed. Brie's hair whipped at his face. He fought to stay upright.

The air stilled. Michael's heart pounded, its rhythm synchronizing with the orchestrated beating of wings. He opened his eyes. A wall of emerald light surrounded them. It shimmered and swirled, illuminating them in a green glow.

Brie lifted her face at the circular swatch of blue heaven above them. Downy feathers garlanded her curls. Flecks of emerald sparkled in her eyes.

She placed her fingers against his cheek. The overwhelming sense of fear and helplessness that paralyzed him, drained from his body. Brie rested her head on his shoulder.

The wall of birds twisted into darkness and then peeled away, leaving a windless void. The starlings coiled and spun themselves into the shape of a tornado racing west.

Brie's breath blew warm against his neck, her pulse strong beneath his fingers. Mac pushed off the ground and set his hand on Brie's back. When her lashes fluttered open, sunlight caught the specks of emerald in the blue of her eyes. Her cheeks were rosy, her lips pink.

Nurses and orderlies helped the fallen to their feet. Duncan sat at a table while a nurse cleaned the scratches on his face. Colin and Grace emerged from the café.

Grace clutched her hand against her chest as she looked at Brie.

Colin pulled a feather from Brie's hair, considered it for a moment, breathed deeply, and smiled. He anchored his arm around Grace. "Let's head over to the ER. Get Brie discharged."

"I most certainly will not."

"You might have to sign a 'Discharge Against Advice of Doctor' form but, I assure you, you will. And if you refuse, I'll do it. You're not the only grandparent Brie has." He turned to Michael. "Take Brie home, where she belongs. Your attorney can sort things out later."

Dorothy approached. "Glad you were able to heal your daughter, St. Michael."

"It was Brie," he said, "who healed me."

Michael and Mac stood in silence. The cerulean sky stretched for miles. A translucent moon hung high, reflecting the light of the sun.

"It's a sky," Michael said, "that almost makes you believe in God."

Mac raised his brow.

"I said almost."

His deep chuckle echoed the courtyard.

Brie straightened, placed her hand over Michael's chest, and smiled.

Oh, god. Anna's smile.

A tear escaped his eye, slid down his cheek. His heart smiled back. "Love you too, Bee."

Chapter 29

"'Winter will pass, the days will lengthen, the ice will melt in the pasture pond. The song sparrow will return and sing, the frogs will awake, the warm wind will blow again. All these sights and sounds and smells will be yours to enjoy, Wilbur — this lovely world, these precious days.'."

Michael stretched his back against the bale of hay, then closed Anna's copy of *Charlotte's Web* and set it on his lap. Brie, curled up like a cat on the floor beside him, had fallen asleep in a patch of sunlight. Gog rested his head on Brie's leg, Baa lay near her shoulder. The rest of the barn's inhabitants served as guardian angels from their stalls.

Grace walked through the door in a skirt and heels, a newspaper tucked under her arm. "Thought I might find you two here. How'd Brie's appointment go this morning?"

"Dr. Eply said there were no signs of trauma from her ordeal yesterday. We have an appointment tomorrow for an MRI and an EEG. Any news from Colin?"

"The hospital won't pursue legal action. They don't want any negative publicity. Colin donating one-hundred thousand to their building fund may have swayed their decision." She flicked her hand at a buzzing fly. "You'll still have to face assault and battery charges for punching the orderly. And there'll be repercussions involving the older gentleman and his stolen car."

"I'll accept the consequences. Brie's home, where she belongs."

Grace drew her shoulders back, clasped her hands. "I'm no longer seeking custody of Brie. I only wanted what was best for her. I can see now that you…this place…these animals," she paused and looked around the barn, "are what's best for Brie." She stood rigid, as if expecting a tirade. When he simply nodded, her face softened, her body relaxed.

"I need to know, Michael, what happened yesterday."

"Could you be more specific?"

She unfolded the *Chicago Sun-Times*, showed him the cover photo. A sky full of starlings filled the page. The headline:

Black Cloud Dances Over White City

Grace cleared her throat and read:

"Thousands of starlings descended upon downtown Chicago Sunday afternoon, giving the city a mesmerizing aerial ballet, what scientists call the murmuration of birds. Their focus: St. Mercy, a small private hospital on the southwest side. One spectator exclaimed 'The birds were twisting and turning like some shape-shifting cloud.

It appeared they were flying as one entity. A collective soul.'

"According to Bill Walton, a specialist with the National Audubon Society, the European Starling was introduced to the states in 1880 by a Shakespeare enthusiast and, although the birds flourished in our environment, their population never exploded to where you'd see tens of thousands flocking together. Maybe a few hundred near farming areas, but never the city. After Walton reviewed a video, he said he found no evidence of a predator within their ranks, which is why scientists believe the starlings murmurate to begin with. 'A red-tailed hawk, a Merlin, even a Peregrine falcon can cause this cloud response, yet there were no signs of danger whatsoever.' Which leaves us wondering," Grace said, as she lowered the paper, *"what caused this massive number of starlings to converge upon St. Mercy?"*

A pervasive silence hung in the barn. The animals remained motionless, peering at Michael as if awaiting an explanation.

"Michael," Mac said as he entered the barn. "Have you seen—Oh…ah…sorry, Grace." He slid his cap off and glanced at the newspaper. "I'll come back later."

Grace pinned Mac with her gaze. "Maybe you can shed some light on what happened yesterday."

He scratched his beard and glanced at Michael. "Couldn't say."

"Apparently," Grace said, folding the newspaper, "I'll get no answers from you two, so I'm headed to the house to make lunch for Brie."

"You know," Mac said, after Grace left, "she's not giving up that easy."

"I'm well aware," he replied.

"You'll have to explain eventually."

"Once Grace starts listening with her heart, she'll figure it out." He wrapped a coil of Brie's hair around his finger. "How are we going to protect her, Mac? We can't keep her locked in the barn. And the world won't change overnight."

"No, probably not. But if the wingbeat of one bird can synchronize the flight of thousands, maybe the voice of one child can change the course of a nation."

A starling darted into the barn and perched on a rafter. Mac gestured to the bird. "We're not the only ones protecting Brie."

Brie stirred. Gog crawled closer to her, stretched out by her side. She curled her fingers into his coat and fell back to sleep.

"She's a miracle," Mac said, smiling down at the wonder that was Brie Russo.

Michael traced the tiny creases in Brie's hand, the rising moons beneath her nails, the heartbeat in her wrist. "All children are miracles. But this one," he said, brushing Brie's cheek, "Is Godsent."

Author's Note

The genesis for *Safe Haven – Where Hope Lives* came after visiting The Farm Sanctuary in Watkins Glen, New York, and volunteering at Sasha Farm Sanctuary in Manchester, Michigan. After experiencing firsthand the emotional lives of these amazing animals and the compassion shown by those who cared for them, I wanted to find a way to spread a message of hope. Telling Brie's story became my passion.

I am not a doctor, lawyer, priest, child development specialist, or speech pathologist. Every effort was made to present authentic events and realistic facts through research and interviews; however, given the fact the novel took place 30 years ago, this task was a bit daunting. I apologize and accept blame for any errors or omissions.

The people and events in this story are purely fictitious. Any attempt to discredit a story simply because something doesn't ring true goes against the very nature of what fiction is: Literature created by the imagination, not presented as fact, though it may be based on a true story or situation.

Thank you for reading Brie's story. I hope it entertained and moved you.

Dear Reader,
Thank you for reading my book. If you enjoyed Brie's story, please consider leaving a review on Amazon. Your feedback helps other readers discover my book. Visit my book page on Amazon, scroll down to reviews, click on **Write a Customer Review**, and share your thoughts.

Warmest Regards,
Elizabeth

You can use the QR Code to scan from your smartphone.

Visit my author's website to learn more about Brie's journey and Farm Sanctuaries at

elizabeth-stiles.com

Acknowledgements

First and foremost, I'd like to thank my husband, for this book would not exist without him. He believed in me when I doubted myself, provided me courage when mine faltered, and chased the relentless inner editor from my head. His unconditional love and unwavering support over the ten years that it took me to write this book were a Godsend. I love you more than words could ever express.

Heartfelt thanks and love to my family, who have always been my cheerleading section.

I'd like to thank the instructors at Gotham in New York for their guidance and advice, and my classmates for their critiques. Much appreciation to my mentor and coach, Lisa, for her time, expertise, and knowledge. I would have given up long ago if it weren't for her optimism and support.

Thank you to Brooke at Inked Voices for providing a platform for writers to collaborate, and to all the aspiring writers who helped me along the way. Sincere thanks to Cheryl for helping with flow and structure; Dana for answering my endless questions about neonatal care, speech and language development with patience and detail, as well as sticking with me all these years; and Doug, master crafter extraordinaire, for helping me find my voice.

I'd also like to thank the members of The Tennessee Authors Guild for their encouragement. Special thanks to

Cheryl and Bill for helping me master the art of Amazon KDP.

And last, but not least, I would like to acknowledge all those who work to make the world a more compassionate place for God's innocent creatures. You are truly my heroes.

About the Author

Elizabeth Stiles is a retired teacher, avid reader, award-winning author, mother of hounds, lover of all creatures great and small. She was born and raised around the lakes of Michigan, but currently resides in the hills of Tennessee.